ELECTION DAY

JA Armstrong

CHAPTER ONE

April 30ᵗʰ — Pennsylvania Primary
Pittsburgh, Pennsylvania

L oud cheers erupted in the hotel suite. Jameson's attention immediately fell on Candace. She'd expected to be met with a jubilant smile. Amid the fervor, Candace remained composed. Michelle, on the other hand, was bouncing. Jameson laughed.

Dana sidled up to Jameson. "What's funny?"

Jameson gestured to Michelle. "I was just thinking the twins could probably use helmets in there."

Dana joined in the laughter. Candace's daughter, Michelle was due to deliver twins in just over a month. She'd had to beg both her wife and her mother to let her make the trip to Pennsylvania. "She wouldn't dare go into labor and miss this victory speech."

"Probably true." Jameson's lips curled into a smile when she saw Candace approaching. Before she could offer Candace her congratulations, Candace's lips found hers. "What was that for?"

Candace wiped a smudge of lipstick from the corner of Jameson's lips with her thumb. "I think you know."

"I didn't do anything," Jameson said.

"Yes, you did." Candace turned her attention to Dana.

"Congratulations, Governor."

"Still a long road ahead," Candace replied.

Dana nodded. By all accounts, Candace had just clinched the Democratic nomination. To call the moment historic would have been a massive understatement. No woman had ever traversed these waters. The fact that Candace Reid was a lesbian added a layer most would never have imagined possible. Candace understood the gravity in that distinction. Dana knew that. Dana took Candace's hand and squeezed gently. "And, everyone in this room will be there to travel it with you."

Candace nodded her thanks.

"Are you going to address the troops?" Jameson wondered.

"In a minute." Candace pulled Jameson aside into the kitchen.

"Are you okay?" Jameson asked.

Candace smiled. "I'm better than okay. I need a minute."

Jameson moved to take Candace in her arms. "I thought you'd be on cloud nine."

"I can't afford cloud nine."

"Candace, let yourself enjoy the moment. You deserve it."

Candace sighed. "No; they deserve it."

"So, do you."

"Maybe. I don't want to lose sight of what comes tomorrow."

Jameson placed a gentle kiss on Candace's forehead. "You won't."

A relieved sigh escaped Candace's lips. She let her head fall against Jameson's chest. The moment that the news declared her the winner of the Pennsylvania primary, Candace's heart began to pound. She struggled to calm it. Every poll had predicted the outcome. For days, major news outlets had speculated about the general election match-up. It seemed inevitable that Governor Candace Reid would face business tycoon Bradley Wolfe. Candace had not permitted herself to buy into the press. A game was not over until the buzzer sounded. George Keyes had served as a formidable opponent throughout the primary season, and sometimes a thorn in her side. He'd challenged her patience at more turns than she had anticipated. It served as excellent preparation for the next leg of the journey. Candace also knew that the road ahead would be littered with every piece of debris Bradley Wolfe and his team could find to throw in her way.

"Candace?"

Candace pulled back and smiled. "I know."

"You know?"

"I know what you're thinking. I am happy. I just know what tomorrow looks like."

Jameson nodded. Bradley Wolfe's campaign had been running against Candace for months. The self-proclaimed business guru had yet to seal the nomination. He'd successfully banished four people from the field of potential candidates. Kansas Governor Luke Revere was still standing shoulder to shoulder with Wolfe. Wolfe would need to win California. Jameson was sure that Candace would prefer to run against the governor of Kansas. Wolfe was not a career politician. He was a master manipulator. Jameson wondered if anyone in Wolfe's sphere possessed an ounce of decency.

"You know, Revere could still take California," Jameson offered.

"Doubtful," Candace said.

"Maybe this win for you will…."

Candace shook her head. "He's so deeply entrenched, Jameson. Wolfe's people don't believe in boundaries."

"Candace, you have to know that we are all with you."

"I do know. I do. I am happy. I just need to keep my feet on the ground."

Jameson understood. She pulled Candace close again and held her.

"Mom?" Michelle walked into the kitchen. "Seriously? Bible study now?"

Candace chuckled. "No one is quoting scripture."

Michelle detected something unusual in her mother's voice. "Are you okay?"

Candace stepped back from Jameson, stretched her back and smiled. "I'm fine, Shell."

"You disappeared."

"I just needed a minute," Candace explained.

"When do you want to go down to address everyone?"

"I need a few minutes. You know the drill."

"Twenty minutes?" Michelle guessed.

"Give or take."

Michelle nodded her understanding.

"Let me guess," Jameson said. "You need to call Cassidy."

Candace smiled. "I do. I just want to run a couple of things by her before I go down."

Jameson placed a kiss on Candace's cheek. "I'll see you in a few."

"Yes, you will."

———— ◆●◆ ————

Pearl placed the phone back in its cradle and closed her eyes. *Not now.*

"Grandma?" Marianne's voice echoed.

Pearl turned to the sound.

"What is it?" Marianne asked.

"That was your Uncle David."

"What's wrong?"

"It's your grandma."

Marianne took a deep breath, expecting the news. "Is she?"

"They rushed her to the hospital. It looks like a stroke. She's… Well, without support… They're going to wait for your mother. David didn't want to call her and spoil tonight."

"Are you going to call Mom?"

Pearl cringed. "I'm going to call Jameson."

"Why now?" Marianne sighed. "How do you think she'll take it—Mom, I mean?"

Pearl's lips curled into a somber smile. "It will break her heart, just a little bit."

Marianne was genuinely surprised at Pearl's observation. Candace had never enjoyed a close relationship with her mother. Marianne had a few fond memories of the woman, but Marjorie Stratton had never been a doting, cookie baking kind of grandmother. Visits with Grandma Stratton had always been defined by polite conversation at an elegant dinner table. Marianne had always been able to sense her mother's unease during those visits. Pearl had acted as Candace's mother and she had assumed the role of a grandmother for Marianne and her siblings. Marianne noted tears in Pearl's eyes.

"Grandma? Are you okay?"

"Oh, you know, sure I am."

"Worried about Mom?"

"I always worry about your mother."

"She'll be okay, Grandma."

"I know she will. Doesn't mean I like seeing her hurt."

"Do you want me to call JD?" Marianne offered.

"No, Spitfire; you go on up to bed. I'll take care of it."

"Excuse me," Jameson stepped away from Dana to answer her phone.

"Hey, Pearl."

"How is everything there?" Pearl inquired.

"Uh-oh. What's wrong? Don't tell me that roof is leaking again."

Pearl sighed through a chuckle. "No leaks," she promised.

"Uh-huh. I can hear it in your voice. You didn't call to congratulate Candace. What's going on?"

Pearl took a deep breath. "David called me a few minutes ago. He didn't want to call you two while you were there."

"Okay?"

"It's Marjorie, Jameson."

Jameson sucked in a nervous breath. Candace's mother had been battling dementia for years. She was confined to a wheelchair, and most days she had no idea who Candace was. Even with her declining health, Jameson had witnessed the woman's ability to reduce Candace to tears. Nonetheless, she was Candace's mother. Jameson also understood that a part of Candace always had and always would yearn for the woman's love and acceptance. She was confident that Pearl knew that too.

"What happened?" Jameson asked.

"Looks like a stroke. It's not good, Jameson. They're… Well, they are just waiting for Candy."

"Shit."

"I know. I'm sorry."

"I'll tell her after she makes her speech."

"Jameson, if you want me to…"

"No," Jameson put the thought to rest. "I'll give David a call now. How about you?"

"Me? I'm all right," Pearl promised. "You just take care of Candy and let me know what you need."

"I will." Jameson rubbed her temple for a minute before placing a call to Candace's older brother. "David?"

"JD?"

"Yeah. Pearl just called. Candace is in the other room getting ready to go address the crowd."

"I'm sorry. I debated whether I should wait to call until morning. I figured Pearl would know best."

"You did the right thing," Jameson assured him. "Candace would be furious if you had waited."

"Maybe, but this is a big night for her. I hate to have anything taint it."

Jameson smiled. She liked Candace's brother. David was far more stoic than Candace. He had a reputation for being rigid. Jameson had seen a different side of him. On occasion, he would tease and taunt Candace as if they were still small children. He knew every button to push where his sister was concerned. One thing Jameson had recognized, David Stratton adored his sister. He might not have been demonstrative, but the affection that lit his eyes when he looked at Candace was evident to Jameson.

"She'll be okay," Jameson promised. She heard David sigh. "She will."

"It will be the hardest for her, JD."

Jameson was surprised by David's summation. "I…"

"She talks a good game. You know Candy. Our mother was always hardest on her. Candy did everything she could to please her."

True. "I'm sorry, David. Are you sure…"

"The machines are keeping her here," he replied. "We won't do anything without Candy."

"Where are you?" Jameson asked.

"St. Peters."

Jameson closed her eyes. "Okay. We'll be there as soon as we can."

"JD…"

"You know her. She'll insist on leaving as soon as she steps off that stage."

David chuckled. "Just do me a favor."

"If I can."

"Tell my sister that we're all proud of her."

"You can tell her yourself," Jameson said.

"I will."

"I'll have her call. I'm sorry, David. I really am."

"I know. I am too."

Jameson disconnected the call and sighed. *Fuck.*

"Hey? Jameson? What's wrong?" Michelle grabbed hold of Jameson's arm.

Jameson looked up and saw Candace emerging from the bedroom. "Not now," Jameson replied. She straightened her posture and smiled.

"Yeah, right," Michelle muttered.

"Not now, Shell," Jameson cautioned. She caught Candace's gaze and winked. As soon as Candace turned her attention away, Jameson sighed.

"JD? Come on, what is going on?" Michelle pressed.

Jameson grabbed Michelle's arm and pulled her into a corner. "It's your grandmother."

"Grandma Pearl…"

"No."

"Grandma Stratton?"

Jameson nodded. "I just talked to David. She's on life support."

Michelle's eyes closed and she bit her lip.

"You okay?" Jameson asked.

Michelle shook her head. "I'm okay," Michelle promised. "I really am, JD."

"I'm sorry, Shell."

"It's okay." Shell looked over at her mother. "Poor Mom."

"Well, let's give her the space to address the troops."

"You're going to wait to tell her?"

"Yes."

"JD…"

"Trust me, Shell. Your mom will understand. She needs to be clear-headed up there tonight. No sadness until later."

Shell shook her head. "JD, I don't usually argue with you about Mom. You're wrong this time."

Jameson was stunned.

"Listen to me; the press will find out that grandma was there and they'll either accuse Mom of acting like it didn't matter or they'll make a case that our family is in crisis. You have to tell her before she goes up there. You have to."

Jameson's heart plummeted in her chest. *She's right. Damnit.* Jameson clasped Michelle's hand. "Thanks."

Michelle watched Jameson navigate the cluster of staff in the hotel suite until she reached Candace. "Shit." With a deep breath, Michelle began to make her way to her mother.

"Jameson?" Candace questioned an undistinguishable expression on Jameson's face.

"Candace, we need to get moving," Glenn Freeman urged.

Jameson addressed him directly. "I'm afraid I have to steal the governor for a moment."

"JD, we," he began to argue.

Candace's gaze grew concerned.

Jameson remained firm. "We'll meet you in the hall."

"JD," he began again.

"In the hall, Glenn," Jameson said.

"Jameson?" Candace's voice quivered.

"I'll go get the crowd ready," Michelle offered. She kissed her mother on the cheek. "See you in a minute."

Jameson nodded her thanks when Michelle closed the door.

"Jameson?" Candace urged again.

"I wish there was an easy way to tell you this."

"Tell me what? Jameson, what is going on?"

"It's your mother."

"What?"

"David called. She's…. It looks like a stroke."

Candace collapsed into a chair and let her face fall into her hands. "Is she…"

"She's alive," Jameson replied. She knelt before Candace. "But she's on life-support. He didn't want to tell you…I didn't want to tell you until…"

"I'm glad you did."

"I'm sorry."

"I know," Candace said. She took a deep breath.

"Candace, if you need to…"

"Tell me this—is this it? Do they think she…"

Jameson squeezed Candace's hand gently. "They're just waiting for you."

Candace nodded. She sucked in another deliberately long breath and exhaled it slowly. "Let's go." She reached for Jameson's hand.

Jameson silently followed, caressing the back of Candace's hand with her thumb. Candace needed to stay focused. She needed to be in control. Jameson mentally prepared herself for the collapse that would ultimately follow. *Why can't it ever be easy?*

Candace held up her hands to quiet the crowd. She decided to stick to her original speech before delivering the news about her mother's health. The crowd gathered was, as Jameson had put it, "on cloud nine." She hated diminishing the energy in the room. In Candace's mind, her personal life was closely mirroring her professional world. Candace was elated by the result in Pennsylvania. The reality that awaited her tomorrow provided gravity. That's how life was. Candace had learned that over the years. Once you reached your intended summit, you were inevitably faced with a trek downward. Candace was happier in her personal life than she had ever been. Her marriage to Jameson served as her life's anchor. She was awaiting the birth of two more grandchildren, making her a Nana six times over. And, she reveled in being Cooper's mommy. Now, she would face loss—again. Cycles— life ran in cycles, just like elections.

Candace took a deep breath as the crowd began to quiet. Her smile remained, but her posture grew rigid. She clasped the sides of the podium and began to address the crowd again. "I want to thank you all again for your enthusiasm and your hard work. I also want to let you know here—before it hits any airwaves that Jameson and I will be headed back to Albany tonight to be with our family." Candace paused. She often thought it a strange reality that silence could be more deafening than sound. "As most of you are aware, my mother has not been well for a few years. Earlier this evening, she suffered a major stroke. For the next few days, my campaign appearances will be on hold. Believe me; the campaign continues," she added. She stretched out her hand for Jameson.

Jameson moved a few steps closer and took Candace's hand with a reassuring squeeze.

Candace felt more than heard the audible sigh that reverberated through the room.

"We love you!"

Candace smiled at the faceless declaration. "And, I love all of you," she promised. "And, together we are going to march on toward that big house on Pennsylvania Avenue!"

A new round of cheers filled the ballroom. Candace tugged on Jameson's hand and led her to the front of the small stage to wave to the crowd.

"You really are something," Jameson whispered.

Candace chuckled. "That could mean many things," she muttered.

Jameson leaned into her wife's ear. "I heard that. It means I love you."

Candace turned and pulled Jameson in for a sweet kiss.

A roar of applause and whoops erupted in the room. Candace chuckled at the rosy tint that crept up Jameson's cheeks. She waved back at the crowd one final time before leading Jameson off the stage. She stopped abruptly and took Jameson's face in her hands.

"What did I do?" Jameson asked.

"I love you too."

Jameson let her lips brush across Candace's forehead. "Let's get you home."

"There aren't going to be any flights to Albany tonight. I need to call David," Candace said.

"I know. I'll figure out the best plan to get there."

"Jameson..."

"Stop," Jameson said. "You go back to the room and call David. I'm going to find Glenn."

Candace nodded her thanks. "Don't take too long."

"Promise."

"Mom?" Michelle caught up with her mother.

"How are you feeling?" Candace asked.

"I think I should be asking you that."

"I'm all right," Candace said as they made their way to the elevator.

"What can I do?" Michelle asked.

Candace put her arm around Michelle. "Having you here is enough."

"Mom, I..."

"Tea."

"What?"

The elevator door opened and Candace chuckled. "Tea," Candace repeated. "I need to call your uncle. Make us some tea. That's what you can do for me."

"I'm sorry, Mom—about grandma."

Candace offered Michelle a smile. "Me too, sweetheart."

"We need California."

Lawson Klein reclined on the large leather sofa and smiled.

"Lawson, this isn't a joke. I haven't secured anything yet," Bradley Wolfe reminded Klein.

"You will."

"And, then? Jesus, did you see that?" Wolfe pointed to the television. "Listen to them!"

Klein sat up, grabbed the remote from a table and clicked off the television. "Stop listening."

"Stop listening? That's your solution? Her momentum just keeps building!"

Klein leaned back again.

"Lawson!"

"I heard you."

"And, you're not worried?"

"She's running for her base," Klein said. "She's not running for ours."

"Right. And, her base is never going to cross over to me."

"Not likely," Klein chuckled.

"This amuses you?"

"Maybe it does."

Bradley Wolfe's patience was wearing thin. Candace Reid's momentum in the primaries had steadily gained strength. Had the Democratic party adopted a winner-take-all scenario, she would have secured her party's nomination by the beginning of April. He massaged his brow forcefully. He'd yet to secure the nomination. That gave the governor weeks to jump into a general election strategy while he was still battling with his party. He would never garner the support of those on the left, and she would never gain votes from those decidedly on the right. That meant that a general election came down to two things: voter turnout and who could command the center.

"I'm afraid I don't find the humor in this."

Klein shrugged. "She's got you rattled."

"I'm not rattled, I'm concerned."

Klein laughed. "No, you're rattled."

"Give me something."

"You have everything you need. Just keep following the narrative."

"And what is the narrative?" Wolfe challenged.

"Accuse her of anything and everything."

"And, when the press proves it's false?"

"Attack them," Klein replied. "Some of it *always* sticks. You don't need all of it to stick to everyone. You just need some of it to stick to enough of them."

"Hasn't worked yet."

Klein shrugged again. "Sure, it has."

"And, when she comes at us?"

"She won't."

"How can you be so sure?"

Klein grinned. "She can't. She's running as the *holier than thou* candidate. That's the liberal platform."

Wolfe pursed his lips doubtfully. "Something tells me they'd argue the other way."

"They can argue anything they like. They want to play the sanctimonious card. It'll backfire. She won't come at you. They'll label her a bitch."

"And, when she's attacked over and over they'll label us misogynists."

Klein laughed.

"That's funny?"

"It's always better to be a sexist asshole than a bitch. Trust me."
Wolfe shook his head. "I hope you're right."

"I am."

Jameson looked over at Candace. The fastest way home turned out to be driving. She was certain that Candace was exhausted. Five hours into a seven-plus hour ride and Candace had yet to close her eyes. She'd been busying herself with reading and reviewing campaign notes and news articles.

"Candace," Jameson called for her wife's attention.

Candace looked up from her tablet.

"Maybe you should try and rest for a while," Jameson suggested.

"I can't."

Jameson searched Candace's eyes for some clue as to what she might be thinking. "Want to talk about it?"

Candace sighed and set the tablet on the seat beside her. "Yes."

Jameson waited.

"I don't know what to say," Candace confessed. She closed her eyes and let her head fall back onto the seat. "You always think there will be more time. No matter how much time passes, no matter what you *know*, you always think there will be more time."

Jameson took hold of Candace's hand.

"What do I say?" Candace asked.

Jameson was puzzled.

"To my mother," Candace clarified.

"Whatever feels right."

Candace shook her head. "Nothing has felt right between us for years."

"Candace, just tell her whatever you need to for you. It's not about her right now. It's about what you need to have peace."

"I just wish I knew what that was."

14

Jameson pulled Candace closer until Candace's head fell onto her shoulder. "You'll know when the time comes."

"I hope so."

"You will. Close your eyes," Jameson said. "You can rest for a couple of hours. You need it."

"Do I look that bad?"

"Never."

"Right." Candace chuckled.

"You look worried and tired because you are. Just close your eyes for a while."

"What about you?"

"I'll close my eyes too."

"Ah, I see your master plan now."

Jameson kissed Candace's temple. "Rest. That's my entire plan, governor."

Candace nestled closer to Jameson and let herself start to relax. The only way she'd found to quiet her thoughts was distraction. She had thought she was prepared for news that her mother had passed. After all, Marjorie Stratton's quality of life had diminished measurably in the last few years. She hadn't recognized any of her children in over a year. She had battled pneumonia three times, a bout with Shingles, and had managed to fall twice despite being relegated to a wheelchair. Her behavior was erratic and her musings seemed senseless most days. Candace had brought her to the farmhouse for a Sunday dinner that summer and it had turned disastrous. Marjorie had fallen into a fearful fit, screaming that people were trying to kill her and pointing the blame at Candace. Jameson had stepped in, and to Candace's surprise had managed to calm the older woman. The episode had shaken Candace to her core, and she had not attempted to bring her mother home since. David had experienced a similar issue at Thanksgiving. He hadn't even been able to get Marjorie in the car. In many ways, Candace felt her mother's life had become inhumane. Marjorie Stratton had been a debutante's debutante. She was fastidious, her closets sized and colorized, her home pristine, and her hair coiffed and styled elegantly, and her hands manicured to perfection. Candace's mother was a shadow of herself. Somehow, that did not seem to quell the ache in Candace's heart.

"Rest," Jameson cooed.

Candace sighed deeply. *There's never enough time.*

––––––◆◆◆––––––

"Hey, babe," Melanie answered her phone. Shell was silent on the other end. "Shell? Are you okay?"

"I don't know."

Melanie's heart sped up instantly. "Are you feeling…"

"I'm sorry, Mel. Yes, I'm fine. I didn't mean to scare you. I'm a little tired, but I'm fine. Looking forward to coming home tomorrow."

"Okay? What's wrong? I can hear it in your voice."

"I guess you weren't watching Mom's speech."

Melanie groaned. "I'm sorry. I was working on some things."

"It's okay."

"Did something happen with her speech? I mean, she did win; right?"

Michelle couldn't help but chuckle. "You really were tuned out."

"I'm sorry. I just want to get this stuff done before you get home."

"I know."

"What happened? You sound upset. I thought you'd be bouncing."

"I was until I found out about Grandma Stratton. She had a stroke earlier today."

"Oh no. How bad?"

"JD and Mom left for Albany already. It's not good. I guess they are just waiting for Mom before they turn off the machines."

"Shit."

"I know. I feel awful. I wanted to go with them. Mom refused to let me."

"She probably can tell that you're tired."

"I am tired," Michelle admitted. "I wish I was home."

"You will be tomorrow."

"That seems so far away."

Melanie rolled up the plans in front of her. "Regretting the trip?"

"No. I just hate that I am so limited," Michelle explained. "I know it will all be worth it. I know Mom was right. I don't think I could have handled that car ride tonight."

"Are you sure you're feeling okay?"

"I promise," Michelle replied. "I'm just tired. I think this will be my last adventure until these two arrive."

Melanie was relieved. She'd struggled not to hold Michelle back. The doctor's permission for Michelle to make the trip to Pennsylvania was the only reason Melanie had agreed. She hoped that Michelle would slow down once Candace secured the nomination. Michelle was due to travel home with Glenn the following day on the campaign bus. It was a long drive, but the bus was comfortable, far more comfortable than a sedan would have been. She was positive that Candace understood that, and she also knew that Candace had been reluctant to have Michelle make the trip to Pennsylvania. She heard Michelle sigh on the other end of the call.

"I just feel awful that I didn't go with Mom."

"Your mom wasn't thrilled with your determination to make the trip in the first place," Melanie reminded her wife.

"No, but this is different."

"Shell, you said it yourself, you need to slow down."

"You didn't see Mom when they left."

"I'm sure she's upset. It is her mother."

"Grandma was always kind of mean to Mom," Michelle said. "Even in front of us."

"I know."

"I don't know," Michelle mused. "Mom should've been so happy tonight. It's her night; you know? I know that it's not Grandma's fault, but it just feels like she's spoiling it again. Mom's face..."

"Your mom will be okay," Melanie interjected. "She will. She has a lot to look forward to. Maybe it's better that you aren't there."

"How can you say that?"

"Because maybe it is. JD will know what to do. And, besides, it would just make your mom more stressed worrying about you making that drive tonight while she tries to deal with losing her mother. At least she knows you are safe and you can get some rest."

Michelle chuckled. "That's almost exactly what she said."

"So, maybe you should take her advice and get some rest."

"I will. I just wanted to watch some of the coverage first."

You really are a junkie, babe. "Pretty sure they will still be talking about it in the morning," Melanie offered.

"Yeah, but right now it's fresh. They haven't had time to censor everything they want to say."

"Don't stay up all night."

"I won't."

Melanie laughed. "Yeah, you will."

"I promise, I won't."

"Good. I know you, and you're apt to get yourself all pissed off about something someone says and then you won't sleep at all. Go to bed, Shell. You know your mom would tell you the same thing. It'll be there tomorrow. Let Glenn and Grant worry about what's going on now."

Michelle closed her eyes. She was exhausted. The twins had been incredibly active on and off all day, she couldn't get comfortable no matter what position she tried to sit or lie in, and her feet hurt. Nevertheless, she feared she might miss something important if she tuned out. She only had a few more weeks to engage in the campaign before she'd be welcoming the twins. Even Michelle knew that the arrival of what Melanie had dubbed "the Dynamic Duo" would change everything. As excited as Michelle was, change could be scary. For the moment, she desired to hang on to what she knew, to be in control of her body and her time. "I'll try."

"Shell," Melanie softened her tone.

"I promise. I promise I will go to bed soon."

"I miss you."

Michelle smiled. "I miss you too. I'll see you tomorrow."

"You will. If you're really that worried about your mom, call her."

"I don't want to disturb her."

"Call her, Shell or at least, text JD. It'll make you feel better."

Probably so. "I'll think about it. Do me a favor?"

"If I can."

"Take the advice you gave me," Michelle said. "Put away your work and get some rest. You're going to need it soon too."

Melanie laughed. "Why is that? You're breastfeeding, right? Kind of lets me sleep."

"Uh… no way. I'm putting that three-hundred-dollar breast pump to good use."

"If you can figure out how to use it."

"Ha-ha. If two lesbians can't make that work, no one can."

Melanie laughed. "Only you, babe. Get some sleep. I'll see you tomorrow."

"You will. I love you, Mel."

"I love you too."

Michelle put her phone on the table and rubbed her belly. "She thinks I was kidding. I'm not kidding," she spoke to her unborn children. "What do you two think? Sleep or MSNBC?" A swift kick to her ribs made Michelle chuckle. "Definitely my kids. MSNBC it is."

———◆●◆———

Jameson hesitated to wake Candace. She was grateful that Candace had allowed herself to slip away into sleep for a few hours. She also knew that the rest of the day would be fraught with anxiety and grief. She kissed the top of Candace's head and jostled her gently. "Candace."

Candace let out a heavy sigh. "I'm awake."

"Listen, if…"

Candace sat up and smiled. "I'm all right—honestly."

Sure, you are. Jameson stepped out of the car and met Candace on the other side. She reached out and silently took Candace's hand. *Why now?* She led Candace through the doors of the hospital running through a million thoughts in her mind and berating whoever might be listening to her questions for adding any stress to Candace's life. Tonight was supposed to offer Candace a moment of celebration and happiness. It didn't matter that there was no one to blame—not to Jameson. Maybe the universe was to blame. It didn't seem fair.

Candace felt tension pouring off Jameson. She didn't require any explanation. She squeezed Jameson's hand lightly. *So protective.* Often, life seemed unfair. Death was an unavoidable part of life. No matter when it arrived, it always seemed too soon. And, regardless of how many times Candace had told herself she was prepared for death's arrival, she knew that was a lie. No one was prepared for the death of a loved one. She'd watched people die from illness and she had suffered through tragic unforeseen loss. One thing Candace knew, loss always felt sudden. She entered the elevator and allowed Jameson to press the button for the floor her brother had directed her to. She closed her eyes when the door closed and took a deep breath.

"Whatever you need, you let me know," Jameson said.

Candace nodded and pressed her lips to Jameson's cheek. "I will."

I hope so.

CHAPTER TWO

"Calling me at 7:30 A.M. the day after Candy clinches? This can't be good," Dana answered Glen's call.

"Depends on your view of good."

Dana poured herself a cup of coffee and sat on the chair in her hotel room. "Okay, I have another coffee in my hand. Let me have it."

"That piece Candy's been working to keep out of the press?"

"Which one?" Dana asked.

"The one about Klein and Rusnac."

Dana took a sip from her coffee cup. *I might need something stronger.* "What about it?"

"Doug got a heads-up early this morning. It seems someone leaked a classified document to *The Washington Post.*"

Shit. "What kind of classified document?"

"FBI—from what I understand."

Shit. "Any idea on who leaked it?"

"Doug's working on that. I made some calls. But, Dana; I'm worried someone is trying to make it appear that someone in our camp leaked it."

Dana sipped her coffee again. Doug's assessment made sense. After all, several members of The House Committee on Intelligence were publicly insinuating that Candace and others had leaked classified information during her time in the Senate. It seemed an unlikely coincidence that classified information regarding Candace's best-known adversary would occur the day she clinched the Democratic nomination. Ironically, it had been Candace who had worked to keep the story out of the papers, even when Dana had offered her opinion that the story was fair-game.

Petru Rusnac was a Moldovan oligarch, connected to the highest power brokers in Russia, Ukraine, and Serbia. Dana didn't know all the details of Rusnac's dealings. She'd heard the name over the years while working with Candace. She understood that Rusnac was sympathetic to what many referred to as "the old guard" in the region, namely The Soviet Union. That had been the extent of her knowledge until one of her sources at *The New York Times* contacted her about a story that landed on his desk. He'd been curious if Candace had any insight as to its validity. That's when Dana had learned that Lawson Klein had a lengthy history of dealing with Rusnac, and that an investigation into their connection had been continuing for several years. Rusnac was suspected of numerous illegal and unethical activities including money laundering and extortion. Dana had heard those allegations before. That was a matter of public discussion in international policy circles. This story didn't focus on Rusnac's shady business practices or even his unsavory alliance with Russian autocrats. The allegation that *The Times* was investigating involved human trafficking. Horrible on its face, it was made worse by a plausible connection to real estate investments and purchases made involving Lawson Klein.

At first, Dana had been inclined to dismiss them. As she considered her response to Glenn's news, she recalled Candace's reaction to the story.

"I know, it's crazy," Dana said. "I thought you should know."

Candace licked her lips and sighed.

"What?" Dana inquired.

"It might not be as crazy as you think."

"Klein involved with Rusnac? Come on, Candy; this is somebody's idea of a great novel after the election."

Candace nodded. "Sit."

"I'm not going to like this, am I?"

"I don't know if Klein is aware of Rusnac's business practices. I can't say. I can tell you that Rusnac has been involved in almost every unethical and evil practice

you can imagine. And, I can say with certainty that Klein has done business with Rusnac. He's also done business in Moldova."

"Okay, but what does that have to do with Rusnac trafficking women?"

Candace was reluctant to elaborate on the story. If the paper had anything tangible, Dana would find out along with the rest of the world. Candace was not inclined to allow that to happen. Laura was part of the rest of the world. Learning that your father had been befriended by a man who enslaved innocent women was not something anyone with a shred of morality would want to hear. Finding out that your father might be beholden or worse, complicit in that practice would be devastating. As much as Candace Reid would have loved to eviscerate Lawson Klein in the press, this was not the method she would choose.

"Candy?" Dana asked.

"I can't say what Klein knows or doesn't, Dana. He sold some property to Rusnac."

"Lots of people sell property to foreigners."

"True. If that property became a place to filter women into the country who…"

"Oh, my God."

Candace shook her head. "I know."

"Why doesn't someone shut it down?" Dana wanted to know.

"If only it were that simple," Candace replied.

"I would think that getting women out of slavery would be simple."

Candace nodded. "So would I. Not much that pertains to Rusnac is simple, Dana. That's all I can tell you."

"What do you want me to do? What do I tell him?"

"Lead him to think he needs serious vetting of the source."

"Does he?" Dana asked.

"It's always best to know who the source is."

"Can I ask you something?"

"Sure."

"Are you worried about this breaking because of Laura or is it something else."

Candace offered an unconvincing smile. "Yes."

"Dana?" Glenn called for his friend's attention. "Did you hear me?"

"I heard you."

"Can you stall it?" he asked.

Dana groaned. "It's been a long time coming," she said. "Probably not. We need to know who's pushing it."

"Do you want me to call Candy?"

"No. She has enough to deal with today."

"Maybe, but if they break this…"

"I know. I have a flight back to New York at 1:00. I'll make my way to Candy. I don't think a call is the way to deliver this news."

"Doug will try to keep it at bay a while longer."

"Do what you can. Find out who is determined to get this out now."

"We'll try, but does it matter?"

"Oh, it matters."

"Candy has her enemies. It could be…"

"Whoever it is, they aren't just Candy's enemy, Glenn. Whoever it is has a grievance with Lawson Klein too. Find out who it is." *Shit. Is it too early for scotch?*

Candace sucked in a deliberately long breath and stepped through the door to her mother's hospital room. The moment it opened, her eyes met her older brother's.

"Candy." David made his way to his sister and embraced her. "You should've gone home and gotten some rest," he whispered.

Candace took a step back and smiled as best she could. "I needed to come."

"I know."

Candace looked over her brother's shoulder at her mother. She closed her eyes momentarily to process the scene. *Oh, Mom.*

"JD." David moved around Candace and extended his hand to Jameson.

"Hi, David. Sorry about your mom."

"I know. It's strange. We all knew this day was coming."

"What you know doesn't change what you feel," Jameson offered.

Candace opened her eyes. She didn't turn to the sound of voices behind her but she smiled genuinely. One more deep breath and she made her way to her mother's bedside. Candace studied her mother for a moment and shook her head. *Oh, Mom.*

David followed Jameson's gaze across the small room. "I'll give you some time," he said.

Jameson nodded her thanks. She moved to Candace's side and put her hand on Candace's shoulder.

Candace reached up and took Jameson's hand.

"I think I'll join David," Jameson said. "If you need me…"

Candace's reply came in the form of a gentle squeeze of the hand holding hers. She waited until Jameson's footsteps passed through the door. Her hand reached over and brushed her mother's hair aside. The woman lying in the bed was a shadow of the woman Candace recalled as a child. It broke Candace's heart. For all the acrimony that permeated their relationship, Candace loved her mother. Marjorie Stratton, the debutante, differed in countless ways from Candace Reid, the politician. Mother and daughter had seldom seen eye to eye whether it had been regarding attire, education or family.

Candace's hand moved to hold her mother's. She'd always marveled at the older woman's poise. She'd come to realize in the last few years how much her mother had influenced her. It wasn't a topic she discussed with others—not even with Jameson. Pearl and Candace's grandparents had shaped the way Candace saw the world. The compassion, tenderness, and affection that she had always been shown on her stays in Schoharie as a child shaped Candace's view of people. More than that, her time in what was now her family's home had given her direction and purpose in life. For many years, Candace had scoffed at the notion that Marjorie Stratton has provided her with anything but frustration and feelings of inadequacy. That perception had changed measurably. Candace felt the warmth of flowing tears fall over her cheeks.

"I wish I knew what to say," she confessed. She looked upward as if some voice might bequeath her with an answer. Slowly, her attention returned to her mother. "Something tells me you can hear me. I hope you can. I know you haven't always agreed with me." Candace chuckled. "Actually, you probably never agreed with me." She sighed. "You did teach me some things that I didn't realize until recently. So much is happening, Mom. I wish—I wish that you had been able to *know* Jameson. I think she would have changed the way you see so many things. She's certainly changed the way I see life. She reminds me what matters most. You would've liked her, even if you didn't admit it. Marianne didn't want to admit it at first either. Now? I think Jameson's the best friend she's ever had. I know she's mine." Candace chuckled again. She closed her eyes to calm her rising emotions, blew out a forceful breath and opened them again. "So much is happening, Mom. Some days I don't know what direction I'm supposed to take. Some days I just want to throw in the towel and forget all of it—escape to Schoharie, be with the kids." Candace sighed as her tears fell without restraint. "What am I doing, Mom? I think I know, but I don't know. I don't know anything more today than I did yesterday. Every answer just seems to bring a thousand more questions."

Candace's eyes fell closed again. Her tears were threatening to turn to sobs. She sucked in a ragged breath and willed her emotions to obey her commands. Another deep breath, and another—one more, and she opened her eyes. A smile graced her lips and she gripped mother's hand tenderly. "That's what you taught me, Mom. I didn't pay attention, did I? I couldn't do this if you hadn't taught me how to stand tall—how to appear confident and poised when inside every part of me is quivering with uncertainty. Jameson sees that. You saw that. I know you did. I didn't understand that until now. Now, I understand. Someone is always watching—I understand." Candace leaned over and brushed her lips across her mother's forehead. "I love you, Mom. I hope you know that. I do. I'll miss you."

Candace's head fell onto her mother's shoulder. Marjorie had never been demonstrative. As Candace laid there, her thoughts wandered until they fell on a memory long forgotten. She soaked in the image. She couldn't remember how old she had been—five or six, she thought. David had punched her during an argument. Her lip had split open, and blood had trickled down her chin. That memory had always been vivid. For some reason, she had forgotten the scene that followed. Now, she remembered with such clarity, she thought she might be transporting to a different time.

"David!" Marjorie yelled. "What on earth were you thinking?"

David shrugged. "She wouldn't stop!"

"And your answer was to hit your sister?"

He shrugged again.

"Go to your room. Your father will deal with you later."

"Mom!" David whined.

"Now."

Candace sat on the ground with her face in her hands. Marjorie shook her head and scooped Candace up.

"Shh," Marjorie hushed her daughter. "Let's get you cleaned up."

Candace clung to her mother as she was carried to the kitchen.

Marjorie kept her daughter in her embrace while she retrieved some ice from the freezer and wrapped it in a towel. She grabbed a cloth and wet it with some warm soapy water, placed Candace on a chair and knelt in front of her. Gently, she wiped the blood from Candace's mouth and chin. She smiled sympathetically. "I know it hurts," she said. "Candy," she continued. "Remember that sometimes people will knock you down so hard you won't want to get up. That's when you need to stand up the straightest. Don't you ever let them keep you down. You hear me? When they hit you, you stand up and you smile right back at them. You show them you are stronger even if you don't feel that way." She placed the cold towel against Candace's lip and kissed Candace's forehead tenderly. "You are stronger," she whispered. She took hold of Candace's hand and placed it over the makeshift ice-pack. "Now, stand up straight, go walk past your brother's room, and give him a smile."

Candace's tears fell on her mother's shoulder. Her arm wrapped as best it could around the woman, and she held on as if willing the memory to linger.

Jameson stepped up to the door and looked through the window. Her heart rose in her chest, nearly choking her. Few people would ever realize who Candace truly was. Jameson had seen the woman behind the stateswoman immediately. She'd recognized Candace's inner child, the longings of a woman's heart that most people never took the time to see. Those were the parts of Candace that Jameson loved the most—the raw vulnerability beneath the controlled surface Candace always managed to portray. She stepped back from the window. Candace needed time. Jameson would not intrude. When she was ready, Candace would emerge the picture of calm readiness even as sorrow tinted her expression. Jameson understood.

"She okay?" David's voice asked.

"Not even a little bit," Jameson answered honestly. "But she will be."

"It's going to print," Dana told Glenn. "I can't stop it. Candy's managed to hold it for months. They're confident about the sources. Where are we on that front?" she asked.

Glenn groaned. "Stalled indefinitely."

"What's Doug's gut say?"

"It could be anyone, Dana. You know how this all works. Might be someone who wants Candy in their pocket."

"Yeah, well, that won't work. We both know that. Who would want this story out about Klein? Doesn't seem to me that Wolfe would. Klein's been lining the campaign's pockets since the beginning."

"Grant is digging."

Dana sighed.

"Still don't trust him?" Doug surmised.

"Right now, Glenn, the number of people I *trust* is shrinking by the minute."

"I understand that. We both know this was inevitable."

"Maybe so. The timing is what worries me. Somebody's got an agenda. I'd like to know what that is and who's behind it."

"Yeah, I got that. Working on it. You do know that Candy will have the best idea what those answers are."

"I know, but I'd prefer to go to her *with* those answers rather than ask her *for* them—particularly now."

"I know, the timing sucks."

Dana laughed. "Accurate."

"Are you headed straight to Candy's?"

"No. I'm stopping home first. JD called a little while ago. They're all heading back to the hospital this afternoon around 4:00. Then, I guess it's just a waiting game. She said the doctors told them it could be minutes or even days. I guess, their best guess is it will be minutes to hours. I just can't believe this is happening now. They've never been close. It's still her mother."

"She'll be okay, Dana. Candy's tough."

Not as tough as you think. "Yeah. I told JD to let me know when they're headed home. I'll talk to Candy then, not while they're at the hospital."

"You realize if she sees it and no one…"

"I'll make sure she's aware," Dana said.

"Can't you get them to just hold off one more day for Christ's sake?" Glenn asked.

"Not this time."

"Assholes."

Dana laughed. "Accurate again. I'll be in touch. You let me know if there's anything else I need to know."

"You'll be the first."

Dana put her phone in her lap and closed her eyes in the back seat of the car. "It never ends."

<hr />

Candace turned and looked back at her mother. She closed her eyes for a moment, took a deep breath and let it out slowly. *It's time.* She placed her hand on the door and closed her eyes one last time, willing herself to walk through it. In a few hours, she would return. She'd already said her goodbye; now, she would support her family as they said theirs. Another breath and she walked to the other side of the door. The short walk to the family waiting room seemed endless to Candace. The moment she opened the door Jameson's eyes met hers. She smiled.

"Hey."

"Where's David?" Candace asked.

"David headed down to get some coffees."

Candace nodded.

"Candace?"

Candace made her way to the loveseat Jameson occupied. She took a seat beside her wife and shook her head. "I'm not sure what to say," she confessed.

"You don't have to say a word."

Candace gratefully folded herself into Jameson's embrace. She had no words and she had no desire to search for any. Lately, her days were filled with a constant search for the best way to explain everything from her feelings to her ideas. That was the nature of a politician's public life. At times, that reality flooded into Candace's personal world. She worried about her children's needs and perceptions, about her staff's energy level and enthusiasm. More than most realized, Candace Reid chose her words carefully. Words possessed power. That was a fact that many people liked to deny. It was a reality that Candace had come to understand early in her life. Words served as a vehicle to shape perception. That gave speech the power to incite action. Candace knew that how she addressed any situation in her life impacted the perception of those around her. She couldn't censor her emotions and her beliefs, she could control how she expressed them to others. Jameson provided her safe place, the place where all pretense could evaporate and Candace could speak freely. Now, she had no words to express the feelings that rolled through her in waves. The only thing she desired was the safety of Jameson's arms.

"You need a little rest," Jameson observed.

"I'm okay."

"You're full of shit," Jameson replied.

Candace chuckled. She pulled away slightly and placed a kiss on Jameson's cheek. "Is that your politically correct way of telling me I look like shit?"

"Nope."

Candace raised her brow.

"You can fool the masses, Candace; you don't fool me."

"I don't want to."

The door opened and David walked back into the room. "Sorry," he apologized, feeling a sense of intrusion.

Candace pulled her focus to her brother. "Don't be. Jameson was just letting me know I look like shit."

Jameson rolled her eyes. *Already at it.*

"I've seen you look worse," David teased.

Candace laughed genuinely. "Thanks."

"Are you going to be okay coming back here this afternoon?" he asked.

Candace sighed. "No," she admitted. "Are you?"

"Not really," he said. He handed Jameson and Candace each a cup of coffee from the tray he carried. "Carol called while I was downstairs. The kids are here."

Candace peeled back the lid on her cup and took a sip. "We need to talk about arrangements."

"Yeah," he agreed. "Why don't you let me take care of that?"

Candace nodded. "We can have the reception at the house."

"Candy, you don't have to do that. You've been on the go for months. We'll just get a banquet room."

Candace shook her head. "No. Who feels comfortable in a banquet room? Other than Mom?"

David laughed. "Are you sure?"

Candace nodded again.

"I'll take care of it," Jameson offered.

Candace opened her mouth to protest.

"I will take care of it," Jameson repeated. She looked at David. "I'm sure Pearl will help."

"I'd count on it," he said. "Are you going to head back to Schoharie?"

"No," Jameson answered before Candace had the chance. "The kids will meet us at the Governor's Mansion. It's closer. In fact..." She looked at Candace. "I took the liberty of getting some food delivered later. It'll be there whenever—well, whenever anyone needs a break from this place or when..."

David smiled. "Thanks, JD. I'm going to head home. See you in a few hours?"

Candace made her way to David and hugged him. "I'm sorry."

"Me too," he said. "See you in a bit. Take your time, Candy."

"Promise."

"I mean it," he said. "Don't rush back here. We'll wait for you."

Candace watched her brother leave and sighed.

"Candace," Jameson stood and placed her hands on Candace's hips.

"I'm okay."

"Sure you are."

"I am." Candace turned in Jameson's arms. "Thank you."

"I didn't do anything."

"Yes, you did."

"I'm sorry," Jameson said.

"I know you are. I am too. I'm okay. At least, I will be."

"Let's go home so you can sleep for a bit."

Candace cupped Jameson's face in her hands. "I'm not sure that's in the cards for me."

"I figured as much. Mom should be there with Coop by now."

Candace smiled. *You always know what I need.* "Thank you."

"It's what I do."

Candace laughed and took Jameson's hand. "Get me out of here."

"At your service."

"You really are a lunatic; you know that?"

Jameson shrugged. *If it makes you smile.*

———————◆●◆———————

"Is Mom here yet?" Jonah asked Marianne.

"Nice to see you too," Marianne teased.

"Sorry."

"Don't be sorry," Marianne said. She handed her daughter a sippy-cup of juice and directed Jonah to have a seat. "Where's Laura?"

"In the other room with Grandma and Maureen."

"They commandeered that baby, huh?" Marianne guessed.

Jonah grinned.

"Figures. Want some coffee?"

"Have any beer?" Jonah asked.

"At ten in the morning?"

"Why not?"

"You okay?" Marianne wondered.

"Worried about Mom."

"JD called about half an hour ago. I'd guess that they'll be here any minute."

"How is she?"

"JD?"

"Mom!"

Marianne smiled. "I didn't talk to her. I'm sure she's exhausted. They drove through the night to get to the hospital."

"This sucks," he groaned.

"Yeah, it does." Marianne handed her brother a beer. His eyes widened. "What? You're of age."

"You seem to be taking this well," he noted.

Marianne took a seat across from her brother. "What can I do?" she asked rhetorically. "Grandma hasn't been well for years, Jonah. I guess—if I'm honest—I see this as a blessing."

"I guess. I just wonder how Mom is. I mean, Grandma was never all that nice to her."

"One thing I have learned over the last few years, don't be too sure you know what exists between two people, no matter what you think you know or who they are to you."

"What does that mean?"

"It means exactly what I said. We all view people through our relationship with them to some degree. Grandma is who she is. Mom is who she is. That doesn't mean they don't love each other."

"Your sister's right," Pearl's voice agreed as she stepped into the room. "Drinking already?"

Jonah shrugged.

"Don't worry so much about your mother," Pearl advised. "Just be there for her."

"How do we do that?" Jonah said.

"Same way you always do, I'd imagine."

"You mean keep our crap off her plate," he guessed.

"Nope. I mean just the opposite."

"Huh?" Jonah looked at Pearl as though she'd lost her mind.

Marianne snickered.

"I mean just what I said—just be you. That's what your mother needs more than anything right now. Everything else is changing around her. You fools are the consistency in her life—craziness and all."

"What about you?" Jonah asked.

"Takes a crazy person to run this asylum as your mother would say."

"Yes, I would," Candace agreed as she walked in through the back door. "And, I learned from the best."

Marianne immediately reached her feet. She embraced Candace. "I'm sorry, Mom."

"I know you are," Candace said.

"Sneaking in the back?" Pearl teased.

"Something like that," Candace admitted.

"Where's JD?" Jonah asked.

"She's outside talking to Scott," Candace answered. "He pulled in behind us."

Jonah nodded and looked down at the beer between his hands.

Candace met Marianne and Pearl's gazes without comment. Both understood the silent request.

"I think I'll go find Coop. I know he's been waiting for you," Marianne said.

"I'll go with you," Pearl offered. "God only knows what those two boys are into up there."

"Let's just hope they haven't made any modifications to the upstairs in the last hour," Marianne laughed.

Candace waited until she and Jonah were alone and took the seat Marianne had vacated. "Jonah?"

"I'm sorry, Mom."

"I know you are. We all are."

Jonah sighed.

"Jonah?"

"I just don't get it," he said.

"What's that?" Candace wondered.

"Why this shit has to happen just when things are going great."

Candace smiled at her son. "I think it just feels that way sometimes."

"Feels that way a lot if you ask me."

"I guess it does. It's just life, sweetheart. I wish it wasn't."

"Can I ask you something?"

Candace nodded.

"Grandma... I mean, she was always kind of—I don't know—mean to you?"

"Mean? Oh, I don't think Grandma was *mean* to me."

"You don't?"

"No," Candace replied honestly. "And, she was never *mean* to you."

"No," Jonah agreed. "But she wasn't like Grandma Pearl."

"Not at all." Candace chuckled. "But I'll bet you have some fond memories of her."

Jonah thought for a minute. "She used to tell Marianne and Shell to stop behaving like monkeys and act like ladies." Jonah laughed. "Then, once? She made Shell put on this pink dress to go to church when you and Dad were away. That pissed Shell off."

"I'll bet it did."

Jonah laughed at the memory and then grew quiet. "She used to sneak us cookies when you weren't around."

Candace's brow arched. "Did she?"

"Yeah. Macaroons."

Candace laughed. *Well, well, Mom, you are full of surprises.*

"She said you hated them."

"I never hated them." Candace kept laughing. "She loved them. I swear, if it hadn't been for Pearl the only dessert we ever would have had were those damn macaroons. Ask your Uncle David if you don't believe me. *He* hated them—still does to this day."

"I love them."

Candace watched Jonah closely. Her mother had always gravitated to Jonah. Jonah was quiet. He was also patient and he excelled at listening. It hadn't been a frequent occurrence that Candace's children spent alone time with her parents. Most of the time when Candace traveled, Pearl had stepped in and stayed with the kids. There had been a few times that Candace's father and mother had taken the three for a long weekend. Candace had never heard any of them speak about those times with either affection nor with antipathy. She wondered as she listened to Jonah if they had avoided discussion with her because of how they perceived her feelings for her mother.

"I never knew you loved macaroons," Candace commented.

"Yeah. Grandma used to let me eat them in bed."

Candace's laughter filled the room. Jonah looked at her in astonishment.

"She did," Jonah said. "She would read *Curious George* to me and she said the closest thing she had to a coconut was a cookie. I never really got that."

Candace kept laughing. Jonah's innocent admission filled her heart in ways she was sure she could never hope to explain. Every person had layers. Candace knew that. She sometimes lost sight of that fact where her mother was concerned. "Thank you," she said as she took Jonah's hand.

"What is going on in here?" Jameson inquired. Scott followed her through the door. Jameson looked at the beer on the table. "Are you getting your mother drunk already?" she asked Jonah.

"What? No!" he answered.

Candace fell into another fit of laughter.

"Mommy!" Cooper ran into the room.

"Speaking of monkeys," Candace said.

"I'm not a monkey!" Cooper giggled. He climbed into Candace's lap.

"You sure about that?" Marianne asked.

"Nana!" Spencer flew to Candace's side and hoisted himself into the chair beside her.

"Two monkeys," Candace teased.

"Yeah, just like Marianne and Shell," Jonah agreed.

"I am positive I don't want to know what you are talking about," Marianne said. "Where is my sister anyway?"

"Probably practicing pumping her breast—or both," Jonah guessed.

Marianne and Candace both laughed. Michelle had been obsessing over the notion of breast pumping for months. Marianne understood that her sister's antics stemmed from nervousness, but she couldn't help that the obsession amused her. "Wouldn't surprise me. She keeps going this way, those things will run dry before she delivers."

Candace burst out laughing at the blush that crept up Jameson's cheeks.

"Not so sorry you missed all that with me now, huh?" Candace whispered to Jameson.

Marianne decided to step in and save Jameson. "Personally, I love that Jonah and Shell will have *double* diaper duty and I'll be free," Marianne said.

"Yeah, well, just remember *you'll* be *in* them sooner than either of us," Shell's voice echoed as she entered the room.

Jameson rolled her eyes. "Welcome home," she said to Candace.

Candace pulled Cooper to her and kissed his head. *Lunatics.*

CHAPTER THREE

Dana walked into the room and forced a smile onto her lips. "Hi, JD."

"Dana. Why do I think this isn't a social call?"

Dana shook her head regretfully.

Jameson sighed. "She's had enough today. Can't this wait?"

"I'm sorry, JD. It can't—not this."

Jameson ran her hand over her face with frustration. By the time everyone had said their goodbyes at the hospital it had been approaching 7:00 P.M. Two hours later, Marjorie Stratton had quietly passed away with Candace and her brothers at her side. Now, everyone had descended on the Governor's residence. It was nearly 11:00 P.M. and Jameson still could not see the end of the day arriving anytime soon. Candace was running on sheer will. Jameson took some solace in the notion that Candace needed to be surrounded by the people she loved. Dana counted in that equation. Unfortunately, Jameson knew that Dana's visit regarded something more than condolences and friendship.

"Now? Dana, can't it wait until morning?"

Dana shook her head.

Candace caught sight of Jameson closing the door behind Dana and ushering her in.

"What's that about?" Michelle asked.

Candace smiled. "Nothing you need to worry about."

"I'm worried about you," Michelle said.

"Don't be. You should go home and get some sleep," Candace advised.

"Do I look that bad?"

"No," Candace chuckled. "You look tired, Shell. Have Mel take you home and get your feet up. It's been a long day for you."

"Yeah, well, they seem to get longer by the day." Michelle rubbed her belly.

"It happens. Go on. I'll call you in the morning."

"Mom, we can stay."

"Go," Candace ordered. She kissed Michelle on the cheek and made her way to Dana and Jameson.

"Dana."

"I'm sorry to intrude," Dana apologized.

"You're never an intrusion."

"You might want to hold that thought until later," Dana said.

Candace winked. "Come on; I could use a diversion."

"You might want to hold that one too."

Candace led Dana out of the room and toward her office. She closed the door behind them and directed Dana to sit. "Okay, let's hear the dire news."

"It's not dire. It's just... I tried, Candy."

"Just tell me."

"The story about Klein and Rusnac is running tomorrow."

Candace nodded her understanding.

"That's all? You don't have anything to say?"

"We both knew this was inevitable."

Dana pursed her lips. "I tried, Candy. I know Laura is..."

"Laura knows."

Dana was shocked. "Laura knows about her father and Rusnac?"

"She knows that the story is going to run at some point."

"I didn't think you..."

"I sat down with her and Jonah before I left for Pennsylvania."

"You knew it was going to run."

"No. I'm not surprised, though."

"What do you want me to do? And, Candy? This time they have a classified FBI report. The timing of this—not just the campaign. There are already calls for you to testify. You know there will be assertions that you leaked it."

"I would think so."

"What do you want me to do?"

"Let it run like the wind."

"What?"

"Keep doing what we've been doing."

"Are you serious? Don't you want to know who leaked this? And, why now?" Dana questioned.

Candace reached into the cabinet behind her desk. She retrieved a bottle of scotch and two glasses. She continued the task of pouring scotch into the glasses without comment. She walked to Dana, handed her a glass and took a seat on the edge of the large wooden desk. "You look like you could use that," she said. She sipped from her glass and set it aside.

"I don't understand why you're not more concerned," Dana admitted.

"I never said I wasn't concerned. You asked me if I want to know who leaked this new FBI document. I do."

"I also asked why now?"

"What do you think?" Candace challenged.

"Glenn thinks it's to compromise the campaign or maybe to get a favor from either you or Wolfe down the line."

Candace grinned. "He would." She picked up her glass, took another sip and set it down again. "I didn't ask what Glenn thinks. I asked what *you* think."

"I'm not sure. The timing? Candy, besides taking the wind out of your sails after last night, you know they are probably going to call you to testify in front of the Intelligence Committee."

"No probably about that." Candace stood and began to pace the room to gather her thoughts. She took a deep breath and turned back to Dana. "Why now? You're thinking like Glenn and Doug. Not everything is about this campaign."

"You don't think this is about influencing the election?"

"I'm sure that would be a bonus for some people. But which people, Dana? This story doesn't do anything but fan the flames of our most ardent supporters and detractors. Wolfe's will say this is an assault on Klein by me and my surrogates to discredit them all and strip funding. Mine will say this proves that Klein and the entire crowd he runs with are corrupt hypocrites. It's nothing new."

"Okay, but people on the fence about either of you…"

"How many people do you suppose that is?" Candace challenged. She shook her head. "The ones who are undecided now? They're not the ones reading these stories, Dana. Will it have an impact on the campaign? Everything does. Why now?"

Dana was growing frustrated. Candace's reaction wasn't what she had suspected. "I'm not following."

"How long have you worked with me?" Candace asked.

"What?"

"Well?"

"Over fifteen years."

"Um hum. Stop thinking like Glenn and Doug. That's not what has kept you at my side all this time."

"You think it's a smoke screen?"

"Don't you? Dana, we're in a different ballgame here. This story? This story is going to command the headlines for at least a week. You know that as well as I do. Every news show and network is going to lead with this barring some tragedy. Let them. You let Doug and Glenn obsess over the headlines for the next couple of weeks. Pay attention to the story on page three, Dana. There is a reason this is happening now. It's not about me."

Dana considered the information. "You think they're trying to bury something?"

"Someone is always trying to bury something. Something is being thrown shade. That's what we need to figure out."

"You think whoever did this—you think we can use this as ammunition down the line?"

Candace made her way back to her desk. "I think it's pertinent down the line—yes."

"You're not referring to the election?"

"No."

Dana took a sip of her scotch. "You think this has implications if you win the election."

Candace smiled. "*If* I win? That's not an option. Pay attention to what *would* have made the front page. Trust me."

"What aren't you telling me? Dana asked.

"Can't tell you what I don't know," Candace replied. She raised her glass and then took a final sip. *But I intend to find out.*

Jameson closed the bathroom door and climbed into bed beside Candace. She took the phone in Candace's hands and placed it on the bedside table. "I think that's enough for the day." She removed the glasses from Candace's face and put them beside the phone. "You need to rest."

"I don't know if I can."

Jameson laid back and pulled Candace into her arms. "You never will if you don't try."

"I can't help it. I'm tired. I admit it. I feel so wired, Jameson. There are a million things that I need to take care of and..."

"Stop. Please, stop. I don't want you to crash. We both know if you keep going at this pace, that's what's going to happen. Just close your eyes. Even if you can't sleep, just close your eyes and rest. Please?"

Candace nestled closer to Jameson. "I can't believe she's gone."

"I know."

"Jonah told me that she used to let him eat cookies in bed when he stayed with my parents."

Jameson chuckled. "I think that's every grandmother."

"Maybe so."

"You never thought of her that way," Jameson guessed.

"No. She wasn't that way with us as kids. Jonah—she was always softer with him for some reason."

Jameson stroked Candace's back as she listened.

"I don't know what that was," Candace mused.

"Jonah has that way about him," Jameson observed. "Even now, he's got this innocence. I can't explain it."

"You don't have to. I think I know what you mean."

"You wish you'd seen that side of her," Jameson guessed.

"More like I wish she could have shown that side of herself more—to anyone. I realized today when I was sitting with her, there was always this sadness in her eyes. I guess I was so caught up in what I felt, I never took the time to think about what she felt."

Jameson pulled Candace closer. "She did love you. You do know that?"

"I do." Candace shifted so that she could look at Jameson. "I remembered this time when I was little? I was sitting there with her, and I don't know why it came back to me. David socked me a good one in the face. I was little, maybe six. I never forgot that bloody lip. I don't know how I forgot about my mother."

"What about her?"

"She cleaned me up. I remember her looking at me. I swear, I can see it right now as if she were standing in front of me—clear as day. I was crying. I think my feelings were hurt more than my lip. She cleaned my face up so gently. I remember, she kissed my forehead." Candace felt tears begin to bathe her cheeks. "It's like I can feel them still resting there, Jameson—her lips on my forehead."

"Maybe they are," Jameson offered. "Look, I don't know what happens when people die, but sometimes? Sometimes I think it gives us both permission to let go; you know? Maybe she wanted you to remember that because she always did. Maybe that's her way of letting you know how she still sees you."

Candace kissed Jameson tenderly. "I wish she could have known you before she started slipping away."

"Me too."

"Thank you for everything."

"You don't need to thank me for anything, but if you really want to, you can start by getting some rest."

"Not going to give up, huh?"

"When it comes to you? Never."

Candace settled back into Jameson's arms and closed her eyes. "I love you."

"I love you too, Candace. I love you too."

FOUR DAYS LATER

"Is the governor going to make any comment?"

Dana smiled. "Governor Reid is focusing on her family right now."

"She must have an opinion on this story," a reporter called out. "No statement? Dana, it's been two days since the story broke in *The Post*. Still no official comment? Hasn't Governor Reid read the news?"

"The governor is abreast of all the news. I'm certain if and when she has any thoughts to offer, she will. She's never been accused of shyness."

The media laughed.

"Dana? One last question?"

Dana pointed to a young woman. "Go ahead."

"Is Governor Reid considering Senator Keyes as a running mate."

Yeah, like that would ever happen. "I believe Governor Reid is considering several qualified candidates."

"But is one of them George Keyes?"

"I'm certain she and Senator Keyes have had discussions since the primary in Pennsylvania. I can't speak to what they discussed. Again, the governor is focused on her family this week. She'll be making visits Friday to New York City, New Rochelle, and White Plains early next week to discuss community policing initiatives. I'm sure she'll take some questions then."

Dana made her way up the capital stairs and groaned.

"They are relentless," Glenn offered. "How is Candy?"

"Tired, I think," Dana replied. "I'm heading there later this afternoon after the burial."

"Shitty week, huh?"

"Just a week," Dana said.

———— ◆●◆ ————

"What the hell are you doing about this?" Lawson Klein bellowed.

"Me?" Jed Ritchie laughed. "What do you want me to do about it, Lawson? I can't believe you were stupid enough to leave a trail."

"I'd be careful, Jed."

"Is that a threat?"

"No, just looking out for you."

"Right." Ritchie sat down on the arm of a couch. "You'd better make sure none of the campaign's funds can be traced to Rusnac."

"Give me a little credit."

"A little? Okay. Is it true?"

"What's that?"

"Did Rusnac use that house to pimp out girls?"

"How should I know what he used the house for?" Klein bit back. "I sold him property. He paid cash. Last I knew, I didn't need a reference check for a cash payment."

"You'd better hope this doesn't bite Wolfe in the ass."

"Oh?"

"You think Wolfe is *your* flunky; don't you?" Ritchie chuckled at the consternation in Lawson Klein's eyes. "You have no idea who he is; do you?"

"I know who he is. I wonder if you know who he isn't."

Ritchie's chuckle grew to sarcastic laughter. *No idea, Lawson—no idea at all.*

———— ◆●◆ ————

"I'll be done in about an hour."

"I'll let Pearl take charge of the asylum," Jameson offered.

"Very generous of you." Candace placed a kiss on Jameson's cheek. "If you need me, I'll be in the office."

"I'll make sure no one interrupts you."

"Just come get me if…"

"I know how to pour wine—and scotch."

Candace smiled. "You are talented," she agreed before beckoning Dana to follow her.

"Where's she off to?" David asked.

"Conference call."

"Campaign life never ends," he said.

Jameson's eyes remained fixed on Candace's retreating figure in the distance.

"JD?"

"Nope. It doesn't."

"Everything okay?"

"As okay as it ever is, I'd imagine."

"That doesn't sound encouraging," he goaded her.

"How are you?" Jameson shifted the conversation.

"Grateful you and Candy hosted this."

Jameson laughed.

"Momma," Cooper tugged Jameson's hand.

"Hey, Coop. I thought you and Spence were outside?"

"Spence hurt himself."

Jameson almost groaned aloud. *Again?* "Where's Spence?" As if on cue Spencer appeared, holding his nose. "What happened, buddy?"

"The swing hit him in the nose," Cooper explained.

"Never a dull moment," Jameson muttered.

"I looked for Marianne," Cooper said.

Jameson smiled and put a hand on each boys' back. "She's upstairs with Shell. Come on, let's go clean you up."

"Do you want me to go find Marianne?" David offered.

"Don't worry about it," Jameson said. "She'll appear sooner or later."

***

"Shell? Are you sure you're okay?" Marianne asked.

"Would you two stop fussing?" Michelle scolded her sister and her wife.

"You look a little flushed, babe," Melanie said.

"It's been a long day. I don't get to face it with wine like the two of you."

Marianne rolled her eyes. "Well, just lie down up here for a little while and humor us."

"I'm not dying, you know? I'm pregnant," Michelle reminded them.

"Babe," Melanie urged her wife.

"Oh, for God's sake!" Michelle protested. "Mom's got a conference call now. I told her I'd be there."

"One look at you, and she'll send you to bed too," Marianne said.

"Oh, please. She's done this more than the two of us put together. I'm fine."

Melanie sighed heavily. "You're impossible."

"No, I'm reasonable. You two are impossible. Now, I'm going downstairs to see Mom. You two go do whatever it is you do when you're not harassing me."

Melanie covered her face with her hands. "I give up."

Marianne put an arm around her sister-in-law. "Let her go. She knows her limits."

"Does she?" Melanie questioned. "You know, the doctor told her yesterday that she could go any time now. Twins. She said it's not uncommon."

"She also told you everything looked good, right?"

"Yeah, but…"

"Would it be terrible if she went early?"

"That's almost a month early!" Melanie's voice cracked.

Marianne sensed Melanie's unease was greater than she had realized. Michelle's pregnancy had been uneventful for the most part. Truth be told, Marianne could tell that her sister was fatigued, uncomfortable, and nervous. Michelle's way of handling all three was to deny she felt any of it and keep going. That had always been Michelle's way of dealing with stress—throw herself into a project, make jokes, and avoid thinking about what was bothering her as much as possible.

"She's nervous," Marianne said.

"Not according to her."

"You know Shell. She talks a good game. If I were you, I'd get ready for those two little ones to arrive sooner rather than later."

"Why?" Melanie asked.

"Call it intuition. Shell's a bundle of energy when most women would want a nap."

"And you think that means she's going to deliver early?"

"I think it means Shell senses something."

Melanie turned pale. "Oh, God."

"Mel, relax." Marianne giggled. "Shell's at 36 weeks."

"Which is why she should rest. Doctor Bridges said 38 weeks is optimal."

Marianne tried not to laugh. *Optimal for who?* "Didn't she also say 37 weeks was the average?"

"Yeah. That's why she hesitated to let Shell go to Pennsylvania. It was too much. Now, this—What if…"

"Everything will be okay," Marianne said.

"I'm sorry, Marianne. I don't mean to be dumping on you. You just lost your grandmother."

"And, you're about to become someone's mother. It's okay. I get it. Believe me; I get it. Shell alone could make you nuts. Shell pregnant with twins? Hell, I'd saint you myself if I could."

Melanie laughed. "Thanks."

"What do you say you and I go raid JD's beer?"

"Think there's any left?" Melanie asked.

"I know where she hides the stash. It's not far from Mom's cookies."

"That didn't sound good."

Marianne shrugged. "At least it's not near the Bible."

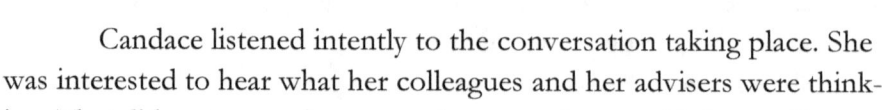

Candace listened intently to the conversation taking place. She was interested to hear what her colleagues and her advisers were thinking. That did not mean that anyone's perception would change Candace's intentions. She would listen.

"It hasn't had any effect on the base—not from our polling," Glenn offered.

"No, but it hasn't had any on Wolfe's either," Doug chimed. "And, right now he's a sure bet to secure the nomination in California. So, we're not getting any wind in our sails from it either. We're running neck and neck for a general. I wish we knew who leaked this and why now."

"There's got to be something we can float to tamp down interest in this story," Glenn said. "Dana?"

Dana cleared her throat. "I suggest we let it a have as much oxygen as it needs."

Candace smiled.

"What?" Doug raised his voice. "Why? We're not getting any messaging out right now with this taking up all the air."

"It's only a few days in," Dana replied calmly. "Let it run its course."

"Candy?" Doug asked for Candace's support over the line.

"I agree with Dana," Candace said.

"You can't be serious," Glenn said with disbelief.

"I'm completely serious. Let it suck up the oxygen. The hotter it burns, the faster it will die out."

"Not if you don't contain it," Glenn argued.

"It's contained," Candace said.

"We must not be looking at the same papers," he said.

"Glenn, let it be. Dana is right. Let it consume itself or be consumed by the next big thing." Candace looked up and saw Michelle as she walked through the door. She tilted her head curiously. Michelle looked a bit unsteady. "What else?" Candace asked.

"You have a call with Reverend Gilford Sunday afternoon before the roundtable of local policing Monday," Doug said. "We need his support."

"We'll have it," Candace said. "Is that it?" She kept her eyes on Michelle as Michelle adjusted her position in a chair.

"I wonder if we should be asking you that," Glenn said. "I can't help but feel there's something you aren't telling us."

"There's always something I'm not telling you," Candace quipped. "The question is whether you need to know it." She chuckled when she heard an audible groan fly from both Glenn and Doug. "Stay focused and on track," she said. "You let me worry about my job. You worry about yours. I'll see you both Monday." She disconnected the call. "Well, that went well."

"Sorry, I was late," Michelle apologized.

"You didn't miss anything," Dana said. "Believe me."

"Shell? Are you okay?" Candace asked.

Michelle offered her mother an unconvincing nod.

"Dana, would you..."

"Sure. I should get home unless you need anything else," Dana replied.

"No, just keep your eyes on what we discussed."

"On it," Dana promised. "See you later, Shell."

Michelle nodded, took a deep breath and released it.

"Feel like telling me what's going on?" Candace asked.

"I'm not sure."

"Okay." Candace made her way around her desk to Michelle. "Something's bothering you."

"Just don't say anything to Mel."

Candace's brow shot up into her hairline. "Michelle, what is going on?"

"I told you; I'm not really sure. I just… Mom…"

Candace sighed. "Are you having contractions?"

"I don't know. Cramps. Kind of. It started a while ago. It's probably all the water I drank."

Candace pursed her lips. "Possibly. How strong are they?"

"Just uncomfortable."

"You need to tell Melanie."

"Mom, she'll have me on the way to the hospital before I even get to say no."

"I'm not so sure that's a bad idea."

"What?"

"No offense, sweetheart, I can tell you aren't feeling like yourself."

"You try having two bowling balls sit on your bladder."

Candace smiled. "I know you're scared. You need to call the doctor."

"She'll tell us to come in too."

"Maybe. Maybe not. And, if she does that is where you need to go."

"It's too soon," Michelle muttered.

"It's only too soon if those two little ones say it is." Candace clasped her daughter's hand.

"Mom, not today. I don't want to make this day worse for you."

"Me?" Candace shook her head. "I know I call you all a bunch of lunatics, but I never thought you were actually crazy. What on earth are you talking about?"

"This—all of this. You have a house full of family, and I know the last couple of days have been…"

"Stop," Candace put the thought to rest. "Stop being my mother. You'll have plenty of practice mothering soon enough." She squeezed Michelle's hand. "Do you want me to get Mel?"

Michelle nodded reluctantly. Candace started to pull away. Michelle tugged on her hand. "Mom, what if…"

"It'll be fine, Shell," Candace promised. "Wait here."

Candace steadied herself as she walked out the door toward the living room.

"Done already?" Jameson caught her in the hallway. "Candace? Did something happen?"

Candace shook her head. "Can you get Mel and come to the office?"

"Are we getting detention again?" Jameson cracked.

Candace sighed. "It's Shell. She's having some contractions."

"Oh, no."

"Not you too," Candace said. "She'll be okay. She needs all of us to be okay."

Jameson nodded. "Maybe you should get Melanie. I'll sit with Mel."

"See if you can get her to call the doctor."

"Me?"

"Yes, you. Where's Mel?"

"She was with Marianne in the kitchen last I saw."

Candace nodded her thanks. "Take a breath, honey. You look almost as nervous as Shell."

Jameson made her way to the office and stopped just outside. "You'd think I would be used to this by now," she muttered. *Here goes.* "Shell?"

Michelle looked up sheepishly.

"How are you doing?" Jameson asked.

"Nervous."

"Yeah, I get that. Your mom's getting Mel right now. Maybe you should call the doctor while we wait."

Michelle bit her lip.

"Shell, come on. You'll feel better once you call."

"I left my phone in Mel's bag."

Jameson took out her phone and handed it to her step-daughter. "Use mine."

Candace heard Melanie and Marianne laughing. She hoped that the jovial atmosphere might help to keep Melanie calm. As adept as Candace had become at placating the fears of others, it remained a challenge with those closest to her. Candace was confident that all would be well with Michelle. She'd accompanied Michelle to her last doctor's appointment. She also understood that this was Michelle's first pregnancy. Michelle's inclination to joke often masked her insecurity. Candace knew that too. Melanie would need to be the voice of reason and calm now.

"Sounds like a party in here," Candace entered the room.

"We found JD's beer," Marianne explained.

"Well, I hate to interrupt the pub tour, but I think Mel is needed elsewhere."

Melanie turned pale.

Marianne smiled and took hold of Melanie's hand while she addressed her mother. "Let me guess, Shell's in labor."

"I'm not sure it's labor," Candace said. "You know how this goes."

"I seem to have some memory of it," Marianne quipped.

Melanie pushed out her chair. "She's freaking out, isn't she?"

Candace chuckled. "A little. She's in my office with Jameson."

Melanie nodded. "Thanks." Without another word, she headed to find her wife.

"She's calmer than I imagined," Candace observed.

"Yeah. I don't think she's that surprised," Marianne said. "How about Shell?"

"She's scared."

"Normal."

"Sure is," Candace agreed. "Want to help offer some moral support?"

Marianne grabbed her beer.

"You're taking that?" Candace asked.

"Hey, I get to have moral support too."

Candace snickered. *Lunatics—all of them.*

Marianne wandered into the kitchen to find Candace at the table sipping a cup of tea. "Shell call yet?"

"About ten minutes ago. The kids go down okay?"

"Yeah. What did she say?"

"They're sending her home—on bed rest."

"Oh, that must've gone over well."

Candace laughed. "Actually, I think she's so relieved, she's okay with it."

"How's Mel?"

"Tired. Sounds like Shell could go any minute. I think they'd like to push it another week or two if possible."

"How's JD?" Marianne asked. "She looked almost as pale as Shell."

"You know her. She worries about all of you."

"Mmm."

"What?"

Marianne sighed. "I think she's worried about you right now."

"I'm all right, Marianne."

"No offense, Mom but for a politician, you are a horrible liar."

Candace toyed with the tea bag in her cup. It had been a long, stressful week. She was used to that scenario. It had also been overwhelmingly emotional. Denying that fact seemed pointless. Marianne would see through it just as Jameson could. "It's been a long week."

"Do you want to talk about it?" Marianne asked.

Did she? Candace had cried plenty of tears in Jameson's arms since her mother's stroke and subsequent death. She'd shared memories and thoughts with Jameson. She hadn't waded into her feelings. Candace wasn't entirely sure what she did feel. The emotions that coursed through her seemed to change like the wind. She'd kept them in check during the day. When evening fell, Candace lost all hope of willing her heart into submission.

"You don't have to, Mom."

"It's not that," Candace replied. "For once, I'm not sure what to say. I know that's hard to believe."

"Not really. That's how I felt when I heard the news about Rick."

"I wish you had never had to go through that. Not the same, honey. Rick was…"

"It's not the same but it's similar."

"I don't think…"

"I know you don't think so," Marianne stopped her mother's protest. "One the hardest parts of losing Rick was having to decide to let him go. I knew that's what he would want. I knew he was already gone. Somehow, that's been the most painful thing to reconcile."

Candace understood. She'd been lying awake every night. Inevitably, the thought passed through her mind that she was responsible for her mother's death. Logically, she knew that wasn't true. Logic failed to reason with the guilt she felt.

Marianne watched her mother closely. She'd had many conversations with her mother after Rick's death. They'd grown closer than they had ever been. Marianne had made peace with her husband's death, as much as any person could. She enjoyed a closer relationship with her mother than ever before. Her friendship with Jameson had blossomed, something she was certain Rick would have loved to see. And, she had met Scott. Scott would never be Rick, but she did love him, so much so that she anticipated they would take their relationship to the next level. Marianne had one benefit that Candace did not. She had always been aware of Rick's love for her. He'd been more than a husband and lover; he had been Marianne's best friend. She had no questions left unanswered about how he viewed her or how he felt about their marriage. Candace had not enjoyed a close relationship with her mother. That left questions unanswered. Marianne imagined those questions had to make Marjorie Stratton's passing doubly hard for her mother.

"Mom, you know those were Grandma's wishes?"

"I know. She wouldn't have wanted to see herself that way. I know that. That doesn't make it easier."

"Not now, but it will. In time, it will."

Candace smiled. "She never wanted me to go to law school, you know?"

"Really?"

"After your father and I got married, she couldn't understand why I would need a career."

"What did Grandpa think?"

"I don't know." Candace chuckled. "What your grandfather thought tended to be overshadowed by what your grandmother told him to think."

Marianne laughed. "She was larger than life."

Candace sobered. *Was she?* "Maybe. It's a funny thing, Marianne—the way you see life as you get older."

"What do you mean?"

"Just that. I'm not sure it's anything that I can explain. Tonight, when I saw Shell, my heart dropped. I just wanted to make it all okay. That never changes. No matter how old your children get, no matter how many children they have themselves, they're still that little boy or girl with the scraped knee."

"I think I get that."

"It's the same with your parents. They've always been there—good, bad, ugly—they've been part of your world since before your first breath. As much as you know they're likely to leave you, you're never ready to let them go. Almost as if you expect them to be immortal."

Marianne listened attentively. She remembered when her grandfather had died. Marianne had been nine. Michelle was only five and Jonah was still in diapers. She remembered her mother weeping in her father's embrace. She hadn't witnessed great affection between her parents often, and that image had stuck with her all these years. Candace's revelations brought the memory back vividly. It left her with a pit in her stomach. One day, she would likely mourn her parents.

"Mom?"

"Yeah?"

"Do you remember when Grandpa Stratton died?"

"Of course. You were nine."

"I don't remember it all that much except seeing Dad holding you in the kitchen while you cried."

"None of us saw that coming," Candace said. "Your father was a rock for me."

"Really?"

Candace smiled. "Your grandmother made a point to be in control. I think she dabbed a few tears at his service. She didn't say much. She made plans. That's who she was."

"And Dad?"

"Your father is a good man, Marianne; you know that. I wasn't good for him and he wasn't good for me. That doesn't mean we didn't love each other."

"Did you? Love him?"

"Of course. I was never in love with him. I think he would say the same. I'll tell you the truth. I was mad as hell at my daddy for leaving me to deal with your grandmother." Candace chuckled. "Daddy was easy. My mother? Impossible to please—at least, for me. Your father knew that. It made me feel awful. She didn't comfort any of us. And, she didn't want us to comfort her. I remember David pounding his fist against the side of the house. He was so angry with her."

"Do you think Grandpa loved her?" Marianne asked.

Candace's eyes glistened. "I do. I don't know how much she let him love her, though. I'm not sure she let anyone love her, Marianne. Maybe that's why this hurts so much."

"What do you mean?"

"You know, your father and I, we weren't always kind to each other. I always knew he cared about me. He still does."

"I know."

"I still care about him. You and your brother and sister mean the world to us both."

"I know that too."

"It's hard for him to show that. He tries. It's hard for him. It was hard for him with me too. In some ways, he reminds me of my mother."

Marianne nodded. Her father struggled to show affection. He'd made a considerable effort to get to know all his children in recent years, but she accepted that he would never be the parent to bandage skinned knees or broken hearts no matter how much he wanted to. He was closest to Marianne, and even she recognized his struggle. "I can see that," Marianne commented.

"He tries," Candace observed. "More now than when he was younger."

"And, Grandma didn't—try, I mean."

"I used to think that."

"And, now?"

Candace sighed. "Now, I wonder who my mother was. I wonder what happened to make her so afraid to love. I spent most of my life angry with her. Now? Now, I wish I had asked that question."

"Do you think she would have answered?"

"I don't know." Candace paused for a long moment. "I tried."

"She knew you loved her."

"Mm. I meant that I tried not to. I think I almost convinced myself that I didn't. I did. I still do. I had convinced myself she didn't love me."

"Mom…"

"I had, Marianne. Then I remembered this time when I was about six. The last few days, I've been remembering," Candace's thought trailed off.

"Mom?"

"Sorry. More like impressions, not memories. She did love me. I wish that made it easier. Somehow, it just leaves me with more questions."

"Well, for whatever it's worth, I love you."

Candace smiled. "It's worth everything." She stood and placed her teacup in the sink. "I should head up. Jameson probably thinks I've polished off the wine rack by now."

Marianne laughed. "Night, Mom."

"Goodnight, sweetheart." Candace kissed Marianne's head. "Thanks for the talk."

Marianne watched as Candace left the room. Her thoughts drifted through memory after memory of the woman who had given her life. She closed her eyes to savor them. Loss had a way of reminding a person to value each moment and every person. Not everyone was blessed with parents they could both admire and trust. Marianne had the privilege of getting to know her mother in a way that many children never would. She recognized the woman that Candace was. She could see the way Candace loved Jameson, the persona she took on when she campaigned, the wisdom of a grandparent, and even the insecurities of the child Candace had been. That didn't change the fact that first and foremost, Candace Reid was her mother.

There was one thing Candace had not expressed that Marianne was positive plagued her mother's fears—the day she would lose Pearl. Marianne found herself offering a silent prayer that it would be many years before she would have to mourn the woman who had given her life. That loss would leave a hole that Marianne found unfathomable. It took her breath away. "I love you so much, Mom."

CHAPTER FOUR

JUNE 1ˢᵗ

"**A**re they really going to call Mom to testify?" Michelle asked as she patted her daughter's back gently.

"Looks like it," Jameson said.

"What the hell? Right before the convention? That's not deliberate," Michelle observed sarcastically.

Jameson shrugged and finished fastening a diaper around her grandson's waist. "What do you think Brody? Nana can handle those good 'ole boys, can't she?" She put Brody down in the portable crib.

"How is Mom?"

Jameson laughed when her granddaughter spit up all over Michelle's shoulder. "Better than you," she said.

"Ha-ha."

Jameson shook her head with amusement. Amanda and Brody had arrived three weeks early—right on time for a pair of what Jameson imagined would be precocious twins.

Michelle handed Jameson the baby. "Can you take her while I change my shirt?"

"Sure. Just don't ask me to pump anything."

"Why not? I'll bet Mom does," Michelle called from the next room.

Jameson rolled her eyes. "Your mother is nuts," she told the baby in her arms.

"I heard that! And, it runs in the family!"

"Can't argue with her there, little one. Just know, that runs on the Fletcher side."

"Sure, it does," Michelle said as she came back into the room. "That's why Mom calls you a lunatic all the time."

"Survival technique."

"Right. So? Mom is really okay with this?"

"You know your mother. She's not going to give them the satisfaction of being rattled."

"What about you?"

"I'm not testifying to anything."

"Very funny." Michelle took Amanda from Jameson and placed her next to Brody in the crib. "I meant your meeting with Dana."

"Oh, that."

"That good, huh?"

"A media relations person? Come on, Shell? Who cares about me?"

"You're kidding right now."

"No."

"JD, seriously? You do realize that when Mom gets elected you will have a staff too? You'll have formal appearances and…"

"Don't remind me."

Michelle sighed. "People want to connect with you."

"Why? Shell, I'm an architect who likes to get my hands dirty."

"Yeah, I'd be careful how you phrase that one. And, leave the Bible out."

"Cute." Jameson groaned. "Hire a media adviser? A press secretary? Who's gonna' want *that* job?"

"How about me?"

Jameson stared at Michelle blankly.

"Thanks for the vote of confidence."

"It's not that. You? Shell, don't you have enough on your plate right now?"

"I hear Gollum is looking for a job if you'd rather give him a call."

"No thanks. I like my ankles in one piece."

"Okay, so let me help you out."

"Oh, I get it. You help me, and that means I get more diaper duty."

"We can negotiate."

Jameson laughed. "Shell, seriously—you have enough to deal with right now."

"Seriously, JD, I love being here with the twins. More than I thought I would—if you want to know the truth."

"I know you do."

"But, it's been three weeks and Mel is ready to kill me already."

"I'm sure that's not true."

"Yeah, it is. I need to help somehow. I can't travel with Mom, not at the pace she has to keep. I can help you. Even Dana thinks it's a good idea."

"Your mom will never agree to this."

Michelle grinned.

"You have got to be kidding me. How did you get her on board with this crazy idea?"

"Wasn't my crazy idea; it was hers."

Jameson's jaw dropped.

"Don't look so surprised. Mom knows you better than anyone. You're going to be forced to make more appearances without her. You know that. I can help you with that. I want to, so let me."

"I can't believe she didn't say anything to me."

"I asked her to let me talk to you about it. JD, look, the truth is I miss you guys. And, I want to help…"

Jameson held up her hand. "You don't have to take anything else on. You've helped your mom plenty."

"I don't see helping you as taking anything else on. JD, I don't want to sit the rest of this campaign out. Believe it or not, I do have some idea what I'm doing. Mom trusts that I can handle this. Dana thinks it's a win. Mel does too. Can't you at least give it a try?"

Jameson did believe that Michelle could handle it. She'd been worrying about her ability to do Candace justice on the big stage. Jameson wasn't a public speaker and she'd never desired public attention. She did need guidance. She trusted Michelle. Jameson understood Candace's reasoning. She resented the fact that Candace had blindsided her. That was not Shell's issue. She took a deep breath. "Okay, Shell."

Michelle smiled. "You'll have groupies before you know it."

"Great."

———◆━◆●◆◆———

Candace took off her glasses and massaged the bridge of her nose. She'd been running at full speed since before the sun came up. Meetings, conference calls, more meetings, legislative proposal reviews, a few more calls, and a convention all needed her attention. She heard the rap on her door and groaned. "I don't want any!"

Jameson opened the door and peered inside. "Okay, I'll take it back."

Candace laughed. "Get in here. What are you doing here? I thought you were at Shell's?"

"You mean you thought I was meeting with my media adviser?"

Candace grimaced.

"Um-hum. When did you plan to tell me about this master plan you two concocted?"

"Jameson, I…"

"I get it. I wish you would have told me."

"Shell wanted to pitch you the idea."

Candace's words struck a nerve. Jameson had been trying to calm her anger on the drive to Albany. "Pitch me the idea? What am I, one of your minions?"

"Jameson…"

"Don't. Don't do that. Don't talk to me like I have no idea what is going on."

"That wasn't my intention or Shell's."

"I know that. I'd rather hear what you're thinking from you and not your daughter."

"Point taken."

"I know that you're stressed. I can see it. Don't shut me out."

Candace sighed heavily. "I'm sorry."

"Don't shut me out, Candace. This isn't easy for me."

"I know that. I want to help."

"You can help by telling me what you're thinking. My God, you discussed this with Dana? Shell? Shell discussed it with Melanie?"

"You made your point," Candace snapped.

"Did I? Are you even listening to me?"

"Are we seriously going to argue about this?"

"We are if you aren't going to take it seriously," Jameson replied evenly.

"Why are you so opposed to this? I know you aren't in love with the idea of making speeches and doing interviews. I was trying to make that a little easier for you. Shell is a pro, Jameson—a pro who loves you."

"I love Shell. That's not the point and you know it."

"What is your point?" Candace asked harshly.

A disbelieving chuckle passed Jameson's lips. "You know what? Maybe you were right when I knocked."

"What are you talking about?"

Jameson turned and opened the door. "I'll leave you to it, Governor. You let me know when my wife is available." Jameson walked through the door and let it close behind her.

Candace threw her head back. "Shit."

<hr>

"Momma?" Cooper called for Jameson's attention.

"I'm sorry, Coop. What did you say?"

Cooper frowned. Jameson had been telling him a story and had drifted into silence after he had asked her a question. "Are you mad at me?"

"Mad at you? Cooper, why would I be mad at you?"

"You're mad."

"I'm not mad," Jameson said.

"Are you mad at Mommy?"

Jameson smiled. *Way to go, JD.* "I'm not mad at anyone, buddy; I promise."

"How come you yelled?"

"When did I yell?"

"On the phone with Grandma."

Jameson mentally slapped herself. Her mother had called when Cooper was in the bathtub. She'd recapped her conversation with Michelle and the argument that followed with Candace. True to form, Maureen Reid had attempted to calm Jameson. Jameson perceived that as her mother siding with Candace—again. Sometimes, they both made her feel like a child. That was not a feeling Jameson appreciated. She was angry. More than that, Jameson was hurt. She accepted what loving Candace meant. That didn't prevent her from struggling with certain realities. Speaking in front of large crowds, giving solo interviews on television—those inevitabilities were far outside Jameson's comfort zone. She was content to stand in Candace's shadow. The spotlight unnerved her. Now, she would be forced to stand in it without Candace by her side. The last thing she needed was to feel pushed aside. It wasn't Candace's idea to have Michelle coach her that upset Jameson. It was the knowledge that everyone had input into the idea except Jameson. When her mother expressed the possibility that Jameson was overreacting, Jameson had cut off the conversation abruptly, not quietly.

"I'm sorry, Coop. I'm not mad. I'm just a little tired."

"Want me to tell you a story instead?" Cooper offered.

Awww, Coop. "I love your stories."

Cooper beamed. "'Kay." He patted his bed. "Lay down, Momma and I'll tell you a good one."

Jameson laid down beside her son and pulled him into her arms. She thought her heart might burst from the gratefulness she felt. Her thoughts immediately spiraled to Candace. She hated being angry. She and Candace seldom fought. This was one of the few instances when Jameson felt the need to hold her ground, even if it tore her apart inside.

"Once upon a time," Cooper began.

Dana was surprised to see Candace at her desk. "You're still here?"

"Why not? You are."

Dana's brow furrowed. Candace tended to be even-tempered. She was sure that Candace was tired; everyone was. Something else was nagging at the governor. "Want to tell me who pissed you off?"

"Not really."

"So, someone did piss you off."

Candace chuckled uncomfortably. "More like I pissed someone off."

"Well, no offense, but that is a daily occurrence."

Candace laughed.

"So? What gives?" Dana asked.

"Jameson gives."

"Come again."

Candace closed her laptop and reclined in her chair. "Jameson—she talked to Shell today."

"She doesn't like the idea of Shell working with her?"

"More like she didn't like the fact that everyone knew about that idea before she did."

"I don't think I…"

"She's right," Candace said. "She usually is."

"I'm not following."

"Well, I brought the idea to you. You thought it was great."

"Right… Shell's been nagging you since she was in the hospital to let her help somehow."

"That's not the issue. I discussed it with you. We brought it to Shell. Shell talked it over with Melanie…"

"Oh, boy… and, JD was the last to hear it."

Candace's brow arched in acknowledgment.

"I think I understand, but no one did that intentionally."

"No, but that's almost worse. I've been so caught up in keeping up that I kept her out."

"What are you talking about?"

Candace rubbed her eyes. "I did. She's right. I shut her out."

"Candy, you have had more on your plate than anyone should have to deal with since you clinched the nomination. Aside from all the everyday responsibilities you have here, you lost your mother; Shell had the twins, you've had the convention and vetting Vice Presidential candidates. I mean—come on, give yourself a break."

"Maybe so. Put yourself in her position, Dana. Jameson has given up everything to support me."

"I don't think she sees it that way."

"No, I know she doesn't see it that way. She's had to compromise more than anyone. The one thing she asked of me was not to shut her out. That's exactly what I did. I made a decision that affects her like I would a decision about a stump speech."

"That's not what you did."

"Isn't it?" Candace shook her head. "I fucked up, Dana."

"So, tell her that you're sorry."

"I don't think sorry is going to cover this one."

"Candy, JD loves you more than anything."

"That's why she's so hurt," Candace observed. "And, she has every right to be."

"Beating yourself up isn't going to make it better."

"Maybe not. I can't help it right now. She's the last person I want to see hurt in any of this craziness. And, I'm the one who hurt her."

Dana often marveled at the change in Candace since meeting Jameson. She did not doubt that if Jameson asked Candace to bow out of the race, Candace would. She'd known Jameson for more than twenty years. One thing Dana was certain of, few people loved each other as completely as Jameson and Candace Reid. To many looking in, the couple appeared picture-perfect. They weren't. They were human. Dana witnessed exhaustion, regret, and pain in Candace's eyes. She also recognized what Candace needed now. "Go home," Dana said. "Tell her, not me."

Candace nodded. "Thanks."

"It's my job."

"And you do it well."

"I'll see you tomorrow."

"You will."

"Candy?"

"Hum?"

"Any closer to making that pick?"

Candace smiled. She hadn't told anyone that she'd settled on a running mate yet. She had. It occurred to her who she needed to share that with now. "I'll let you know."

Dana grinned knowingly. "Night. Governor."

"Goodnight."

Candace peeked into Cooper's room and smiled. Jameson was asleep. Candace was surprised to see Cooper reading a book. "Did Momma put herself to sleep?" she asked her son.

Cooper smiled. "Hi, Mommy," he whispered.

"Why are you still awake?"

Cooper shrugged. "I was telling Momma stories."

"You were?"

"Yep. Mommy?"

"Yes, sweetheart?"

"Are you mad?"

"Mad?"

"At Momma?"

Candace sat down on the edge of the bed. "No, sweetheart."

"Momma was mad tonight. She yelled at Grandma on the phone."

Candace nodded. "She had a long day."

"Yep. Then she was sad."

"She was?"

"Yeah. I could tell."

"So, you told her some stories?"

"Yep." Cooper looked over at Jameson. "I don't like it when she's sad."

"I don't either."

"Mommy?"

"Yes, Cooper?"

"Never mind."

"Cooper?"

"Can you stay with us tomorrow?"

"I wish I could, sweetheart. I have to work tomorrow."

Cooper looked down sadly.

"What about if I promise that we can have pizza tomorrow night when I get home—just the three of us?"

"Really?"

"I promise."

Cooper threw himself into Candace. The motion stirred Jameson from her sleep. She squinted to bring the room into focus.

"Hi," Candace said.

Jameson smiled. "What time is it?"

"It's late," Candace replied.

"Coop put me to sleep."

"So, I heard."

Cooper grinned proudly. "Yep. I told Momma about when Genie drove the train."

"It's a good one," Jameson said as she pulled herself from the bed.

"Mommy says we can have pizza tomorrow."

Jameson nodded. "Pizza, huh?"

"Yep! Just us."

"Just you and Mommy?" Jameson teased.

"No! And you, Momma."

"Oh, I get to have pizza too?"

"Yep!"

"Do I have to make it?" Jameson asked.

"No. You buy it, Momma!"

Jameson chuckled. "All right, pizza boy. Lights out."

Cooper pulled up his blanket and snuggled his pillow.

"Goodnight, sweetheart." Candace kissed Cooper's forehead. "I'll see you tomorrow."

"'Kay."

Jameson flipped off the light and followed Candace from the room.

"We need to talk," Candace said.

"I know. No offense, you look exhausted. It can wait."

"No, it can't," Candace disagreed. "Not this."

"Do you want to go downstairs?"

Candace felt her heart drop. "I'd rather go to our room."

Jameson nodded. She held out her hand to Candace and led her down the hall. She closed the bedroom door and was taken off guard when she turned to find tears in Candace's eyes. "Why are you crying?"

"I'm so tired, Jameson."

Jameson folded Candace into her embrace. "I know that."

"I'm so sorry."

"I know that too. What I don't know is why you're crying."

Candace stepped away. "I told you; I'm tired."

"I can see that."

"You weren't wrong earlier."

Jameson listened.

"I should have talked to you first. I don't know why I didn't."

"Maybe because it didn't occur to you that you needed to," Jameson offered.

"Jameson, I…"

"Just hear me out."

"Okay."

"You're so used to having to direct everyone and everything that I fell into that category. I know you didn't mean for that to happen. That is what happened, Candace. It didn't seem like a big deal. I know it didn't—not to you. You did what you would do with any decision on your campaign. You brought it to the experts."

Candace covered her face. Jameson had nailed it. That's exactly what she had done. "I didn't mean to."

"Yeah, I know. You need to slow down for a minute."

"How am I supposed to do that?" Candace snapped.

Jameson raised her brow.

"I'm sorry."

"I don't want you to be sorry. I want you to take a breath, and not just for me. You can't be everything to everyone all the time. You're running so fast," Jameson stopped and pointed to her head. "Up here. You are always running. You haven't taken any time to be quiet. You aren't sleeping. You can't go on like this. I can't go on like this. You need to talk to me, Candace. And, lately? It feels like you are avoiding that. Ever since your mom…"

"I'm sorry."

"You can't fill up that hole with work."

Candace collapsed in defeat onto the bed and put her face in her hands. Jameson knew her better than anyone.

"What happened with us earlier, that happened because you are on auto-pilot," Jameson said.

"I didn't mean to hurt you. You are the last person I want to hurt."

Jameson sat beside her wife. "I know that. I know you. Candace, everyone is spinning in circles around you. You need be the one to slow that down. I may not be the political wonk in this family. I do know that you can't go on like this. You can't."

"What about you?"

"What about me? I love you. Do you understand why I'm up-set?"

"I didn't mean to make you an oversight."

"That's exactly my point. You didn't mean to, but it still hap-pened. You're on autopilot when you're home lately. The campaign? Your job? Those aren't the cause. Those are your escape. Talk to me."

Candace looked up and met Jameson's expectant gaze. "I can't stop thinking about it."

"Your mother?"

"Not just that. That, but... How did she get that way? What happened to the woman I remember putting ice on my lip? She just disappeared. How does someone disappear when they are still there? What makes a person do that?"

Jameson took Candace's hands with hers. "I think you know that answer."

"Do I?"

"Look at the last few weeks. You're doing the same thing without knowing it. Maybe not the same way. You say, 'I love you.'"

"I do love you."

"You're not listening to me. You're hurting—more than I think I have ever seen you hurt. This has brought it all back up for you—every loss. Tell me that I'm wrong?"

Candace closed her eyes.

"You're scared. You can control this campaign. You can get people marching in line without them even knowing it. You can't control life and death. Don't shut me out. Talk to me."

"I don't know what's wrong with me, Jameson. I look at Cooper and I find myself terrified. What if something happens to me? What was I thinking? I'm sixty. Look at you; you have your whole life in front of you."

"So, do you."

"You know what I mean."

"We've been through this for years. When are you going to let this go?"

"I don't want to let you down, Jameson. That includes leaving you alone. Cooper—the kids. Jesus. Then, I start thinking about my mother again, and then Pearl."

Bingo. Jameson pulled Candace into her arms. "Let it go, Candace. Just let it go."

"I don't know how."

"You're allowed to be afraid."

"Am I?"

"Yes."

"What if…"

"Aren't you the one who always says there are no 'what ifs' in life?"

Candace giggled through a few tears. "Easier to give that advice than to take it."

"You don't say."

"I love you so much, Jameson. I haven't done a very good job of showing you that lately."

"I wouldn't say that." Jameson pushed Candace away so that she could look in her eyes.

Candace pursed her lips doubtfully.

"You are so busy trying to be everything to everyone, trying to show everyone that you do love them, that you aren't letting us love you. I just see it because I'm not caught in that same spin."

"Something tells me you're not the only one who's noticed."

"Marianne may have mentioned she was concerned about you."

"What if I can't handle this?"

"Another what if?" Jameson winked at Candace. "Candace, you can handle anything anyone throws at you."

"I wish that were true."

"It is. You just have to remember *why* that is. You're not your mother. You might never know why she was the way she was. Don't let her sadness become yours. You didn't cause that. If anything, you were probably the thing that kept her going all those years."

"I'm not so sure about that. I do hear you."

"Good."

"I am sorry. I don't want to shut you out. I don't want to see you hurt. I seem to be the one doing that lately."

"We have a lot in common. I don't like seeing you hurt either. Nothing is harder for me than that—nothing."

Candace took Jameson's face in her hands. "I love you, Jameson. I wish I could show you how much."

Jameson laid back on the bed and pulled Candace to her. "You do. You can show me right now by closing your eyes and going to sleep."

"Can I get out of these clothes first?"

"Will that lead to sleep?"

Candace kissed Jameson soundly. "Tonight—yes; tomorrow…"

Jameson smiled at Candace as Candace stood and shed her clothes. "I thought we were having pizza tomorrow?"

Candace climbed back onto the bed and kissed Jameson again. "Don't they have pizza with Bible Study?"

Jameson sensed that Candace had turned the corner she had been resisting. She imagined it was far from the last turn they would need to navigate. She was confident they would always find their way around the curves. "And, you call me a lunatic."

"Maybe I just needed familiar company."

Jameson laughed. "I'll remember that. I love you, Candace."

"I love you too."

"Get some sleep."

"I didn't expect to see you today." Marianne opened the door for Jameson and Cooper. "Hi, Coop."

"Hi, Marianne!"

"Spencer is in his room."

"'Kay!"

"And, he's off." Jameson laughed.

"Not that I'm not happy to see you, but why am I seeing you?" Marianne asked.

"Your mom wanted to get away before next week's chaos."

"Perfect timing with Scott and I taking the kids away this weekend."

Jameson shrugged.

"How is Mom?"

"Better, I think."

"She's taking Grandma's death hard."

"Harder than she would have expected," Jameson agreed. "I think this weekend will be good for her. Big announcement Wednesday. She's headed out of state Monday evening."

"She chose a running mate?"

Jameson nodded.

"Did she tell you who it is?"

"She did—this morning before she left."

"Well?" Marianne urged.

"Seriously? She'll kill me."

"She can't kill you. Granted, as far as I'm concerned, jail would be less stressful than the presidency, but..."

"Not arguing with you there."

"Come on, tell me!"

Jameson was enjoying her game. Teasing Michelle and Jonah was easy. She seldom had the chance to get under Marianne's skin playfully. Candace had told Jameson that she expected the news of her choice to leak to the press later that afternoon. Jameson would never understand why there was such a build-up to big announcements and appearances if the news was going to be deliberately leaked out in advance. That was Candace's department.

"I didn't think you were interested in politics," Jameson said.

"JD!"

"You remind me of Shell right now."

"Are you seriously not going to tell me?"

"Got any coffee made?" Jameson asked.

"Bribery? Really?"

Jameson shrugged.

"No, but I'll make you some," Marianne said.

"Oh, you really are curious. You usually tell me I know where to find it."

"JD!"

Jameson laughed. "Okay! Geez."

"Who did she choose? Please tell me it isn't Keyes."

Jameson shuddered. "After that primary campaign? No, your mother is not a masochist."

"Thanks for *that*."

"You're welcome."

"So?" Marianne set about starting a fresh pot of coffee.

"She said that she wrestled with the final two. She settled on Nate Ellison."

"You're kidding? That's kind of a fringe pick, isn't it?"

"Don't ask me. She said he fits the bill."

It was no secret that Marianne did not share her mother and sister's taste for politics. She did stay informed, particularly about anything that pertained to her mother's career. Nathan (Nate) Ellison was forty-four-years-old, energetic, handsome, a life-long Catholic who served as the junior senator from Nevada. Most people expected her mother to choose a moderate Southerner. Ellison's mother had moved to the states from Mexico when she was two and raised her children to be bilingual. His father had been a decorated Navy officer and pilot before being killed in a car crash when Ellison was in his senior year of college. Ellison was passionate about immigration, far more moderate on gun control than Candace, and widely regarded as a politician who desired to be the people's voice. Marianne imagined that much of her mother's staff would be suffering from heartburn over the decision.

"He's as liberal as she is," Marianne said.

Jameson shrugged. "Well, she knows what she's doing. She did say Doug was pissed."

"I'll bet he was."

"You know her; it's not all about the election."

"Does she seem happy about it?"

"I don't know about happy. She seems confident," Jameson said.

"What about you?"

"Me? Doesn't have anything to do with me."

"Come on; you must have an opinion."

"I like Ellison," Jameson said. "As long as he has your mom's back, he's good with me."

"So, let me guess? She's headed to Nevada next week."

"Looks like it. Then to Arizona and Texas."

"Arizona and Texas?"

Jameson offered Marianne another shrug. "I told you; don't ask me. I go where I'm told."

"So? What about you?"

"What about me?"

"Are you going with her?"

Jameson nodded. "Coop and I will be with her in Nevada—Ellison's family too. After that, I'm headed back. I was hoping I could talk to you about that."

"Ah, the real reason I have the pleasure of your company."

"No. I wanted to be home this weekend, so does your mom."

"The calm before the storm?" Marianne surmised.

"Something like that. Look, feel free to say no."

"JD, just tell me what you need."

"Your mom asked me to make an appearance in Illinois next Friday without her. She needs someone to appear with Congresswoman Mackey at a rally."

"Coop can stay anytime. You should know that."

"Yeah, I do. The thing is," Jameson hesitated. "He's spent so much time traveling with us, I'm surprised they're passing him into first grade."

"Coop's bright, JD."

"Yeah, but he needs to be around kids."

"I told you; Coop can stay here whenever you need him to."

"What about me?"

Marianne's brow furrowed. "What are you talking about?"

"Your mom and I talked late into the night last night. When she's in Albany it's all work, all day. Between her job as governor and the campaign, she's rolling in at 2:00 A.M. and leaving by 6:00 every morning."

"Um, JD, this is *your* house. If you want to stay here during the week, you don't need my permission."

"I know. It's more about Coop. Your mom's going to be on the road constantly after the convention."

"You will too."

"Yeah, I know. We'll take Coop when we can, but when he's not with us—I just want him to have some consistency. I don't want to impose on you or on your time with Scott, neither does your mom."

Marianne poured Jameson a cup of coffee. "Coop could never be an imposition. I seem to remember a time when you stepped in to help with my kids."

"Not the same," Jameson said.

"Yes, it is."

"Thanks."

Marianne winked. "You can thank me by keeping the wine rack and your not-so-secret cabinet of micro beers stocked."

"Deal."

Marianne sipped her cup of coffee. "Sometimes, I forget this is all real. She's really doing it. I mean, Mom might be the president."

"She will be."

"JD, are you ready for this?"

"Nope."

Marianne laughed. "That's what I thought."

"We still have time," Doug said.

"Time?" Candace asked.

"For you to make a change!"

"A change?"

"Candace! Wolfe has clinched the nomination. You can't be serious about this. Nathan Ellison? Have you lost your mind?" Doug asked.

"I guess that depends on who you ask," Candace quipped.

Dana bit her lip to keep from laughing.

"This isn't funny," Doug said.

Candace smiled.

"His concerns are valid," Grant chimed.

"Not you too," Candace said.

Grant held up a hand. "I'm just saying that he isn't the safest pick."

Candace wanted to scream. She respected her campaign advisers. At the moment, they were testing her patience.

"We vetted six possible candidates," Doug said.

"Yes, we did, and Nate is one of them," Candace replied.

"That was for optics!" Doug argued.

"Oh? And, Senator Gray and Governor Blake were for substance?" Candace challenged him. She took off her glasses and set them on her desk. "Optics. Since it's obvious that you need a lesson on the difference between optics and substance, let me give it to you."

"Candy," Glenn tried to reel in the conversation.

Candace shot her campaign manager a silent warning glare. "You expected me to choose the optimal candidate for campaign *optics*. Let me guess; a southern boy who is a fiscal moderate, attends a Baptist or Methodist church every Sunday, and speaks with a charming drawl. And, for some reason, you think that might win us votes where? In the south? You're dreaming."

"We can't lose those swing states," Doug said.

"Um-hum. You think Gray or Blake will secure Pennsylvania or Ohio?" Candace shook her head.

"They wouldn't *hurt* you there," Grant offered.

"And, you think Ellison will?" Candace asked. She heard a collective sigh filter through the room. "I disagree. You want to do what you think is tried and true. If that's the case, why are you working on this campaign?"

"Candy, that's not what anyone is saying," Glenn said.

"Sure, it is. I don't fit that bill."

"That's why Gray or Blake would have been a stabilizing choice," Doug said.

"That's your opinion, not mine. I don't need a 'stabilizing' force to win this election, I need someone who can match the energy we have behind us."

"Blake is an engaging…"

"Blake is a sixty-three-year-old from North Carolina. He's a Harvard educated lawyer whose father served as a senator for five terms. He's a nice man. He's intelligent. Two governors who are Ivy League lawyers by trade? Come on," Candace scoffed. "Could you get more boring? Besides, what does he bring to the table after the election for me?"

Doug sighed. "You have to get elected first."

"Yes, I do. And, when I do, I need someone that I can work with. I need someone who can work with Congress on both sides of the aisle. Blake or Gray would be eviscerated the moment they stepped onto the line, much less try to cross over it."

"You don't think Ellison will be?" Glenn asked.

"No, I don't."

"Your mind's made up," Doug surmised.

"I'm making the formal call this afternoon as planned. Where are we with that, Dana?"

"All set for 3:00 P.M."

"Good. Jameson and Cooper will be traveling with me to Nevada next week for the rally. Now, what's next?"

"Looks like they want you to testify on June 14th," Dana said.

"Flag Day? Fitting," Candace replied. "All right. Let them know that's a go. Clear that day. Dana, see what you can do about getting some idea about the scope."

"Already on it," Dana said.

"Candy, that's a week before the convention," Doug said.

"Yes, I know."

"Can't you get them to postpone your testimony until after?"

"Probably. Why would I do that?"

"Aside from needing to prepare for the convention?" Doug continued. "What about the..."

"Optics?" Candace guessed. "Postponing will only make me look weak. You need to trust me on this. If they think they're going to damper our convention, they've made a grave mistake."

"What about this ongoing story with Klein?" Glenn asked. "You haven't made much comment yet. You know that is going to come up when you and Ellison start making the rounds on talk shows."

"I'll address it then."

"How will you address it?" Glenn asked.

"I have confidence that the allegations are being investigated appropriately. That's the end of it as far as I am concerned. Then, I'll pivot."

"What about Jameson?" Glenn wanted to know.

"What about her?" Candace replied.

"It's only three weeks until she has to make a speech in front of all the delegates. Is she up to that?"

Candace smiled. "Don't underestimate Jameson, Glenn."

"I'm not."

"Good. Moving on."

Candace walked through the door and kicked off her heels. "God, I needed that."

"Hey," Jameson greeted her wife. "I heard the car."

"Sorry, I'm a little late."

"It's okay. Coop was exhausted from playing with Spencer. He took a three-hour nap. He'll be up for hours. No offense, you look like you could use a three-hour nap yourself. Bad day?"

"No. Typical day these days."

"How'd the call go with Ellison?" Jameson asked. She moved to open a bottle of wine and pour Candace a glass.

"It went well."

"Still feel good about it?" Jameson wondered.

"Actually, I do."

"Good." Jameson handed Candace a glass of wine.

"Thank you."

"Want to talk about it?"

"Nope." Candace leaned over and kissed Jameson's lips. "Not tonight."

"Mommy!" Cooper barreled into the room. "Can we get pizza now?"

Candace laughed. "Is that the only reason you're happy to see me?"

"No." Cooper grabbed Candace's hand. "Me and Momma got you a surprise."

"You did?"

"Yep. Close your eyes," he said. Cooper began to lead Candace away.

"Where are we going?" she asked.

"You'll see. Okay, open them!"

Candace opened her eyes and smiled. Cooper had pillows and blankets lined across the living room floor. An old *Scooby Doo* movie was playing on the television. *I can imagine who chose that one.* Candace forced herself not to laugh. Jameson was constantly trying to convince Cooper and Spencer that they should watch *Scooby Doo.* "What's all this?"

"It's a big bed!" Cooper explained excitedly. "So, you can rest while we watch movies and eat pizza."

Candace bent over and kissed Cooper's cheek. "It's perfect."

"Yep. You have to go get ready now. Momma will take you."

Candace looked at Jameson curiously.

"You heard the man," Jameson said. "We'll be right back, Coop. Then we'll order pizza."

"'Kay!"

Jameson chuckled at Cooper as he settled himself into a sea of pillows. She led Candace up the stairs into their bedroom and closed the door. Before Candace could offer a thought, Jameson's lips were on hers.

"What was that for?" Candace asked.

"Do I need a reason?"

"Never."

Jameson reached over to grab a box from the bed and handed it to Candace.

"What's this?"

"Open it."

Candace did as Jameson requested. She raised a brow and removed the contents. "Do I want to know why I am holding pajamas with turtles on them?" she asked Jameson.

"They didn't have Aladdin, trains or dinosaurs in your size."

"Uh-huh."

"I took Coop and Spence shopping before Scott came. I told them they could pick something out for you. That was it."

Candace nodded. She looked at the pajamas and shook her head. "I can't believe I am about to do this."

Jameson grinned.

"What are you grinning about?"

"Oh, I was just thinking about getting you to come out of your shell later."

Candace threw the empty box at Jameson and headed to the bathroom.

"What?" Jameson feigned innocence.

"Don't get too cocky, honey. I have a credit card too."

Jameson frowned. "Damnit. I didn't think of that," she muttered.

Candace heard Jameson's comment and giggled. She shed her suit and slipped into her new pajamas. *The things I do.*

"What are you doing in there?" Jameson asked.

Candace emerged. "Think before you speak," she warned her wife.

"It's a good look on you."

"Glad you approve."

"Ready for pizza?" Jameson asked.

"Wait a minute. Cooper's already in his jammies. What are you wearing to this party?"

"Me?" Jameson asked.

Candace raised her brow.

"What's wrong with what I have on?"

"You need pajamas, Jameson."

"I sleep naked, Candace."

"Well, how about I loan you something?"

"What?"

Candace held up a finger. "Wait here."

"What is she up to?"

A few minutes passed and Candace returned holding a large, pink nightgown with ruffles.

"What is *that*?" Jameson's eyes widened in horror.

"My mother bought it for me years ago one Christmas. It's been in the old wardrobe ever since."

"I am not wearing that."

"Oh, yes you are."

"Candace…"

Candace grinned. "I'll play the teenage turtle; you play the ruffled rose."

Jameson groaned. There was no way she was getting out of this and she knew it. "Fine."

It took every ounce of self-control Candace possessed not to fall over laughing when Jameson walked out of the bathroom. She held out her hand and led Jameson down the stairs. Cooper turned when he heard his parents and immediately began to laugh hysterically.

"Momma!" Cooper laughed harder. "Momma!"

Candace finally laughed.

"Laugh it up, Donatello. You're answering the door for the pizza," Jameson whispered.

Candace laughed so hard she cried. She leaned in and kissed Jameson lovingly. "I love you, you lunatic."

Jameson groaned.

Candace decided to let her off the hook. "As adorable as you are, I prefer you in a pair of sweats. Go change."

"Really?"

"Yes. Besides, I'm pretty sure both Cooper and I will need a diaper if we have to look at you wearing that all night."

"Cute."

Candace pecked Jameson's cheek. "Go on."

"What about you?" Jameson asked.

Candace smiled. She was sure that Jameson had encouraged the boys to pick out her new evening attire. It didn't matter. That was one of the things she adored about Jameson—Jameson's playfulness. Candace would wear a bag over her head if Cooper or any of her grandchildren gave it to her. "I'm fine," she said.

"I'll call for the pizza," Jameson said. "Just sit with Coop. He missed you."

Candace sat down with Cooper while Jameson headed off to change.

"Momma's silly," Cooper said.

"She certainly is," Candace agreed.

Cooper snuggled against Candace happily. "We got you turtles. Momma couldn't find trains."

"I love them." *Not as much as I love you.*

"Momma says we're gonna be home all weekend."

Candace let her head fall onto Cooper's head. She was grateful to be home. For the next two days, she intended to put work aside as much as possible and focus on her family. Balance would always be a challenge. She did need to slow down. Less than a half an hour of being home and Candace found herself wishing she never had to leave. "Yes, we are, Cooper. Yes, we are."

CHAPTER FIVE

Jameson enjoyed watching Cooper run around her parents' yard with her nephew. It reminded her of her childhood. She was looking forward to Michelle and Melanie arriving that evening for a visit. One bonus to Candace's travel—it gave Jameson a reason to spend more time with her mother and Candace's kids.

"Does he ever stop?" Maureen asked.

"Not until he drops."

"When do you two leave for Nevada?"

"Tomorrow morning."

"What about Candace?"

"Tomorrow night."

"Surprised you didn't want to be in Albany."

"She's in meetings all day today and all day tomorrow. We were with her all weekend. She'll catch up with us tomorrow night. It's all good."

Maureen considered Jameson's words. She wondered how Jameson was handling the increasing pace of Candace's schedule and the growing scrutiny of their lives. "How are you, JD?"

"Good," Jameson answered honestly.

"How's Candace holding up with everything?"

"She's holding up. You know her."

"I do. I was surprised by her pick."

Jameson shrugged. "You know me, I stay out of that."

"You must have an opinion. I mean, JD it will affect you too. You'll be traveling with them for the next few months, longer if she wins."

"I like Ellison—from what I know of him. I think they're a good fit."

"He's young."

Jameson laughed. "He's older than me."

"You know what I mean."

"Not really. Besides, I think that worked to his benefit."

"JD?"

"Hum?"

"What do you make of all this press about Candace and Russia?"

"Mom, if I paid attention to the press I'd either be an alcoholic or in a psych ward by now."

"I just don't understand how they can come at her. No senator has that kind of power."

Oh, you'd be surprised. "She's not worried about testifying if that's what you're wondering. And, before you ask, I don't ask about the nuts and bolts of her job. If she offers, I listen. Some things she can't offer."

Maureen considered Jameson's reply. She had always been fascinated by politics. That interest was one of the primary reasons she had decided to teach history. Jameson loved to tease her about having a crush on Candace. Maureen admired her daughter-in-law. She'd watched Candace's career at a distance for years. The last thing she had expected was for Jameson to marry the affable senator. Jameson's marriage to Candace had changed their family dynamic in ways that continued to surprise Maureen. Most of it had been welcome. Maureen enjoyed a close relationship with Candace. They confided in each other about everything from the challenges in marriage to the foibles of raising children. They even discussed policy and politics at length. Candace was open, but also cautious. Maureen hadn't given much thought to how difficult balancing the enormity of Candace's job and the realities of her life with Jameson must be until now. At least, she hadn't considered the fact that Candace would be unable to share parts of her day with Jameson.

"Must be hard," Maureen commented absently.

"What's that?"

"Not being able to talk to your spouse about everything."

"Do you talk to Dad about *everything?*"

"No, but I can."

Jameson shrugged. "She tells me what I need to know to support her. That's good enough for me. I don't know how she handles all of it—the state, the campaign, the kids—me." Jameson laughed. "Probably me most of all."

"I doubt she sees it that way."

Jameson winked at her mother.

"Are you nervous about the convention?" Maureen wondered.

"You mean am I freaking out about speaking in front of the whole country?"

"That too."

"Not freaking out, not yet anyway. Shell's helping me write the speech."

"Shell?"

"Yeah. Why? Do you think that's a bad idea?"

"No, I'm just surprised."

"You know Shell. She can't stay out of it. This lets her be a part of everything without having to travel. Candace always finds a way."

"JD, can I ask you something without you getting mad?"

"That's not a good sign."

"I just wonder if you are doing okay with all of this. You've given a lot up already, and you're a private person. This is…"

"It's my life now," Jameson said.

"But is it the life you want?"

Jameson smiled. She understood her mother's concerns.

"I know how much you love Candace."

"I thought you hopped onto this runaway train long ago," Jameson commented.

"This isn't about me. I love Candace too."

"You don't say."

"Stop it. She'll make a fantastic president. It does alter your life. I knew that. Seeing it unfold—I just wonder how you feel about it."

Jameson's eyes fell on Cooper. *How do I feel about it?* "I never imagined being anyone's Mom."

"What does that have to do with…"

"It has everything to do with what you're asking. You seem to have some idea that none of this was my choice," Jameson said. "It is. If I asked Candace to quit tomorrow, I'm pretty sure she would. Everyone thinks I've given something up. I haven't given up any more than she has."

"JD, you've left your firm. You've agreed to travel and to…"

"I've given up my anonymity. I gave that up when I decided that I wanted to be with Candace. I knew what that meant. I knew where she was heading, Mom. I probably knew it before she did. Do you know why Candace and I work?"

"Tell me."

"Part of it is that I don't care about the Governor's Ball or the spotlight. I don't enjoy that."

"That's my point."

"Would you just listen?" Jameson chuckled. "I don't enjoy those things on my own. I wouldn't seek it out for myself. Being with her? I love those events. You don't get that. I love it because I get to be at her side. I get to watch the way her eyes light up and the way everyone's eyes fall on her the moment she enters a room. You're right. I don't feed myself on a steady diet of cable news. I do love to listen to her dissect a problem."

"And, Candace?"

"Candace? She would have to tell you how she sees it. You don't see the fatigue in her eyes in the morning after she tosses and turns over some bill that she needs to pass or over a call she got late in the night. I see that side of her too. We balance each other. She might complain about me climbing on the roof, but she loves to watch me do it. I know that. I'm not missing anything, Mom. Trust me on that. And, if you want to know the truth, it isn't always easy for us. Sometimes, I want to throttle her for not slowing down. And, I wouldn't blame her if she wanted to scream at how stubborn I can be. Our life isn't like most people's lives—not when it comes to what you see on those cable news shows.

That's only part of it. It's all the other parts that hold us together. I wouldn't change her decision to run this campaign. It's who she is. That's who I want to be with, even if that makes me crazy sometimes."

"I give you credit, JD."

"What do you mean?"

"Candace is lucky to have you."

Jameson laughed. "You definitely have that one backward."

Candace looked out the window of the airplane at the glistening lights below. She felt more rested than she had in months. A couple of days at home had been a balm for her soul. She'd balked at looking at the news or taking calls. She'd been surprised when Jameson pulled her aside Saturday afternoon and told her to take a couple of hours and catch up—surprised and grateful. Jameson's support and understanding gave her focus and strength. She replayed the conversation as the plane began its final descent.

"Go do what you need to do," Jameson said.

"I need to be with you and Cooper."

"I know. We need that too. You're not going to be able to focus on us if you are playing possibilities all day in the back of your mind. Go call Glenn and Dana, catch up on the news you need to for a couple of hours."

"I promised Cooper…"

"I've got that covered."

"Jameson…"

"Go on. Your phone's been buzzing for two hours."

"So, it can buzz."

Jameson smiled. "Candace, I don't expect your undivided attention for an entire weekend. I think we both know that is unlikely to happen—ever."

Candace sighed.

"Stop. When have we not been interrupted by work or one of the kids? It's inevitable. You're here. Trust me, if you're not done by the time we get back, I will hide your phone for the rest of the weekend."

"Where are you going?" Candace asked.

"Coop and I have a couple of errands to run."

"None of these errands involve new outfits for me, do they?"

Jameson grinned. "I can't take Coop into those stores."

Candace swatted Jameson. "Stop."

"Just go. You won't be able to enjoy your time and relax if you don't make those calls. I know you."

"I promise, I will be done when you get home."

Jameson nodded and placed a sweet kiss on Candace's lips. "Just remind all of your little minions that I have a speech to make. Never know what I might say."

Candace laughed. "Leverage?"

"Whatever it takes. I'll see you in a couple of hours."

"I'll be here."

"Hey." Dana's voice pulled Candace from her memory. "You look rested."

"I feel rested."

"That's good."

"Oh, no. What now?" Candace asked.

"It's not that bad."

"That's like saying you have measles instead of syphilis."

Dana laughed. "Want me to add that analogy to your speech?"

"Might work," Candace said. "What is it?"

Dana handed Candace a folder.

Candace reached in front of her and retrieved her glasses. She studied the contents of the folder thoughtfully. Occasionally, her tongue would roll across her lower lip as she processed the information. She sighed, nodded, removed her glasses, and handed the folder back to Dana. "When did you get this?"

"Early this morning. You were with Glenn and Doug."

Candace looked out the window again. She shook her head. "I need you to do something for me."

"Whatever you need—you know that."

Candace nodded and turned back to her friend. "Call Jane Merrow."

"Jane?"

"See if she can make some room in her schedule to meet me in Illinois this week."

"You're not scheduled to be in Illinois; Jameson is."

"Yes, I know."

"Candy, you are supposed to be at a meeting in Albany Friday morning."

"And, I will be. Jane has a fundraiser in Chicago Sunday that she's scheduled to speak at."

"I know, but…"

"Dana, please—make the arrangements. My meeting is at 9:00 A.M. I can be in Chicago by dinner."

"What do you want me to tell Jane?"

"Tell her I want to discuss strategy."

"Campaign strategy?"

Candace smiled.

"Okay, I get it. Why don't you just call her yourself?" Dana wondered.

"Optics, Dana."

"Do you want me to schedule an appearance for the two of you?"

"No. Make it about old friends. She'll understand."

"I'm on it."

Candace's head fell back against the seat. She sighed. "Damnit."

TUESDAY, JUNE 10ᵗʰ

"Momma?"

"What's up, Coop?"

"When's Mommy coming?"

"Mommy will be here tomorrow morning when you wake up."

Cooper frowned.

"I know you miss her, buddy. I do too."

"It's okay. Momma?"

"Yes?"

"Can me and you swim?"

"Cooper, are you sure your name isn't Flounder?"

"No! You're silly. I'm not a fish."

"Are you sure about that?" Jameson teased.

"I just like to swim."

"Like a fish," Jameson said.

"No. I can't stay under the water."

"Oh. Good point."

Cooper giggled. "Can we?"

Jameson had no issue taking Cooper for a swim. Since Candace had secured the Democratic nomination, their lives had changed drastically. Candace, Jameson, and Cooper had 24/7 Secret Service protection. Jameson knew that some of that was procedure. Some of it had to do with the opposition certain factions of people had to their family. She hated that reality. There were crazy people in the world. That much Jameson did know. A simple trip to the hotel pool now required notice. She would need to advise their detail about her plans.

"Tell you what," Jameson said. "I'll go talk to Agent Lamkin, and you go see if you can find your suit. I know Mommy packed it."

"Mommy always packs it," Cooper said. He hopped off the couch and headed for the bedroom.

Jameson made her way to the door.

"Ms. Reid, everything okay?" Jeff Lamkin asked.

"Yeah, it's fine, Jeff. Coop wants to go for a swim."

Lamkin nodded. "I'll call down. Shouldn't be a problem. Pretty quiet here right now."

"Thanks."

"No thanks necessary, Ma'am."

"Jeff, if you want us both to survive this arrangement, call me anything but Ma'am."

Lamkin chuckled. He liked Jameson. He also realized that he'd been hand selected for this detail. Candace Reid had more pull than most people realized. She'd made it clear that she wanted someone with Cooper who knew how to interact with a small child. Jeff Lamkin fit that bill. "I'll take that under advisement," he replied. "I'll knock when we're ready."

"Thanks." Jameson closed the door. *Good thing the White House has a pool.*

———————————◆•◉•◆———————————

"Lawson, you need to lay low for a while."

"Why? Because of some ridiculous story in *The Post?*"

Bradley Wolfe shook his head. "Lawson, just do us all a favor and don't do me any favors right now; okay?"

"Who leaked that document?" Klein asked.

"Don't you think I'd be doing something about it if I knew?"

"I don't know. Would you?"

"You're becoming paranoid. It's fodder. Let it die its death naturally."

"The FBI names me in an investigation…"

"You don't know that. No one knows what that document was linked to."

"It was linked to me! This is that bitch's way of trying to put me down like an old dog."

Wolfe forced himself not to roll his eyes. "Just do what Ritchie told you to do."

"What's that? Keep funneling money to you?"

Wolfe grinned.

"Two can play this game," Klein muttered.

"Lawson, whatever you are thinking, stop."

"You don't pay me, Wolfe. You don't scare me either. You're nothing more than a lowly altar boy holding someone else's chalice. Instead of telling me what I need to do, maybe you should start performing your duty." Klein walked through the office door and slammed it behind him.

"How'd it go?" Jed Ritchie asked.

"Exactly as we planned," Wolfe said.

"Good."

———◆●◆———

The short ride to the hotel felt endless to Candace. Her phone had buzzed endlessly since landing, offering one dire message after another. None of them rated as dire in Candace's mind. All of them ranked at the highest level of importance to someone in her sphere. She had one priority—spending a few hours alone with Jameson. The next day would be harried and hurried. First, there would be breakfast with Nate Ellison and his family. That would be closely followed by a meeting with Candace's advisers and Ellison to pour over campaign strategy, talking points, and schedules. Jameson and Cooper would be given the task of entertaining Ellison's family until Candace and Nate Ellison's first appearance as running mates. There were moments that Candace found herself shrouded in disbelief. Life felt like a strange dream. She'd traveled with presidents. She'd campaigned for presidents. She'd been part of national security discussions and domestic policy initiatives. As governor, she'd been apprised of what were deemed credible terrorist threats and comforted families after tragedies. Pursuing the presidency was an honor. It was also an enormous responsibility. Amid the excitement of crowds, the questions from media, the curiosity about everything from her hairstyle to her children, the demands of her job as governor, and the needs of her family, Candace felt the weight of the future. She was no longer speaking to a small constituency of hopeful citizens. She was addressing the entire world. Her success or failure as a candidate would dictate the course the country would take for the next four years and beyond. Her ability to navigate the minefields of special interest, military and intelligence agendas, the political aspirations of others, the deeply held beliefs of a diverse electorate, and the grievances of old adversaries would determine whether she could prevail not only as a candidate but as a president. She let her eyes fall shut and willed her mind to quiet its thoughts and questions. A few hours away from the rest of the world would refresh her spirit. She replayed Jameson's call to her to slow down. There was little room for quiet in her world. When the opportunity knocked, Candace understood that she needed to take it. Hotel rooms would serve as home for much of the next four months. Jameson was the person who could create that reality into a refuge. *Just get me home.*

———————◆◆●◆◆———————

Jameson heard Candace's voice as Candace entered the hotel suite. She stretched and yawned and headed toward the sound.

"Thank you, Dominick."

"Have a good evening, Governor," Agent Dominick Macpherson bid Candace goodnight.

Candace dropped her bag, closed the door and collapsed against it.

"Rough day?" Jameson asked.

"Not really." Candace made her way across the room and fell into Jameson's arms.

"Not your most convincing argument, Governor Reid."

"Honest, it was just another long day."

"Did you eat?"

"On the plane."

"Feel like a glass of wine?"

Candace shook her head. "What if I told you that all I want is to be with you?"

"That's it? Really?"

"Really. Cooper's asleep?"

"Yeah. He spent three hours in the pool."

"I don't believe it. Jeff must've loved that."

"He's a good sport—for a Secret Service Agent. He's good with Coop. At least he speaks to me—more than three-word answers. Do they send them to stoic school or something? Can you institute a personality class when you get elected?"

Candace laughed. "I'll see what I can do."

Jameson leaned in and kissed Candace. "I missed you."

"Mmm. I missed you too."

"Why don't you go check on Coop? I'll take your things into the bedroom."

Candace placed a light kiss on Jameson's lips. "Thank you."

"For what?"

"I'm just happy to be here."

Jameson nodded. "I'll see you in a few minutes." She watched Candace make her way into the room Cooper had. *You need a break.* Jameson grabbed Candace's bag and brought it into the bedroom. She shook her head. Candace seemed in good spirits, but she was tired. Jameson went to the bathroom and started the water in the large tub. A long, hot bath would help Candace relax. Jameson wondered when the last time Candace had allowed herself the indulgence of some alone time had been. She would gently force the issue of relaxation tonight.

Candace brushed her hand across the top of Cooper's head. *Oh, Cooper, what am I doing?*

"Mommy?"

"It's me." Candace bent over and kissed Cooper's head. "Go back to sleep, honey."

Cooper grabbed Candace's hand. "Can you stay with me?"

Candace's heart ached. She missed all her children. She missed Cooper most of all. She took off her suit jacket and tossed it aside, kicked off her heels and complied with her son's request. He snuggled against her happily. "Did you have a good day with Momma?"

"Yep. We went on the plane and then we went in the pool."

"I heard."

"Yep. Momma made me mac and cheese for dinner. She made broccoli too. She said green is just as important."

"Momma's right." Candace smiled and let her lips brush against Cooper's head. Candace and Jameson were determined to make things as normal as possible for Cooper when they traveled. That meant suites with kitchens and tables where meals could be prepared and shared. Candace found herself musing that she would have given anything to share macaroni and cheese with broccoli with her two favorite people. *Who would have imagined I'd miss that?*

Cooper nestled as close to Candace as he could manage. "Jeff has a nephew just like me."

Candace chuckled. Cooper had only recently begun to grasp that his favorite playmate was also his nephew. She and Jameson had explained it numerous times, but something seemed to have triggered a new understanding for Cooper about who he was to his parents and who Spencer was to him. Candace wasn't sure if it was the birth of Michelle's twins or the amount of time Cooper had been spending with Marianne. He shared a unique bond with his eldest sibling. While Candace knew he adored Jonah and Michelle, Marianne occupied a special place in Cooper's heart. She imagined that a shared understanding of loss had created that bridge. He listened to everything Marianne said as if it were the most important nugget of information he'd ever heard. And, Candace was also sure that Cooper confided in his sister about his feelings. Marianne would only share what she deemed necessary with her mother and Jameson. Cooper was small, but he understood the concept of trust better than most adults Candace knew. Slowly, Cooper was beginning to put the pieces of their large family and his place in it together.

"You like Jeff, don't you?"

"Yep. He showed me a picture. His nephew is seven. That's older than me."

"Only a little bit," Candace said.

"Mommy?"

"Hum?"

"How come Momma doesn't go to work anymore?"

"I think Momma wants more time to spend with you." Candace was positive she could feel Cooper's smile.

"Momma dived in the pool."

"She did?"

"Yep. She said I'm part fish."

"You do love the water."

"I don't know how to do that."

"Dive? I'll bet Momma will teach you."

"Yep. She said so. I think Momma's a whale."

Don't tell her that. "Why is Momma a whale?"

"Cause she spitted too!"

Candace laughed. She hugged Cooper close. Listening to him talk about his day with Jameson reminded Candace how much she loved them both.

"What's going on in here?" Jameson poked her head into the room.

"Cooper was just telling me that you remind him of a whale."

"A whale? Am I that big?" Jameson asked.

Cooper giggled. "No!"

"Do I have a tail?"

"No, Momma!"

"Then why am I a whale?"

"Cause you dived and you spitted!" Cooper laughed.

Jameson shrugged. "I swallowed a little too much water," she tried to explain.

Candace shot Jameson a doubtful gaze.

Cooper kept laughing. "You spitted like a whale!"

"Whales have spouts—and tails," Jameson clarified. The look she received from Candace made her clear her throat. "Okay, Flounder."

"I'm not Flounder!" Cooper laughed some more.

"I think it's sleepy time for you and Mommy."

Cooper groaned and clung playfully to Candace.

"Come on," Jameson gently urged her son. "Let Mommy go. You'll see her in the morning."

"Promise?" he asked.

Candace smiled. "I promise."

"'Kay. I love you."

"Goodnight, sweetheart." Candace placed another kiss on Cooper's head. "Momma and I love you too."

Jameson took hold of Candace's hand and led her from the room. She gently pulled Candace forward until they reached the large bathroom that adjoined their bedroom.

"What's this?" Candace gestured to the bathtub full of steaming water.

Jameson started silently undressing Candace.

"Looking to play whale again?" Candace teased.

Jameson had become lost in a sea of unexpected emotion. It had been weeks since she had made love to Candace. They'd shared reverent kisses and loving embraces. Jameson missed her wife. She missed touching Candace. She missed the way Candace's skin felt against hers. Her eyes roamed appreciatively over her wife as Candace's clothes pooled on the floor.

"Jameson," Candace called softly. She lifted Jameson's eyes to hers. "I've missed you too."

Jameson's fingertips caressed Candace's cheek. She brought their lips together softly. A hint of Chardonnay lingered on Candace's lips, tempting Jameson's senses. She struggled to tame the beating of her heart as her desire to lower Candace to the bathroom floor swelled. She started to pull away but Candace's mouth claimed hers insistently. Thought evaporated in an instant. Emotion flooded any hope of reason. The kiss continued searching, probing, asking permission, promising submission, and begging to be carried away all at once. Seldom had Jameson endeavored to take Candace without warning. Soft, slow, yielding—that had always dictated Jameson's touch. Feeling Candace's hands as they glided up and down her back, Jameson's resolve crumbled like sand. Damn the bath. Forget the bed. She kicked the door to ensure it was closed. She should lock it. Small, curious eyes might wander into this space without warning. *Screw it.* The only thing that mattered to Jameson now was the woman pressed against her. Too many moments were stolen from them every day. She'd be damned if this one slipped into oblivion.

Jameson's lips wandered from the warmth of Candace's mouth over the cool textures of Candace's skin. She nipped at the flesh behind

Candace's ear, enjoying the scent of perfume that greeted her. It conjured brief images of sunflowers, all bright and yellow, an elegant majesty that rolled on in gently swaying rows. *Beautiful.* Everything about Candace was beautiful. Strength and gentleness mingled in the woman she held close. Jameson's lips traveled with abandon as if she had never explored the landscape beneath them.

"Jameson," Candace's voice quivered.

Jameson pulled her T-shirt off and tossed it aside. She lowered her sweatpants and stepped out of them. She needed to feel Candace against her. No words now—Jameson had no desire to waste a moment on words. Something sacred was passing between them. Perhaps that would have seemed strange to most people—making love in the bathroom of a hotel suite. On paper, it sounded like a scene from a bad romance novel. The thought brought a smile to Jameson's lips. Life was stranger than fiction. If lust was the most intoxicating part of living, love was the most peculiar experience life could offer. Combined, the two could easily drown logic from the most stolid soul. Jameson was anything but stoic. And, Candace? Passion burned in Candace's veins. Candace's passion for every moment and possibility life offered elicited a consuming need in Jameson. Her mouth covered Candace's nipple, delighting in the shudder the twirl of her tongue evoked. How much longer could she stand, she wondered? Jameson was pulled under by Candace's presence like a pebble sucked out to sea at high-tide.

Candace's head tilted back. Her fingertips pressed into the flesh of Jameson's hips, desperately seeking support. Her knees trembled. Her body tingled under Jameson's touch. How had they ended up here? Where had they been? Everything had blurred. Nothing mattered but Jameson's hands, her mouth, the sound of Jameson's pleasure as she continued to descend lower. She whimpered when Jameson's teeth raked over her nipple and tugged gently. How much longer until Jameson would release her? Did she want to be released? *No.* Candace looked down at Jameson. Jameson's eyes drifted to hers. Candace made a futile attempt to pull Jameson to face her. Jameson fell to her knees in defiance.

Jameson's hands drifted back up to Candace's breasts, kneading the supple flesh, teasing and taunting, enjoying the sound of Candace's sighs as they grew desperate. She could feel the steady quiver of Candace's legs growing more intense. How many times had she made love to her wife? Hundreds? Thousands? She never tired of touching Candace. Every sensation was new each time they came together. Familiarity could not quell anticipation. She kissed Candace's thigh and let her tongue trail inward.

"Oh, God," Candace grabbed Jameson's shoulders to steady herself.

Slowly, Jameson guided Candace to her knees. She gazed into Candace's eyes lovingly before claiming Candace's lips with a searing kiss. Her fingers found Candace's center. Warmth greeted her, inviting her to enter. She sucked in a ragged breath and moved deeper. Candace's head fell back exposing her neck and Jameson moved to taste it again. Her arm slid around Candace's waist and guided her to the floor. Jameson offered Candace one sweet kiss before descending her body like a cat stalking its prey. Her tongue danced over the dips of Candace's stomach and curves of her hips until finally, Jameson reached the destination she longed to explore. A guttural moan laced with pure desire escaped her mouth at the first taste of the woman she loved. She greeted the rise of Candace's hips with the firm pressure of her hand, forcing Candace into total submission.

"Jameson," Candace pleaded.

Jameson's only reply was an achingly slow swirl of her tongue around Candace's center as her fingers dove deeper. She needed Candace. She wanted to drive Candace over the edge of sanity into a sea of ecstasy. Her fingers thrust steadily in time with the playful flick of her tongue, complimenting each other like the melody and harmony of a haunting ballad. She pressed her weight against Candace's legs, preventing Candace from arching against her touch.

Candace struggled to breathe against a rising tide. The softness of Jameson's tongue, the rhythm of her fingers, the feel of her breasts brushing against Candace's legs—it was all too much. She wanted to touch Jameson, to taste Jameson, to hear Jameson. The hot water in the tub had cooled, leaving a mist hovering in the air. It chilled her skin and stoked the embers of her desire further. Hot and cold, hard and soft, contrast and compliment—Candace's hands dropped to Jameson's head, trying to hold her in place, silently begging for release. The sound of her urgent sighs as they mixed with Jameson's desperate moans sent a rush through Candace's body, greeting Jameson as a final plea.

Jameson drank Candace in. She craved Candace's release. Her fingers twirled inside Candace, delighting in the warm wetness. She sucked gently at first, slowly increasing the pressure of her lips around Candace's need until Candace screamed her name.

Candace's entire body rose to meet Jameson's. She shuddered when Jameson's fingers began to probe again, gently but firmly. "No… God, Jameson…"

Jameson lifted herself and kissed Candace urgently. "Just feel me, Candace."

Candace's eyelids fluttered and closed. She could feel Jameson everywhere. Her entire body hummed like a bee buried in the sweet nectar of a flower. She felt Jameson moving inside her tenderly. Jameson's voice carried softly as they rocked together.

"I want you again," Jameson said. She moved to taste Candace again with abandon.

Candace gave herself over to Jameson. She wanted Jameson to take her. She wanted to lose all control, all hope of conscious thought. She needed to escape—to feel, to be reminded that there was one place she could fall away completely—Jameson. She moved against Jameson's hand until her body erupted again, quaking against her will, loving every delicious moment of the fall.

Jameson slowed her pace. She waited to ascend Candace's body until she felt Candace's quaking give way to faint tremors. Lovingly, she kissed her way back to Candace's lips. "I love you so much," she whispered.

Candace brushed the hair from Jameson's eyes. "I know, Jameson. I know you do."

"I missed you."

"I missed you too," Candace replied. She kissed Jameson sweetly. Her hand dropped between them. She smiled at the warmth between Jameson's legs.

"Candace, it's okay…"

"I need to feel you, Jameson—right now."

Jameson's forehead fell against Candace's. She was positive that the moment Candace began to touch her, she would erupt like Mt. Vesuvius—without warning.

Candace smiled. She'd felt the evidence of Jameson's arousal pressed against her. And, she sensed her wife's desperation as Jameson attempted to grind against her. "Not so fast," she said.

Jameson groaned in frustration.

"I want you to feel you, Jameson. I want to feel you let go of everything."

Jameson closed her eyes.

"You know what I want?" Candace asked.

Jameson did know. Candace loved to hear Jameson voice her desires. She had no intention of relenting immediately. She loved to hear Candace talk, to have Candace solicit those desires from her.

Candace forced herself not to chuckle. She knew Jameson's game. She knew exactly what Jameson wanted, and she had every intention of giving it to her. "Tell me," Candace said. She kissed Jameson's lips. "Tell me what you want."

"You."

"Mm. You have me." Candace sucked on Jameson's earlobe. "Do you want to know how you make me feel?"

Jameson sucked in a ragged breath.

"You do. I know you do, Jameson."

"Please."

"Please what?"

"Tell me."

"You tell me what you want right now, and I'll tell you how you make me feel."

Jameson panted.

"Tell me," Candace ordered.

"I want to feel you inside me."

Candace thrust deeply into Jameson, soliciting a sigh. "Like that?"

"Yes."

"Mm." Candace kissed Jameson passionately and moved in and out of her repeatedly. "I love the way you touch me," she said. "The way your lips slip over my skin."

"Oh, God," Jameson croaked.

Candace's eyes sparkled. She loved to watch Jameson fall away. "What do you want?"

"You. I swear, I want you again right now."

Candace chuckled. She had no doubt that Jameson was being honest. She moved to straddle Jameson's hips and dropped her breasts just above Jameson's lips.

Jameson arched her back, desperately wanting to claim the prize Candace was offering.

Candace pulled back slightly. "Tell me, Jameson."

"Please, please let me touch you," Jameson begged.

"That's what you want?"

"Yes. I want to hear what you want," Jameson said.

"What if I show you instead?" Candace lowered herself. She gasped when Jameson sucked a nipple into her mouth. She pulled back and kissed Jameson's forehead. "I want you right now," Candace said. Without another word, Candace's body glided down Jameson's. She bent Jameson's knee and held it in place with one hand. Her tongue bathed Jameson's center in long, leisurely strokes until Jameson began to writhe beneath her.

"Candace, please... Please..."

Candace answered Jameson's plea happily. She understood Jameson's heart and her body. Jameson had been dangling on the edge of oblivion for what felt like hours to Candace. It was easy for Candace to understand. Nothing would ever arouse Candace more than making love to Jameson, not even Jameson touching her. That was their shared reality, a reality that made these moments together more than erotic.

Love always took control of lust in the end. It left Candace with a feeling of awe and completion. She pulled Jameson closer as the first waves of pleasure began to thunder through Jameson's body. She loved making love with Jameson. God, how she had missed it.

Once Jameson's trembling subsided, Candace moved to kiss her tenderly. "I did miss you, Jameson. I missed you so much." She collapsed onto Jameson's chest, content to lie on the cold tile in the warmth of Jameson's arms. She lifted her head when she heard Jameson chuckle. "What are you laughing about?"

"Nothing."

Candace's brow arched into her hairline.

"Okay. It just hit me that I just seduced the next president in a hotel bathroom."

Candace laughed. "No one can say we aren't classy."

"On that note, what do you say we re-fill that bathtub?"

"Are you suggesting we are dirty?"

Jameson shrugged. "The floor's cold."

"I see. That's your reason, huh?"

"One of them."

Candace grinned. *Something tells me this is going to be a long night.*

CHAPTER SIX

"Where are we going?" Cooper asked.

"We're going with Mommy to a rally, buddy," Jameson explained.

Cooper shrugged and spooned some cereal into his mouth.

"Good morning, sweetheart." Candace kissed the top of Cooper's head.

Jameson handed Candace a cup of coffee and received a delicate kiss as thanks.

"Do I look like I need this?" Candace asked playfully.

"I'm on my third," Jameson replied.

"Momma said since there's no rest for the weary, God made coffee," Cooper offered.

Candace shook her head. "Lunatic."

"I assume that was Glenn who called at the crack of dawn?"

"How'd you guess?" Candace sipped her coffee gratefully. "This is almost as good as…"

"Don't say it," Jameson chuckled.

"What did you think I was going to say?" Candace asked.

"Sleep?"

"I'm sure."

"Ready for today?" Jameson wondered.

"I think so. It'll be interesting to see the reaction."

"It's not like this is the first time you and Ellison have appeared together."

"True, but as running mates? It's a completely different ball-game."

Jameson waved off the notion. "Two attractive, successful people with incredibly good-looking families? What's not to like?"

Candace laughed. "I'll at least agree to the latter part of that statement." She sighed and took another sip of her coffee.

"Let me guess; you have some calls to make."

Candace's smile was laced with regret and apology.

Jameson kissed Candace's cheek. "No worries," she promised. "I promised Coop we could watch some *Scooby Doo* before we have to leave."

"Uh-huh."

"What?"

"I'm sure Cooper appreciates how difficult that will be for you."

Jameson rolled her eyes. "You finished, buddy?"

Cooper wiped his mouth with the back of his hand. "Yep! Mommy, you want to watch Scooby with us?"

"I will try and sneak in for a few minutes."

"'Kay!" Cooper scampered off to his room.

"Are you sure you don't want to come with me to Arizona?" Candace asked.

"I want to," Jameson said. "I do. Candace, I do. I promised Jonah I would look at this new contract he landed. Cooper…"

"I know."

"We both would rather be with you," Jameson said. "It's only for a couple of days."

"Actually…"

Jameson waited for the shoe to drop.

Candace grinned. Jameson clearly expected her to deliver the news that she would be away longer than expected. "Actually, I'm planning on meeting you in Illinois Friday night."

"I was planning on coming home Friday night."

"I know. Your mom is going to make the trip with me and Cooper. I'm having dinner with Jane. I thought maybe we could take Cooper to see the Cubs play."

"Uh-huh. Don't you need to plan ahead for that?"

"Already taken care of. I rented a suite. Marianne and Scott are flying in Saturday morning to join us. Dana and Steve will be there with the boys too."

"Dana and Steve? Let me guess; they're playing The Mets."

"Maybe."

"Ah, the master plan comes into focus. Sneaky, Governor."

Candace shrugged. "Not sneakier than you convincing our son watching *Scooby Doo* is all about him."

"Don't you have a call to make?" Jameson asked.

Candace laughed. "I'll catch up with you in a bit, Shaggy."

"Shaggy? I'd say I'm more like Fred."

"Uh-huh." Candace strolled out of the room.

"Shaggy? Who's she calling shaggy?"

Candace poked her head back around the corner. She gestured to the box of cookies already in Jameson's hand.

"What?" Jameson asked. "You can't watch Scooby without snacks."

"Just make sure you and Cooper go easy on the *Scooby Snacks*. It's only 8:00 A.M. I don't need either of you wired on sugar today."

"Ha-ha."

"I wasn't kidding."

"Go do president things, will you?"

Candace chuckled and walked away.

Jameson looked at the box of cookies in her hand and frowned. She shrugged, reached inside and popped one in her mouth. She sighed again, rolled her eyes, and placed the box on the counter. *I hate it when she's right.*

"Is she here yet?" Nate Ellison asked.

"About five minutes out."

Ellison took a deep breath and blew it out nervously.

"Are you nervous about seeing Candace?"

Ellison looked at his assistant. John Deaver had been an intern on his senatorial campaign. He admired the young man's intelligence and political aptitude. Deaver was inexperienced when it came to presidential politics. In truth, so was Ellison. Nate Ellison gave his assistant a smile. "I'm not nervous about seeing Candace. She's not Candace today, John. She's the party's candidate for president. In a few months, she may be the most powerful person in the world."

"When you put it that way."

"Governor Reid's car just pulled up," a man called into the room.

"I'll get Janine and the kids," Deaver offered.

Ellison took a few deep breaths. He'd shared a stage with Candace Reid a few times. While his star may have been considered as a rising one, hers had always eclipsed his. He imagined that would always be the case. He'd been genuinely surprised when she'd called to inform him that she wanted him to join the ticket. Like most people, Deaver had assumed his vetting had been done purely for the masses; a name that would conjure interest and discussion without ever being thrown into serious consideration. He replayed Candace's call as he waited for her arrival.

"Governor Reid."

"Drop the formality, Nate. If we're going to work together, I think we should be on a first name basis."

Silence hovered.

Candace laughed. "Not what you expected me to say?"

"I.."

"I've spent more hours than I care to count weighing my options," Candace said.

Ellison had no doubt that was true. He'd participated in two lengthy face to face meetings with the governor and several phone conversations. "I can imagine."

"I need someone who balances me—not the way the politicos have been chattering endlessly about for the last month. I need someone who will challenge me, but who respects that the decisions ultimately lie with me. And, I need someone who

wants to take on more than diplomatic pleasantries. The vice presidency shouldn't be a slot filled to bolster votes. At least, it shouldn't be that alone. God forbid anything were to happen to me, I need a partner who can lead seamlessly. I think you're that partner, Nate. That is, if you are still interested in the job."

"I'd be honored."

"Don't be honored, be honest."

"Understood."

"I want you to be sure," Candace said. "The pace will change. It isn't easy. Frankly, this campaign is exhausting. You have two young children. Also, a benefit from my perspective, but a challenge as a parent. You won't be under a telescope anymore. You'll be under a microscope—so, will your family."

"That's your sales pitch?" Ellison joked.

"I don't have any desire to sell this job to anyone who doesn't want it. One thing you will learn about me, Nate, I can blow smoke up the asses of the windbags we know and love with the best of them. I don't bullshit my team."

"In that case, where do I sign up?"

Ellison felt a hand on his back. He turned and smiled at his wife. "Ready?" he asked.

"I'm so proud of you," Janine Ellison said.

"Let's hope I can help her deliver this election."

"You will."

"She's on her way in," Deaver said.

Ellison took another deep breath.

"You'll be great," Janine encouraged her husband.

Candace entered the small banquet room that had been reserved for their luncheon with a smile. She was aware that her presence had the power to both excite and unnerve people. She headed directly for Ellison. "Well, Senator, you ready to go win an election?" she asked.

"Absolutely, Governor."

Candace winked. "It's good to see you, Nate." She took Janine Ellison into an embrace. "How are you, Janine?"

"Proud of this guy."

"You should be," Candace said. She beckoned Jameson and Cooper closer. "You remember my wife, Jameson?"

"Of course," Ellison extended his hand.

"JD," Jameson said. "There are only two people on the planet who call me Jameson when I'm *not* in trouble."

"It is your name, isn't it?" Candace quipped.

"Yes, it is," Jameson agreed.

"And, this is our youngest, Cooper," Candace took hold of Cooper's hand. He offered the group a shy wave.

"Cooper," Ellison offered his hand. Cooper looked at Candace for permission. She winked at him, and he grasped the senator's hand. "Your mother tells me you love trains," Ellison said.

"Yep," Cooper agreed. "But Momma thinks I'm a fish."

"He loves the water," Jameson explained.

"So, do ours," Janine replied. She gestured to her two boys. "This is Derek, and this," she shuttled her younger son in front of her, "is Grayson."

"It's nice to see you again Derek—and Grayson." Candace shook each boy's hand. "You might not remember me."

"You're on TV," Grayson offered innocently.

Candace chuckled. "Once in a while." She gestured to the room behind them. "Why don't we all go have a seat before the horde arrives."

"Horde?" Janine whispered to Jameson.

"That's what she calls the press," Jameson explained.

Janine nodded.

"How are you doing with all this?" Jameson asked Ellison's wife.

"To tell you the truth, I'm not sure what to expect."

"The unexpected," Jameson chimed.

Janine laughed. Jameson put her immediately at ease. She looked ahead to find both her boys regaling Candace and Cooper with a story. Cooper was grinning while he clasped his mother's hand. Candace seemed fully engaged and attentive to the story she was being told.

"The boys like her."

"Most people do once they meet her," Jameson said.

Janine smiled. "Somehow, I don't doubt that, JD."

One thing Jameson never tired of was watching Candace address a crowd. She stood just off stage with Janine and the boys, watching as Candace and Nate Ellison walked onto stage to the boisterous cheers of the crowd. She glanced over at Janine and chuckled. "Not like most of the rallies you've been to."

"Not really."

"The good news is they love her here."

"The bad news?" Janine asked.

Jameson turned back to the stage. People in the public either adored Candace or they loathed her. It remained a difficult fact for Jameson to understand. Jameson had told Janine Ellison the truth earlier that day. People who had the chance to meet Candace or talk with her almost always ended up in her corner. Not everyone desired to take the time to interact with Candace Reid. There were some people—more than Jameson cared to admit who had a visceral aversion to Candace as both a candidate and as a person. Jameson would never grasp that. She could easily understand disagreeing with Candace's policies. There were times she disagreed with her wife on issues both at home and in politics. But Jameson knew that Candace made her decisions based on what she thought would benefit the most people. The people in this arena felt that from their candidate. Jameson reveled in watching Candace soar. She also knew that on the other side of the walls protestors would be holding signs spouting vile rhetoric and hateful names about the woman she loved. Strange reality.

"Hello, Nevada!" Candace called out.

As if on cue the crowd called back. "Hello, Candace!"

Jameson grinned. Somewhere along the campaign trail, the crowds had adopted the process of returning Candace's greeting. It had become a hallmark of every rally. She listened as Candace began to speak.

"You know, I had a lot of names thrown at me over the last few months. I talked to some of the smartest and most experienced people we have as leaders today. I kept asking myself one question: Who will make me a better president? The answer I came up with time and again was Nate Ellison."

Dana sidled up to Jameson. "Hell of an introduction," she whispered.

"She means it," Jameson said.

"I know she does."

"What's up?" Jameson asked.

Dana cringed.

"Do we need to step away right this minute?" Jameson asked.

Dana nodded.

"Excuse me for one minute," Jameson apologized to Janine Ellison.

Dana gently pulled Jameson aside.

"What's going on?" Jameson asked.

"Marianne just called."

Jameson froze.

"It's nothing serious."

"Then why are you pulling me away?"

"Pearl fell."

"What do you mean Pearl fell?"

"She's okay. Marianne just wanted you to call her as soon as you can."

"How long do I have?" Jameson asked.

Dana looked down at her iPad and up to the stage. "Probably about fifteen minutes before they wrap and call you up there."

Jameson nodded. She pulled out her phone. "Where can I…"

Dana beckoned one of the volunteers over. "Take Jameson around the corner to the booth."

"I'll be right back," Jameson promised. "Where's Coop?"

"He's still with Glenn. I'll have him here when you get back," Dana promised.

Jameson followed the volunteer to a small corner that housed a soundproof room. "Thanks." She lifted her phone. *Please, do not let this be anything that will upset her.* "Marianne?"

"JD? I'm so sorry to call you today."

"Don't worry about it. What's going on?"

"Grandma Pearl took a tumble."

"How bad?"

"She's okay, JD. Her wrist is broken."

Shit. "Do you need me to fly home tonight instead of tomorrow?"

"No. They want to keep Grandma tonight."

"Keep her? For a broken wrist? What aren't you telling me?"

"It's just that her heart's been pretty fast while she's been here."

"Shit."

"She's okay, JD. I swear. She didn't want me to call."

"I'm sure."

"I've got it under control here. But after Grandma Stratton… You know Mom is…"

"I'll handle your mother. Seriously, do you need me to come home early?"

"No. But I thought you should know. You know how everything is. God forbid Mom finds out somehow and thinks that no one called…"

"I know. Listen, I have to go."

"I know, I'm watching in the waiting room."

"Who's with the kids?"

"Shell has them."

"Shell? With the twins?"

"Yeah, I know! Crazy!"

"Are you sure there's nothing you haven't told me?"

"I promise."

"You know, your mother's going to want to come home."

"Grandma will kill me and then kill her. Tell her that."

Jameson chuckled. "I will. Call you in a bit."

"JD," Dana opened the door.

"Ready."

"Everything okay?" Dana asked as they walked back toward the stage.

"I don't really know. I think so. It might not be when I tell Candace."

Dana sighed. *It never ends.*

"What do you mean Pearl is in the hospital?"

"Candace, take a breath."

Candace glared at Jameson.

"She fell and broke her wrist."

"How?"

"I don't know. I didn't have time to get all the details. She's okay. Marianne is with her. They're going to keep her tonight."

"For a broken wrist?"

"Candace…"

"I'm flying home."

"No, you aren't."

"What?"

"No. Pearl will have all our heads if you do that."

"I don't really care."

Jameson licked her lips and took a deep breath. "Just take a breath."

"Governor Reid!"

"Go," Jameson said.

"I'm not going anywhere. They can wait."

Jameson took gentle hold of Candace's arms. "Do you trust me?"

"What? Of course!"

"Then let me handle this right now. Go and make the rounds with Nate. I promise when you get back I will have all the details, okay? I promise. If you still feel you need to go home, we'll go together."

Candace's entire body was shaking with fear. The thought of losing Pearl was more than she could bear.

"Candace, she's okay. Marianne would have told me. Go on."

Candace nodded. "You come get me if…"

"Go." Jameson waited for Candace to disappear into the crowd gathered outside the small room. *Deep breath, JD.*

———————◆●◆———————

"I'm not staying here."

"Grandma."

"Don't you 'Grandma' me," Pearl said. "For heaven's sake, I have a broken wrist, not brain damage. I swear, you become more like your mother by the day."

Marianne chuckled. "They just want to make sure your heart slows down a little."

"Slows down a little? Marianne, no one my age wants her heart to 'slow down a little.' That's like saying someone your age wants to wear Depends."

"You're impossible. You know, Mom is going to insist you do what the doctors say."

"Don't tell me you called her?!"

Marianne grinned sheepishly.

"Marianne!"

"What did you expect me to do?"

"Take me home for starters. I have two hands, you know. I can't believe you called your mother."

"I didn't."

"Well, good."

"I called JD."

Pearl rolled her eyes.

"Grandma, come on, please just do what they ask."

"I have stayed in the hospital twice in my life. So, unless some miracle has occurred and I am about to give birth for a third time, I'm going home."

Marianne groaned. *Mom, help.*

Candace said her goodbyes to Nate Ellison and his family, promising to see him the next morning for their appearance in Arizona. She turned to look for Jameson.

"Hey," Jameson caught up with her.

"What did you find out?"

"She's okay, Candace. She was furious that Marianne called."

"I would have been livid if she hadn't."

"She knows that too. She's been pushing Marianne to take her home."

"I thought they wanted to keep her?"

"They do," Jameson said. Candace's lingering nervousness was evident. "Listen, it's not uncommon. They did a few tests. She doesn't have any significant blockages that need to be addressed. She might need some blood pressure medication. I guess that was a little high, and maybe a blood thinner. She's okay. To tell you the truth, I suspect part of the reason they are being so cautious is you."

"Me?"

"Seriously? Candace, everyone knows that you consider Pearl your mom. Do you really think they want to let her go and take any kind of chance that something might happen? They are crossing every 'T' and dotting every 'I' with a fine point."

Candace huffed.

"If you go rushing home all it will do is upset her. She's already embarrassed."

"Embarrassed? Why?"

"From what Marianne said, Pearl was talking on her phone to Shell, and she wasn't paying attention to where she was walking. She tripped over one of Spencer's trucks."

"That could happen to any of us."

"Exactly, but all of us would feel the same way. You know that's true. Just do me a favor and call her? But calm down a little first? Marianne sounds like she's about to have a stroke. If anyone is going to get Pearl to see reason, it's you."

Candace nodded. *I wouldn't count on that.*

———◆◆◉◆◆———

"Candy…"

Candace softened her tone. "Mom, please."

Pearl closed her eyes in defeat. "You're not playing fair."

"I'll play it any way I need to if it will get you to stay put and behave. Just humor me, please?"

"Don't you come flying back here."

"Don't worry, Jameson hid my broomstick."

Pearl laughed then grumbled. "I feel fine."

"Just stay put or you're apt to have Marianne in the bed beside you."

"What about you?" Pearl asked. "I missed part of that show today while I was getting this cast. How'd it go?"

"I think it went well."

"How's Jameson?" Pearl asked.

Candace glanced across the room. "I don't know what I'd do without her."

"You don't say."

"Yeah, well, I don't know what I would do without you either."

"I'll try not to trip over any toys for a while."

"At least it wasn't Jinx this time, and maybe it's good that you did."

"What on earth are you breathing out there?" Pearl asked.

"You said yourself that they are putting you on some new medicine. Maybe this is a blessing in disguise."

Pearl sighed. "Maybe it is."

"That was tough to admit, wasn't it?"

"You have no idea."

"Let Marianne help until we get home," Candace requested.

"I have another hand, Candy."

"Just let her help."

Pearl chuckled. "Anyone ever tell you that you're kind of bossy?"

"Learned from the best."

"I don't want you worrying about me," Pearl said.

"Too late."

"Candy…"

"Don't tell me not to worry. Just do what the doctors say and let the kids help you for a change."

"The kids have enough with their kids."

"Mom…"

"Okay, I get it. Don't you dare tell any of them I admitted that."

Candace laughed. She felt a thousand times lighter after talking to Pearl. "I wish I wasn't so far away."

"You can make it up to me when you get home."

"Oh? What is my penance?"

"I don't know yet. I'll think of something."

"I've no doubt." Candace closed her eyes. News of Pearl's mishap had shaken her to her core. As grateful as Candace was to know that Pearl was in good health overall, her emotions remained raw. "I love you, you know?"

"Of course, I know. I love you too, Hellion."

"I'll call you tomorrow," Candace promised.

"If you have time."

"I'll have time."

"Speaking of time, go spend some with your wife and son," Pearl said.

"I will. Call if anything…"

"Goodnight, Candy."

"Night, Mom."

Jameson made her way over to the couch. "Feel better?"

"I do. Know what would make me feel even better?"

Jameson smirked.

"You are impossible." Candace swatted Jameson's knee.

"Let me guess; Chinese food."

"That would be a bonus. I was going to say a quiet night with you and Cooper and…"

"*Scooby Doo?*"

Candace laughed. "Why not? It beats another night of Aladdin."

Jameson got up from her seat.

"Where are you going?"

"To see about Chinese food."

Candace smiled. She made her way to the door and opened it.

"Governor Reid," the Secret Service Agent greeted her. "Did you need something?"

"Actually, I was going to tell you that we're ordering in. Anything you gentleman would like? Jameson's ordering Chinese."

"Not necessary, Ma'am."

Candace shook her head. "Agent Macpherson, we are stuck with each other. Call me Candace."

"I can't do that, "Ma'am."

Candace chuckled. "Call me anything but Ma'am. And, Dominick?"

He looked at her.

"Get used to Chinese food. It's serious business in this family."

"I'll make sure we check everything," he deadpanned.

"Good. Make sure they don't forget my fortune cookies."

"I meant for safety," he said.

"So, did I," Candace quipped. She was certain she saw him smile. *Ha-ha, gotcha!*

Friday, June 13th

"Nervous?" Congresswoman Mackey wondered.

"Is it that obvious?" Jameson asked.

"Not really. Just be yourself, JD."

"Easy for you to say."

"Not really." Congresswoman Elena Mackey squeezed Jameson's arm in reassurance.

Candace sat in front of the TV with Dana, Marianne, and Pearl watching the live feed from Chicago, waiting for Jameson to take the stage. "Cooper," she called to her son. "Momma's going to be on in a minute."

Cooper ran over and sat between his mother and Marianne.

"Is she on yet?" Michelle blew through the front door with Amanda in her arms.

"Aunt Shell!" Spencer slid across the floor toward her.

"Hey, Spence."

"Where's the other half of your duo?" Marianne asked.

"Mel's coming with Brody now. Did we miss it?"

"No. Any minute," Marianne said.

"Why's Momma on TV?" Cooper asked.

"Jay Jay is helping Nana," Spencer told him. He positioned himself on his mother's lap.

Michelle made her way over and squeezed in beside Pearl. "Did this couch shrink?"

Three sets of eyes simultaneously rolled at Michelle's question.

"What? It seems smaller."

"It's all the kids you keep adding," Candace commented.

"Hey, you're the chief contributor," Michelle replied.

"She's got you there," Pearl said.

"There's Momma!" Cooper pointed to the screen.

"Did I miss it?" Melanie stepped through the door. A collective "shhhh" served as her reply.

Candace concentrated on the screen as Jameson began to speak.

"I have to admit, I was surprised when Candace asked me to make this trip. She'd be the first to tell you that I am more comfortable climbing on roofs or designing them than I am speaking in front of a crowd."

Soft laughter rolled through the room.

"But this is a topic that I feel strongly about, just as she does. I was raised in a family full of police officers. My grandfather, my uncles, great-uncles, and two of my cousins served on the NYPD. I could tell a million stories from the dinner table and holiday gatherings. I can also tell you that I remember the expression on my grandmother's face, and the tears that my mother cried the night my Uncle Patrick was shot. You don't forget things like that. I know that each time an officer puts on his or her uniform, it is knowing that anything might happen that day—that at any moment they might be faced with a choice to fire their weapon or risk not seeing their family again."

"Did you write this, Shell?" Marianne asked.

"I only helped."

"I've heard people say that Candace is soft on crime, too interested in reforming criminals and not interested in supporting law enforcement. I've seen her after she's consoled the family of a fallen officer and I've watched her as she's held the hand of the mother of a teenager who has died on the street. Neither is acceptable to her."

Jameson took a breath.

"Some people criticize my wife for shedding any tears, others claim that she lacks heart. Candace has more heart than any person I have ever known. Her commitment to community policing is founded on her belief that every person has value, and that as partners we can change the communities we live in."

The crowd began to clap. A voice rang out and Jameson strained to hear it.

"She supports cop killers!"

"Uh-oh," Shell mumbled. "Ignore it, JD—just like we talked about."

Candace remained focused on the screen.

Jameson took a deep breath. She smiled and continued. "No," Jameson said. "She doesn't support any kind of violence." She watched as security began to remove the man and held up her hand. "No, no," she called out. "He's welcome to stay."

Candace smiled.

"This is exactly why Candace wants to see an investment in community policing. If we can't talk and listen to each other, how will we ever stop this cycle?"

"God, I love you," Candace said without thought.

Marianne exchanged a smiled with Michelle and Pearl.

"Like I said when I stepped out here, I was surprised when Candace asked me to come here. I welcome the chance to tell you about what she wants to do and why. I'm bias, but I believe she'll be the kind of president who values more than just Main Street or Wall Street. She wants to make a difference for every neighborhood in America. That's what this is all about—not just the idea of community policing or her campaign—her entire life."

"That wasn't in the speech," Michelle said.

Candace chuckled and hugged Cooper. "Your Momma is an amazing lady, Cooper."

"You should be glad she doesn't have any political aspirations," Marianne said. "She might give you a run for your money."

"I have no doubt."

LATER THAT EVENING

Jane waited for the waiter to leave. She'd secured a small private room for her and Candace to enjoy a leisurely dinner and assure that they could speak freely. "Jameson certainly held her own today with that crowd."

Candace beamed with pride. "She sure did."

"How are you both doing with everything?" Jane wondered.

"You mean the constant attention and protection?"

"For starters."

"It's not easy."

"No, it isn't," Jane agreed.

"I have to believe it's all worth it."

"It is. How are the kids?"

"Good—all of them. All this press surrounding Klein hasn't been easy for Laura, and that upsets Jonah."

"I can imagine. He's not the first vile man to end up with a great kid," Jane observed.

"No."

"I'm glad you had Dana call. I've been thinking that we were overdue for a sit-down."

"Long overdue."

"So? Ellison."

"You approve?" Candace asked.

"Savvy choice."

"I thought so."

"What is it you want to know?"

"I'd like your perspective."

"On?"

"Whether I should let him know *all* the reasons I chose him."

Candace was widely regarded as an intelligent and charismatic politician. What many people failed to realize was that Candace could be as cunning as the most adept intelligence agent. The governor preferred the high road. Jane admired that in her friend. Candace understood that if she hoped to successfully navigate the presidency far more than colorful rhetoric and shrewd negotiation skills would be required. National security had become a byline for foreign policy. Most people would never grasp the reality that national security encompassed every decision a president made in his or her capacity as the leader of the free world. Every speech, every signature, every interaction, every State dinner, every diplomatic overture ranked in equal importance to any activity a president engaged in as Commander in Chief. Every decision and each word that passed a president's lips had a direct effect on his or her success or failure. And, there would always be someone looking to undermine a president's agenda. There were reasons Candace Reid had chosen Nate Ellison as her running mate. Jane was sure that many aligned with the public narrative. She was also positive that Candace possessed a deeper motivation in putting Senator Ellison on the ticket.

"You haven't told him that you know," Jane surmised.

"No."

"And you want to know if you should?"

Candace sipped her wine. "I've already decided that I will. What I want to know from you is whether you think that should occur before or after the election."

Jane lifted her wine glass and sipped thoughtfully. *Excellent question.* She set it down and offered Candace a wicked grin.

Candace snickered. "You have an evil streak."

"No, but I do enjoy a good game of chess," Jane replied. "You're inviting his family for the barbeque on the fourth, I assume?"

"Of course."

"Tell him on your playing field."

Candace raised her brow.

Jane's smile broadened. "He won't see it coming. Alex and Cassidy will be there?"

"They will be. Claire and her partner too. Jameson's kept in touch regularly with her."

Jane nodded. "Well, that will send him a message on its own."

"Do you think he knows about Alex?"

"Alex and Jonathan are known entities in the intelligence community—broadly. There's no way he doesn't know about their affiliation. He certainly knows about Alex's past at the NSA. That's a matter of public record now. How much he knows, that I can't say."

"Will it compromise him? My telling him that I know his background is deeper than it appears?" Candace inquired.

"You mean as an intelligence operative?"

Candace nodded.

"Absolutely."

Candace nodded again.

"In the appropriate way. Right now? Right now, he thinks you've chosen the handsome golden boy, someone to bolster votes and help you win this election. That gives him power with the people who positioned him in the first place."

Candace sipped her wine thoughtfully. "I want him to understand that he works for my administration. Whatever agenda he was given before this is null and void unless I deem it otherwise."

Jane's eyes sparkled. "He won't see it coming."

"What do you know about his agenda?" Candace asked.

"Hard to say," Jane answered truthfully. "His father worked in military intelligence and consulted with the NSA. Nate? Well, he's a legal eagle with twelve years at DOJ before seeking public office. You know the story on paper. He worked high profile money laundering cases. If I had to guess, he was encouraged into public office to trace or to hide money trails."

"But whose?" Candace said.

"That's always the question," Jane said. "I'm not sure that matters anymore. Follow your gut. Let him know who is pulling his strings now. He's not the first intelligence operative highly placed. He'll be the first deliberately placed by a civilian. Even if he has distanced himself from his past as much as possible, the people he reported to will see his nomination to the ticket as an opportunity to further their agenda. Once in intelligence, always in intelligence. You never get to fully divorce it." She chuckled with delight. "I would love to be a fly on the wall when you tell him. Something tells me that's not the only reason you wanted to meet."

"No, it isn't."

"Should we order another bottle?" Jane raised her glass.

Candace laughed. "Tempting, but I'm not sure the image of Agent Macpherson carrying my drunken form out of here would do much for my prospects in the general."

"Fair point. So? What's on your mind?"

Candace sobered measurably. "Klein's connection to Moldova…"

"Disgusting."

"I agree. We didn't leak that document," Candace said

"I didn't think so."

"That means someone on Wolfe's team did."

"Likely," Jane agreed.

"Interesting timing."

Jane smiled. "You've been digging."

"Didn't have to dig deep to find the reason. Page three in *The New York Times* the same day did that for me."

"Ah, yes—Wolfe Industries' investment divestments."

Candace nodded. "Two medical companies, three investment brokerages—what I haven't been able to discern is why."

"But you have a guess."

"I do. You'd be hard-pressed to find a country he doesn't do business in."

"True," Jane agreed.

"He's divesting interests and investments in the Mediterranean. I'm not certain that would have made page one without the Klein scandal."

"Probably not."

Candace continued. "But the Klein scandal focuses on Moldova. That puts eyes squarely on Russia and Serbia. It feeds directly into their narrative about John and by extension, me."

Jane sighed. *Exactly on point.* "Are you sure there isn't something you haven't told me?" Jane joked.

Candace chuckled. "I'm not 007 or 0015 for that matter. You and I both know that this country is one of the worst offenders in the money laundering game. There's a reason he's peeling those off. The Mediterranean? It's a pipeline. We both know that too."

"Always has been."

"And, it's largely ignored—publicly speaking."

"Also, true. You want me to see what I can find out about those investments he's suddenly keen on divesting," Jane guessed.

"I wouldn't say no if you offered."

"I'll see what I can find out."

"Jane? The Moldova story?"

"Which part?"

"The women."

Jane sighed. "It's true, although I'm certain the women were used for much more than earning a few dollars in the bedroom."

"I was afraid you'd say that."

"You think the two stories are related," Jane surmised.

"I think it's all related."

Jane nodded. "Listen, I told you; there's a reason certain corners want Wolfe in The White House. You let me do the legwork for what you need come November. I promise, I will keep you in the loop. You need to concentrate on keeping him off Pennsylvania Avenue. This conversation tells you all the reasons why."

"Well, they certainly are determined to get him there by any means possible."

"They are. They're also set on crippling your ability to lead should you prevail. The Ellison move was wise. Play that hand. Make him your asset before anyone else tries to deploy him."

"You think his handlers are in Wolfe's corner?"

"I think Ellison thinks he's one of the good guys. Make sure he knows what that entails. You know more than he does already, Candace. I'd bet my life on that. He's not paid to ask questions. What he does in front of a camera or a crowd is not indicative of the agenda he has in his office or committee. It might be feeding information to someone. It might be influencing outcomes. He's *your* source now. I'll work on finding out who's been pulling his strings."

"I must be crazy to think I can do this."

"You're already doing it, Candace. John would love to be here to see you now."

"Do you honestly think any of it will ever change?"

Jane sighed. "Change is a relative term. Things change by the minute. Truthfully? Not in our lifetime. We can influence it—all of it. You can make a difference, Candace. You know as well as I do that there will always be greedy people. There will always be someone deluded by power. Until you figure out a way to change people, the world will struggle with all these issues. But, that doesn't mean we don't have to make the effort."

Candace raised her glass. "Touché. What about Drury and Stevis?"

Congressman Drury and Congressman Stevis were thought to be Candace's main detractors in the House. They both sat on the House Committee on Intelligence, and Candace was positive they were driving the call for her testimony. It was not a secret that they wanted a Republican in The White House. Candace wanted to know why they had both seemed hell-bent on Bradley Wolfe. Knowing their reasons would both help her tweak campaign strategy and prepare for the Oval Office.

Jane topped off her glass with some wine. "Drury has investments everywhere. I mean, everywhere—including in several of Wolfe's holdings. Stevis? He's the GOP's flunky, always has been. He doesn't have a mind of his own. That much I can tell you for certain. Alex could tell you more about Stevis. Talk to her."

"Alex?"

"Mmm. When she was at NSA, she was involved with some investigations into campaign funds—specifically, the diversion of campaign donations to other entities. Stevis was on the radar. That much I do know. They never pinned him or his campaign, but if she was digging into it; there was a reason to dig."

"Do you think Wolfe was involved?" Candace asked.

Jane raised her glass.

Candace shook her head. "What have I gotten myself into?"

"A beautiful mess," Jane said. She winked at Candace. "None of it surprises you."

"No. Maybe some part of me hoped…"

"Keep hoping," Jane said. "Just don't close your eyes."

Candace nodded. "I won't."

CHAPTER SEVEN

June 14th — The United States Capital

"Y ou seem calm," Dana observed.

"I have nothing to hide. Besides, I know something the congressmen don't."

"You usually do. Lots of press in there waiting for you."

"For once, let's hope I bore them to tears."

Dana laughed. "And they say nothing changes."

"Did you talk to Mom this morning?" Michelle asked Jameson.

"I talk to your mom every morning." Jameson held a bottle for Brody. She was intent on studying him as he ate.

"How was she?"

"She's fine, Shell."

"JD?"

"Hum?"

"Can I ask you something?"

"Can I stop you?" Jameson quipped.

"I'm serious."

"I'm sorry. What is it?"

Michelle fidgeted with the laundry she was folding.

"Shell?"

"Do you think Jonah and Laura are okay?"

"What do you mean?"

Michelle looked at Jameson with concern. "When you were in Nevada with Mom? Mel said Jonah was slamming things around at work. Laura showed up here that afternoon in tears with the kids. She wouldn't tell me what happened."

Jameson considered how to reply. Her relationship with each of Candace's grown children differed. In many ways, Marianne had become Jameson's best friend. Shell was like a little sister to Jameson. As strange as it might have seemed to some people, Jonah viewed Jameson as his parent, and when Jameson took the time to examine it, she loved Jonah in much the same way that she did Cooper. She was protective of the entire family. She loved them all equally, but her relationship with Jonah was something that she could not easily explain. He'd been struggling recently with balance. How could he support his wife fully when he hated her father? How could he support his mother when he wanted to publicly call out Lawson Klein?

"I think Jonah is trying to figure out how to support Laura."

"You mean because of her father."

"I do."

"He has to remember that it *is* her father, JD. I get it. I hate the guy."

"You might understand how he feels, Shell but you aren't the one living it. It's not just your mother he wants to protect. It's also his wife and his kids. That's a lot to handle."

"I guess, I'm just surprised."

"Surprised?"

"Yeah, at his temper. Jonah's always been the one to be cool-headed."

Jameson chuckled. "Living with you and Marianne, I doubt he had much choice."

"Ha-ha. Come on; he tells you everything."

"Not everything," Jameson said.

"You're not worried?"

"I worry about all of you," Jameson replied honestly.

"I just hope Klein doesn't succeed in breaking them up."

Jameson smiled. "I wouldn't worry too much about that, Shell."

"I don't know, JD. Laura was a mess that day. She wouldn't say why. She just said she needed some company."

"Shell, Laura's got a lot on her plate. You of all people should get that. She's got two kids, a father who insults her family publicly, a husband who is carrying more weight at work than he ever has, and a mother-in-law who is running for president. Cut her some slack. Maybe she just needed to be with an adult other than Jonah."

"Maybe."

"Don't project issues that aren't there."

"I'm not."

Jameson shook her head. She loved Michelle, but sometimes Michelle's emotions ran away with her mouth. "Let it be, Shell."

"Oh, God, you sounded just like Mom!"

"Good. Maybe then you will listen to me."

"I always listen to you."

"Yeah, right."

A sly grin crinkled the corners of Michelle's mouth as she sought to change the subject.

"What are you up to?" Jameson asked.

"You know how you said you don't want any babies?"

"I am sure I don't want to know where you are going with this."

"Hey, everyone has two kids now except you."

Jameson blinked and shook her head. "What?"

"What? It's true! Marianne, me, Jonah—we all have two. You are slacking, JD."

Jameson would have smacked her forehead if Brody hadn't been in her lap. "You need to get out more."

"What are you talking about?"

"How do you have time to play marriage counselor and fertility specialist with two babies to deal with?"

"Very funny, JD."

"I wasn't being funny. Are you that bored at home that you need to obsess over Jonah's marriage and my ovaries?"

"Who says it has to be *your* ovaries?"

"Oh, my God!" Jameson laughed. "Where is this coming from?"

"I told you. Don't you think Cooper should have a sibling?"

Jameson kept laughing. "Last I checked, he has three."

"His own age, JD."

"Your mother and I are not having a baby, Shell."

"Heard that before."

Jameson rolled her eyes. If nothing else, Michelle was consistent. "Out of curiosity, why do you always bring this up with me and not your mother?"

"Why? Think it'd work?"

"I think you need a hobby—one that doesn't involve me."

Michelle shrugged. She loved to tease Jameson. Her teasing was laced with a degree of truth. She was positive that Jameson thought about the subject more than she let on. She suspected that her mother had as well. She had to admit that she doubted they would ever act on their musings, but Michelle wanted them to know that they would be supported no matter what. She watched as Jameson lifted Brody to her shoulder.

"Stranger things have happened, JD."

"Not really," Jameson said.

"You ended up married to a candidate for president with three grown kids and became a grandma before forty," Michelle said.

Jameson paled immediately.

"See? Stranger things," Michelle said.

Jameson laughed. *Not really, Shell—not really.*

Candace sipped from the glass of water in front of her. She had sat on the other side of this room a few times when she was a congresswoman, and she had done her share of questioning as a senator. Testifying on the other side of the table was a new experience.

"Governor Reid, as the ranking member of the Intelligence Committee you were privy to numerous pieces of classified material; yes?"

"Correct."

"And, did you at any time share any of that sensitive material outside of the committee?"

Candace smiled. "Of course."

Congressman Drury's ears perked. "You did?"

"Outside of the Intelligence Committee? Of course, I did."

"You're admitting that you have shared classified information with parties not authorized to receive it?"

"No."

"I don't understand. You just told us that you shared classified information."

"Congressman, your question as I recall was whether I have ever shared classified information outside of the Intelligence Committee. The answer to that is yes. That is common protocol."

"It's common to share sensitive information outside a secure environment?"

Candace wished she could laugh. Congressman Drury's intention was to catch her off guard, to trap her with her words. It was a familiar game. He'd yet to realize that she'd turned the tables on him. Rookie.

"Governor?"

"I've never shared classified information with anyone who was not already aware of that information."

"That contradicts your statement," Drury responded.

"I don't believe so. You asked if I shared classified information outside of committee. There are numerous committees and people privy to that same information, Congressman. That includes the majority and minority leader of both houses, members and ranking members of committees on Foreign Relations, Homeland Security, Armed Services— among others. While not every member of the Senate or the House may have access to sensitive materials, I can assure you there are more than you might imagine."

"I don't need a lesson in congressional protocol."

Candace nodded.

"So, you've never shared classified intelligence with an unauthorized person?"

"No."

Drury took a breath. "In all your years, you never once slipped up at a family dinner."

Candace chuckled. "Congressman, I have four children and six grandchildren. Between wiping up spilled milk, inspecting castles made of my couch cushions and changing diapers, I'm lucky if I get to finish a glass of wine at dinner."

Muffled laughter filtered through the chamber. Candace resisted the urge to gloat. She had expected Congressman Drury to test her patience. So far, he had amused her. And, Candace was "privy," as the congressman had put it to much more information that he was ever likely to confront. She had no intention of sharing an ounce of it with the junior congressman. She was sure that he had no idea that just down the hall, Senator Blake Fitzgerald and Senator Pat Duncan were holding a press conference. What Candace was certain of, was that when Congressman Drury and his cohorts got the news, they would be both humiliated and furious. She found herself secretly hoping someone would come and whisper in the congressman's ear.

"Thank you for coming," Senator Fitzgerald greeted the press. "Considering the decision made by the House Committee on Intelligence to conduct hearings regarding policy decisions made during the Merrow administration, Senator Duncan and I felt we should address the issue publicly." The senator gestured behind him to a cluster of other senators. "Senators Wilcox, George, Abbot, and Burroughs are also present." Blake Fitzgerald took a deep breath. "Represented here today is the bi-partisan leadership of the Senate Intelligence, Foreign Relations, and Armed Services committees. At this time, none of the Senate committees intend to conduct any hearings nor any investigations pertaining to policy initiatives nor covert actions taken during the Merrow administration with regard to Russia. Each committee has conducted a review of the pertinent documents and no Senate committee has found any indication of improprieties by any member of any committee nor of any surrogate of the Merrow administration. To be clear, our leadership consists of both senators who served during that time and who are new to these committees."

"Will you testify?"

Senator Fitzgerald smiled. "We will testify at the request of the House Intelligence Committee. A couple of questions."

"Senators?"

"Daryl," Senator Fitzgerald acknowledged the reporter.

"Do you believe these hearings are a witch hunt?"

Senator Fitzgerald smiled. "I don't think I would classify an inquiry as a witch hunt."

"Congressman Drury and Congressman Stevis have levied some heavy accusations in the press about Governor Reid's relationship to President Merrow," the reporter chimed.

Senator Fitzgerald cleared his throat. "The House has the right to conduct hearings as it sees fit," he replied.

"How much of this is a ploy to hinder the governor's chances in the fall?" another voice called.

Senator Duncan stepped up to the microphone. "Look, folks, this is an election year. We all know that and a lot of things are said during campaigns."

"But it isn't a campaign making the allegations, it's two congressmen," the reporter said.

Duncan smiled. "As Senator Fitzgerald said, our partners across the hall have the right to conduct hearings and investigations as they deem necessary. We do not feel it is either necessary nor advantageous to hold hearings or investigations in the Senate, at least, not in these committees."

"Is that a unanimous decision?"

"It is," Senator Duncan replied.

———————◆•●•◆———————

Candace remained determined not to show any signs of fatigue. She was facing the last "interrogation" of the day. Her opinion of Congressman Phil Stevis was dwindling by the second, and it hadn't been high to begin with. He'd chosen to reiterate all of Senator Drury's musings and questions albeit with a bit more flair. She had to give him that much, Phil Stevis possessed a strange magnetism. As it was with all magnetic personalities, the congressman either served to attract or repel anyone who crossed his path. Candace was his opposite and that was perfectly acceptable to her.

"I'm sure you're tired, Governor Reid," Congressman Stevis said.

Of you. "I'm used to long days, Congressman."

"I'm sure. Before we wrap up today, I am curious about your relationship with President Merrow."

Candace remained stoic. *Be careful, Congressman.*

"You spent quite a bit of time alone with the former president."

"We were friends for years."

"Yes, you served in the Senate together."

Candace did not comment.

"And, he extended an offer originally to you, didn't he?"

Candace waited.

"A cabinet appointment?"

"No."

"No?"

"No. We had discussions about cabinet appointments during his transition. He never offered me a position."

"Really?"

"Really."

"Did that surprise you?"

"No."

"So, one of your closest friends and allies becomes president and he doesn't extend you any gratitude. That didn't irritate you?"

"Not at all."

"I see. That didn't stop him from sharing information with you."

"Not if he thought it was something I needed to know."

"Or?"

"Or if it was something he wanted an opinion on."

"I see. And, was any of that classified?"

"I'm certain it was."

"So, the President of the United States chose to share classified information with you."

"As a senator, of course."

"And, you didn't find that inappropriate."

"Not in the least."

"Because it was information you would have already been given in your capacity?"

"In most cases."

"In most cases?"

Candace nodded. "Yes."

"What about in other cases?"

"Those would be a privileged conversation."

The congressman bristled. "The president isn't here to assert executive privilege."

"No," Candace agreed. "Nor would he need to."

"You won't share that information with the committee?"

"What's the question?" Candace asked.

"Did President Merrow confide classified information to you at any time that you were not already aware of?"

"Yes."

"And, would you share that with the committee?"

"No."

"Why is that?"

"It isn't germane to the topic at hand nor have you been authorized to hear it."

"As a matter of course…"

"As a matter of law, the President of the United States has the right to share information as he or she deems in the best interest of the execution of his or her duties."

"But you cannot share that with us now?"

"I'm not the President of the United States."

Congressman Stevis offered Candace a sly grin. "Earlier you said that President Merrow never extended an offer to nominate you to a cabinet post."

"That's right."

"But you were extended an offer later, isn't that correct?"

Candace took a deep breath. It was common knowledge throughout these halls that President Wallace had extended Candace more than one offer to join his team. She'd always publicly denied the rumors that she had been his first choice as a running mate. She had been his first choice. She had not been the party's first choice, and she had made it clear that she had no desire to be Vice President. After his election, President Wallace had courted Candace repeatedly, almost aggressively to join his team. She was sure she could have picked her post had she been inclined to accept. The president's desire to nominate Candace to serve as Attorney General or Secretary of State had become a talking point since Candace announced her candidacy. She had not weighed in. President Wallace made no denials repeatedly telling anyone who asked that he would have loved to have Candace Reid on his team. For months, Candace had known she would eventually be forced to comment. She had not expected it to be in this forum.

"I was," Candace acknowledged.

"And, you declined?"

"I did."

"Why?"

"Personal reasons."

"Personal reasons?" Congressman Stevis scoffed at the reply. "Would any of the 'personal reasons' be related to your conversations with John Merrow?"

"No."

"So, you expect us to believe that as an aspirational senator you turned down a cabinet post for personal reasons?"

"I don't expect you to believe anything. That doesn't change the truth. It was my decision to accept or decline. I chose to decline."

Stevis' eye twitched perceptibly. "President Merrow was a *personal* friend to you."

"He was."

"He confided in you."

"I'd like to think we confided in each other," Candace replied dryly.

"Might those confidences have compromised you in a different administration?"

Candace shook her head. "I don't know that answer. I can't imagine how that would be. It certainly was not part of the equation in my decision."

"I see. President Merrow had close ties with some Russian actors. His administration sanctioned multiple covert missions that arguably emboldened Soviet era militant groups, one of whom is believed to have engineered the attack on our embassy in Moscow—an attack that claimed the lives of twenty-two people including Ambassador Russell Matthews."

"I would call that speculation, Congressman."

"Which part?"

"That any of the Merrow administration's policies or any of the intelligence operations conducted during that period *emboldened* the groups you reference. Those groups were emboldened long before President Merrow took office."

"That's your opinion."

"I suppose it is." Candace noted the smug look on Stevis' face. *Think I'm done?* "It's an opinion based on years of intelligence information, military assessment and political wrangling. And, it's an opinion shared by the majority of military leaders, diplomats, and senior members of Congress."

"So, you would mitigate your role as a surrogate for the Merrow administration in the embassy bombing?"

"I hardly think President Merrow would have deemed me a surrogate."

"Are you saying you never used your influence in or out of committee to further his agenda?"

"Of course, I used my influence—when I believed it was appropriate. That's part of the job, Congressman. There's no point in accepting a leadership position if you are unwilling to lead."

"And, President Merrow? Did he listen to your counsel?"

"Most of the time." Candace laughed. "He wasn't always keen on my opinions or advice."

"What was he keen on, Governor Reid? Would lining his pockets with profits or maybe the pockets of the DNC from ASA be one of those things?"

Candace took a deep breath to control her temper. ASA or Advanced Strategic Applications was a Russian energy company. At least, that was its front. ASA dealt in weapon development, arms sales, and almost every unsavory venture imaginable that could earn a profit. The company lined the pockets of the Russian government while empowering oligarchs across the region. Candace didn't doubt that ASA played some role in the tragedy at the embassy. What that role had been remained cloudy at best. She did know that John Merrow had no illusions about what ASA engaged in, and no affection for it nor its efforts. Sometimes, things were not as they appeared. The Merrow administration had done business with ASA. It was not her place, nor was this the forum to discuss the reasons why. She had only just begun to gain a clearer understanding of the intricacies involved in the bombing. Convoluted didn't begin to cover it. The layers of deception, the hundreds of operations, and the numerous assets still deployed across the globe were not pieces of intel that a congressman the likes of Duncan or Stevis would be entrusted with. Beyond that, Candace resented the innuendo the congressman's question held.

"Congressman," Candace addressed him calmly. "I'm not sure I understand what it is you hope to achieve here today."

"How about the truth?"

"The truth? The truth is that I'm not 'privy' to as much as you seem to believe. The information that I do have in no way supports the notion that President Merrow was lining his pockets from any corporation anywhere on the planet."

"The DNC certainly was enriched after his assassination."

Candace reached her limit. "That tends to happen when a party loses its leader in a senseless, violent, reprehensible act."

"The upside to assassination?"

Candace's expression darkened. *Too far, Congressman.*

"Perhaps I should rephrase that."

"Oh, I don't think that's necessary. I certainly don't believe the death of a human being has an upside. I've been at this a long time." Candace glanced around the room and let her eyes meet with several people. "These halls, these chambers—they see their share of discussion and debate—and, in the interest of truth, they also see a good deal of divisiveness. That's part of our political process. Occasionally, that all falls away. There are moments when rhetoric takes on depth and divisiveness gives way to attentiveness. Partisanship has no place in safeguarding this nation. Behind the closed doors of offices and meeting rooms, that's the part the public doesn't see."

"I don't see what that has to do with this hearing."

"It has everything to do with this hearing. John Merrow served this country with distinction long before he ran for office. You are free to disagree with his policies. You have the right to question his decisions. To suggest in any way, implicitly or explicitly that President Merrow acted in his best interest before the interest of this country is out of bounds."

"I'm not suggesting anything. I'm merely trying to get to the truth."

"Truth is a funny thing, Congressman. Two people can dissect a fact and come up with drastically different perceptions about its meaning. In the end? Facts fade in the light of the meaning we give them."

Stevis narrowed his gaze. "So, you are telling this committee that you don't believe your actions in any way hindered or compromised the security of this country or any of its allies or assets?"

Candace sighed. "No. I'm sure I've made decisions and cast votes that have resulted in negative consequences. I doubt there is anyone here that can truthfully claim otherwise. Hindsight is always 20/20, Congressman. An embassy bombing, a mass shooting, a railway accident share one major thing in common."

"What's that?"

"With hindsight, we can always find things we should have noticed, could have changed—mistakes, missteps, but none of us has the benefit of hindsight. We make the most informed decisions we can and when we suffer the inevitable tragedies, we learn from them."

"Congressman," Chairman Vasquez spoke. "That's your time."

"I just have one more question," Stevis said.

"The Governor has been kind enough to…"

"It's fine," Candace offered.

"Very well. Last question, Congressman Stevis."

"Governor Reid, looking back, would you change any of the recommendations you made while serving on the Intelligence Committee?"

"Looking back, there are many things I would change," Candace admitted. "I'm not sure that any recommendation our committee made—that any action the committee approved or for that matter, any legislation either house passed during my tenure would have prevented the attack in Moscow. I do know that had John Merrow lived to see the embassy destroyed, it would have torn him in two. Hindsight teaches us, Congressman. It does not give us guarantees nor absolution."

Congressman Vasquez stepped in. "Thank you, Governor, for taking the time to appear here and answer our questions. We all know how busy you are these days."

Candace smiled.

Vasquez continued. "This hearing is adjourned. A note for my colleagues, we are due in general session for a vote at 2:30 P.M."

Candace slid her chair back and grabbed her briefcase.

"That was interesting," Dana said.

Candace rolled her eyes.

"Wine?" Dana guessed.

"Scotch. Straight up."

Jameson peeked in Cooper's bedroom and laughed. He had taken his latest Lego creation to bed with him. *Priceless.* She wandered down the stairs in search of Candace. They hadn't had much occasion to spend time at the townhouse in Arlington since Candace became governor. At one time, Jameson had thought that this might become her primary residence. She'd started to plan for a second office in the DC area. Those plans had been tabled after Candace announced her candidacy for the governorship. After Jameson's discussion with Shell the previous day, she'd begun to mull over recommending to Melanie and Jonah that they follow through with that idea.

Candace was sitting on the sofa in the living room typing on her computer. Jameson stopped in her tracks when she realized that Candace was also on a call.

"Candace, if you think it's over the top, change it."

Jameson recognized the voice immediately as belonging to Cassidy Toles.

"It's not over the top."

"But?"

"I don't know, Cassidy. I just wonder if I shouldn't give the foreign policy angle more of a punch in this speech."

"It's your speech," Cassidy replied.

"That's the problem."

"That it's your speech?" Cassidy asked.

"Maybe I'm just too close to all of it."

"You are."

Candace laughed. "Thanks for your honesty."

"You're welcome."

"Tell me."

"Tell you what?" Cassidy asked. "Do you want me to tell you what *I* think or what I think you want to hear?"

"Touché." Candace sighed. "Tell me what you think."

"I think you should be yourself. This isn't a policy speech. This is you showing the world who you will be as a leader. Don't get tied up in what happened today. You didn't while you were testifying. You spoke above the politics. You spoke above the details in policy. That is what this speech should be. You know it. You're just so busy convincing yourself that you should listen to the people around you that you aren't listening to yourself."

Candace laughed. "Tell me again why you aren't running?"

"Oh, no—no thank you. I'm happy working for you."

"I don't know what I'd do without you."

"You'd be fine."

"I don't know, Cassidy. The more I learn, the fewer people I trust."

Cassidy sighed. She'd been close enough to the inner workings of presidential politics to know what Candace meant. And, Cassidy had the inside track on the intelligence concerns Candace was dealing with. "Just don't let anyone make you lose trust in your judgment, not when it comes to a speech or policy," Cassidy advised. "Don't let them, Candace. God knows, someone will always try."

Candace did know. "Thanks."

"Anytime."

"We'll go over this again next week?"

"Whenever you want," Cassidy promised.

"Cassidy?"

"Yeah?"

"I hope you and Alex will still be able to make it that night."

"I wouldn't miss it."

"Talk to you later."

"You will. Tell Cooper and JD we send our love."

"I will."

Candace collapsed back against the sofa with a thud.

"Cassidy, huh?" Jameson made her entrance.

"I don't know what I would do without her; I swear."

"So, I heard. Problems with your speech?"

"Not really," Candace said. "I needed to get out of everyone else's head."

"Mmm."

"Cooper go down?"

"He's sleeping with that Lego monster he built."

"Let's hope it doesn't lose its head in the night."

Jameson laughed.

Candace closed her laptop and let her head fall into Jameson's lap. "How did things go with Shell yesterday?"

"Depends on which things you are asking about?"

"Uh-oh."

"My speech? Fine."

"What happened?" Candace asked.

"To tell you the truth, I'm not really sure."

"Want to talk about it?"

"I don't know—she was worried about Jonah and Laura."

"Jonah and Laura, why?"

"He's been stressed out at work; I know that. All the drama with Klein—you know, it's hard for him to keep quiet about the guy."

"I understand that."

"She thinks that signals some doom for them or something. I guess Laura showed up at Shell's in tears."

Candace sighed. "I know. She called me."

"Laura?"

"Yeah. It wasn't Jonah, though. She was upset about me."

"You?"

"She thought that her father would get dragged into my testimony."

Jameson groaned. "I really hate that guy."

"Jameson? What aren't you telling me?"

Jameson groaned again. "Shell has some crazy idea about us having a baby."

Candace laughed. "She would."

"At first, I thought she was just busting my chops."

"At first?"

"I don't know, Candace. I think she's really stressed out about all the changes."

"You mean being home with the twins?"

"Not exactly. I think she's feeling kind of lost, though. Some of it is how much Mel has had to deal with recently. She's been traveling a lot."

"I know."

"It got me thinking."

"About?"

"Maybe Jonah and Mel should revisit my idea of opening an office down here."

"In DC?"

Jameson nodded.

"Are you thinking that one of them should move here?"

"Candace, I think that we will be."

"Jameson, there is no guarantee I will win this election."

"No, I know. I think you need to stop that, though."

"Stop what?"

"Quantifying things. We both know nothing is guaranteed, not even tomorrow. If I did place bets, I'd lay all the odds in your favor. You're going to win."

Candace pivoted. "Who are you thinking should come here?"

"At first, I was thinking Shell."

"And now?"

"I think Shell needs to be close to Marianne. I think Marianne needs that too."

Candace listened.

"Jonah and Laura? Candace, I think Laura misses you even more than Marianne, and that's saying something. She needs you. It's great that she has Mary, but to her? To her, you are her mom."

"I know."

"And, Jonah?"

"Jonah misses you," Candace said.

"I know. They could take this place."

Candace smiled. "I suppose they could."

"What?"

"You miss Jonah," Candace said.

"Yeah, I do."

"If you really think it's a good idea for the firm, talk to them."

"What do you think?" Jameson asked.

"If I had my way, I wouldn't be far from any of them."

Jameson nodded.

"Jameson?"

"Yeah?"

"Did Shell's baby talk get you thinking?"

"Yeah. It did. It got me thinking that she needs meds."

Candace laughed. "That's not what I meant."

"I know." Jameson took a deep breath. "I'll always think about it," she admitted. "That doesn't mean I'll ever want to do it."

Candace reached up and stroked Jameson's cheek. "I know. Me too."

"Want to go upstairs?"

Candace shook her head. "Would you mind if we just stayed here for a while?"

"Not at all."

Candace closed her eyes. "You're a terrific mom, you know?"

"I've had terrific teachers."

Candace tenderly caressed Jameson's hand as it held her. "Thanks."

"For what?" Jameson wondered.

"For thinking about it."

Jameson bent over and kissed Candace's forehead. She leaned back and let her eyes fall shut. "Right now, I don't want to think about anything—including any of the kids."

A smile graced Candace's lips. "We could try."

Jameson opened one eye. "You want to try and knock me up?"

Candace giggled.

"The apple definitely did not fall far from the tree."

"What?" Candace asked.

"You're as crazy as Shell."

"Probably so," Candace agreed. "Still love me?"

"More than anything."

CHAPTER EIGHT

June 21st — Democratic National Convention

Jameson paced in the kitchen of the hotel suite rehearsing her speech.

"You know, it will be right there in front of you," Marianne said.

"Maybe. I'd feel better if I memorized it."

"JD, you're going to be great. Look how you handled that rally in Illinois."

"That was a lot smaller. The whole world wasn't watching."

"True, but this will be a room full of Democrats. Everybody in there is on Mom's team. You've seen them the last couple of days. They're all going to be excited to see you."

Jameson appreciated Marianne's support and encouragement. Tonight was Candace's night. Aside from Election Night and potentially her Inauguration, tonight would likely be the most momentous night in Candace's career. That was not lost on Jameson. The last two days had been filled with nervous excitement. Jameson could feel the energy throughout the convention hall. She had been in the hall with Michelle for the roll call as each delegation cast its votes for Candace. She'd been surprised at the way her heart raced. It wasn't as if she didn't know the outcome. Something about the process made her feel as though she were sitting on pins and needles.

Jameson had the opportunity to introduce her wife. Candace's acceptance speech would follow. She'd been reluctant at first, suggesting that Michelle might be a better choice; perhaps even Marianne would be willing. Dana had assured her that if she felt uncomfortable, Candace would understand. But Dana had also told Jameson that she believed no one could make an introduction as earnest, heartfelt, and moving as Jameson. No one knew Candace better. After talking it over with her mother, Pearl, Candace, and even with Cassidy, Jameson agreed. She'd spent hours with Michelle hashing out the right words. She'd been practicing all morning. Hearing them over and over, Jameson worried that her sentiments might be inadequate.

"I don't want to blow this," Jameson said.

"You won't." Marianne squeezed Jameson's hand. "I've heard it. It's all you. It's the truth, isn't it?"

"Every word."

"Then, trust me; it will be everything it's meant to be."

I hope so.

Maureen Reid's face dropped to her hands in defeat.

"Mo?" Duncan Reid called for his wife's attention.

Maureen looked up with unshed tears.

"Hey, what's wrong? I thought you'd be excited."

"I don't know what to do."

"Do about what?"

Maureen shook her head. "Colleen just called me."

Duncan's brow furrowed. Colleen was married to Maureen's brother Jerry. Maureen had been distant from her brother's family for years. Jerry was an outspoken critic of many things—not the least of which was Jameson.

"Jerry… Duncan, he's started giving interviews about JD."

Duncan's jaw tightened. "What do you mean he's giving interviews?"

"I don't know! Colleen was so upset she could barely talk. You know how he is. He's been like this ever since Craig died."

"I'm sorry about Craig; we all were. That was not JD or Scott's fault. I don't care how much pain he has; he doesn't have any right to hurt Jameson."

"What am I supposed to do?" Maureen asked.

"What exactly did Colleen say?"

"Only that he's supporting Bradley Wolfe any way he can and that he's going to help him any way he can. God! I never thought he would take things this far!"

"You don't know what he's doing," Duncan said.

"We both know what he's capable of."

Duncan scratched his brow. Jerry Donnelly had never been known for his patience. In fact, Duncan had always suspected that his freeness with his fists had led to his son Craig's desire to spend as much time as possible away from home. After Craig's death, Jerry had started drinking with greater frequency. When Maureen's eldest brother, Patrick died of cancer, Jerry had gone off the rails. Duncan had tried to talk to him. Maureen had tried to reason with him. Even Scott had attempted to reach his uncle. Nothing seemed to work. Jerry Donnelly had become a bitter old man before his time.

"Let's just hope whatever he does, JD doesn't see it."

Maureen looked at her husband doubtfully.

"You need to get ready," Duncan said. "JD will kill us both if we're late. Don't let him spoil today, Mo."

Maureen smiled. It wasn't every day a mother got to watch her daughter introduce the woman who would likely become the next president. "Not a chance."

Candace had commandeered a small conference room in the hotel for a meeting with her Chief of Staff and New York's Attorney General. It was a monthly conference call with her Lieutenant Governor, federal and local partners, and the Superintendent of the New York State Police regarding threat assessments and readiness for the state. Not even the convention slowed the business of the State of New York. No matter where Candace was, there were things that required her attention.

"Any other concerns?" Candace asked.

"Nothing from me," Superintendent Foster replied. "Unless any of our local representatives have something."

A short chorus of no's poured over the open line.

"Excuse me, Governor?"

Candace turned to the sound of Dana's voice.

"A moment?" Dana requested.

"Now? Can't it wait?"

Dana shook her head. "I'm sorry."

Candace studied Dana's expression and determined whatever needed to be discussed required privacy. "Give us the room, please. We'll pick this up again on the next call. If anyone has concerns feel free to bring them to Dan or myself at any time."

Dana stepped inside, offering the departing attendants a silent acknowledgment as they passed her. "I'm sorry."

"This had better be good."

Dana pulled out her phone. "I'm not sure good is the word I'd use." She opened a video and pressed play.

"What am I watching?"

"I think it's better if you see for yourself."

Candace took a deep breath and focused on the screen.

"So, you've known Jameson Reid most of your life."

"Since we were teenagers."

"And, what made you come forward now?"

"It's like her Uncle Jerry said, she's not who she pretends to be."

"Do you care to clarify that?"

"You know, she's not really gay."

"That seems like a crazy accusation to make."

"Well, she wasn't gay when she was with me. A little drunk, maybe—not into girls, if you know what I mean."

Candace's blood began to boil. She noted Jameson's Uncle Jerry in the background. Her hand balled into a fist as the interview continued.

"Ms. Reid's been in the public eye for years. What made you start talking about this now?"

"I heard her Uncle Jerry, you know? Talking about how she led her cousins into trouble. JD was always with them. And, they liked to party. Now, all of a sudden, she's the poster child for sobriety and gay rights? People have a right to know who she really is."

"I've seen enough." Candace pushed the phone away. "When was this?"

"About twenty minutes ago at a Wolfe Rally in the city."

Candace sat silently, brewing over how to proceed. "Who is he?"

"His name is Jed Tyler."

Candace pushed out her chair and smoothed out her blazer. "Find out everything there is to know about Mr. Tyler. If he so much as blew through a stop sign at sixteen, I want to know about it."

"Candace…"

"Do it Dana, or I'll find someone who will." Candace headed toward the door.

"Where are you going?"

"I need to find Jameson—now."

―――――――――◆●◆―――――――――

Candace walked without comment through the hallway toward the suite she had.

"Governor Reid," Agent Barclay addressed her.

Candace smiled. "I'm sorry Gil. I didn't mean to ignore you."

"No Ma'am, I was just wondering if you planned on heading back to the conference rooms soon."

"Not immediately—no."

Agent Barclay nodded to the Secret Service agents placed outside Candace's suite. "If you change your mind…"

"You'll be the first to know," Candace promised. The moment she walked through the door Marianne approached her. Candace needed no explanation. Jameson had seen the video. "Where is she?" Candace asked.

"She stepped out onto the balcony for some air."

Candace took a long, deep breath.

"You saw it, didn't you?" Marianne guessed.

"Unfortunately. I was hoping I would get here before Jameson did."

"Mom, she's—I've never seen JD like that."

Candace nodded. "Where's Cooper?"

"Scott took the boys downstairs to the pool so JD could work on her speech."

"Someone went with them?"

"Of course," Marianne said. "You know, they won't let JD or Cooper leave the room without an escort."

"Good."

"Mom, are you worried about Cooper's safety?"

"I'm worried about a lot of things. Do me a favor?"

Marianne guessed what her mother's request would be. "Clear out for a few?"

"Catch your sister before she comes storming through the door. She should be here any minute. And, see if you can reach Maureen. They're probably on route."

"I'll do my best."

Candace offered a smile as her thanks and went in search of Jameson. She noted a crushed soda can sitting on one of the tables in the common room. *That's not good.* She stopped before making her way through the sliding glass doors to the balcony. Jameson was standing with her hands gripping the railing. Candace took a deep breath and ventured forward.

"Jameson."

Jameson didn't move. "It wasn't enough back then?"

"Jameson." Candace walked forward and put her hand on Jameson's back. "I'm so sorry, honey."

Jameson shook her head. She couldn't face Candace. She couldn't face anyone yet. Her initial reaction to seeing Jed Tyler on television was disbelief. Shame and guilt immediately followed. Anger simmered beneath it all. "It's a lie. Just like it was then. It's a lie."

Candace closed her eyes against an onslaught of raw pain. Jameson had only been intimate with one man in her life. She had confided the details of her first-time to Candace. It was an experience Candace had listened to many women recount—someone taking what they had no right to take. Jameson's only fault had been trusting the wrong person. Jed Tyler had taken advantage of that trust, and he had taken Jameson's innocence. He'd just violated her again. "I'm so sorry."

Jameson finally turned. "This isn't your fault, Candace."

"Maybe not, but you are caught in the crossfire because of me."

"Bullshit. My asshole uncle just found a way to put the screws to me again. I don't even know how he found out about Jed. Where the hell did he dig that up?"

"My guess is he didn't."

"He was right there!"

"I saw."

"What the hell, Candace? What do I do now? I'm supposed to walk out on that stage tonight and introduce you. How the hell do I do that?"

Candace held Jameson's arms. "You do it exactly the way you planned before you saw that video."

"How?"

"Jameson, listen to me—please. No one who matters is giving that show that happened earlier today an ounce of credence—no one. You don't owe anyone an explanation. You have *nothing* to feel self-conscious about."

"Oh? Aside from being called a whore and a liar?"

"We both know you are neither of those things."

Jameson shook her head. "I thought that was over. Do you have any idea how many times that memory still comes back?"

"I do."

"Son of a bitch!"

Candace could feel Jameson trembling beneath her touch. "Jameson, I know how much this hurts."

"Candace, the kids will hear that. Cooper will see that one day— he's going to hear people saying that."

"The kids love you—all of them. I love you. And, believe me when I tell you that there are millions of people who have already fallen in love with you too. Don't give him this power. You are not a sixteen-year-old girl afraid of who you are. You're a successful, beautiful, strong woman. Don't give him that power, Jameson. It's not his to take."

Tears streamed over Jameson's cheeks. "Why would Jerry do that? Why would anyone do that?"

Candace pulled Jameson to her and held her. "I don't know, honey." *But I promise you, I am going to find out.*

Candace kissed a sleeping Jameson on the temple. "I love you so much," she promised. She was relieved that Jameson had calmed and was resting. Candace found herself torn between wanting to hold Jameson close and finding a way to eviscerate Jerry Donnelly and Jed Tyler. She had no doubt that Jameson would emerge that evening as the picture of strength and confidence. She also understood that the earlier display had hurt her wife deeply. Candace had spent years as the target of hateful rhetoric and innuendo. None of it had ever come from her family, not publicly. Jed Tyler's two minutes of fame would have been painful on its own. The knowledge that Jameson's Uncle Jerry had been a party to it, perhaps even solicited it was unfathomable to Candace. She kissed Jameson again sweetly. Marianne had called and informed Candace that Maureen was on the verge of flying home and confronting her older brother. Candace reluctantly pulled herself from the bed and straightened her attire. A day that should have centered on celebration had taken an unexpected turn toward damage control. *Tell me why I'm doing this again?*

"Candace," Maureen accepted Candace's hug. "I'm so sorry."

"You don't have anything to be sorry for."

"I can't believe he would do that."

Candace nodded sadly. "I know. Jameson wanted me to explain."

"She doesn't need to explain anything."

"I know that too. I'm not sure that she's ready to talk about this with anyone."

Maureen's heart lurched in her chest.

Candace took her mother-in-law's hand. "I don't think Jameson has ever told anyone except me."

"Told them what?"

"Jed Tyler."

"She went on a few dates with him back in high school."

Candace nodded. "She did. One of those dates," Candace paused and inhaled a deep breath for courage. She could imagine how she would feel if Maureen were telling her the same story about Marianne or Shell. She sighed. "He took advantage of the situation."

Maureen thought she might be sick. "Are you telling me he raped her?"

Candace's solemn smile gave the answer.

"Why didn't she tell us?"

"She was a sixteen-year-old girl struggling with her sexuality."

Maureen's eyes filled with tears. "Oh, JD."

"I know that you want to lash out at them, I do too. That isn't what Jameson needs right now."

"I can't believe Jerry would... I mean, he's always been hurtful—long before Craig's death."

"I've heard."

"But, this? My God, Candace." Maureen shook her head. "Is Jameson…"

"She's resting. She's okay—just okay."

"Is she still planning on introducing you?"

Candace smiled. "She is."

"She was already nervous."

Candace was aware that Jameson was nervous about speaking at the convention. She also believed that the day's events would instill a unique resolve in her wife. Jameson needed to step onto that stage more now than ever. She would claim the power that Jed Tyler had tried to take from her. And, that would empower her in new ways. Candace was confident of that fact.

"She needs to do this," Candace said. "Not for me, for her."

Maureen nodded. "I swear to you…"

"Trust me; I know how you feel. I need you to also trust me that I will not take this lying down."

Maureen offered the first hint of a smile. *Oh, I have no doubt about that.* "I wish I could say I feel sorry for them."

"Not a sentiment they deserve," Candace replied.

"No, it isn't."

— ◆●◆ —

Marianne hadn't made any attempt to wade into what she was positive were tumultuous waters. Jameson had gone to Michelle and Melanie's room to escape the constant flow of advisers and family in and out of the hotel suite.

"How's JD?" Marianne asked Candace.

"She's okay."

"What about you?"

"I'm all right, Marianne."

"No, you aren't. I can tell."

Candace smiled. "I will be. She will be too."

"What did Maureen say?"

Candace sighed. Jameson's mother was beyond furious. Maureen Reid's fury had managed to calm both Jameson and Candace. Candace had found herself talking her mother-in-law off a ledge. Jameson hadn't told many people about what Jed Tyler had done to her in the backseat of his car. Jameson had wrestled with guilt for years. Her body had responded without her permission just as Jed Tyler had continued to touch her without her consent. The entire situation made Candace sick. Maureen, upon hearing the details was ready to kill both her brother and Jed Tyler.

"She was upset," Candace said.

"I don't blame her. I'd like a few minutes alone with those assholes myself."

Candace chuckled. *You are so protective.* "I think Jameson might let you."

"Is JD going to be okay tonight?"

"She's practicing with Shell now," Candace said. "She'll be great."

"She must be a wreck."

"Oh, I think she might just surprise everyone," Candace said. She patted Marianne's knee. "I have a couple of calls I need to make before Jameson gets back."

Marianne watched her mother go.

Melanie had brought the twins to Candace and Jameson's suite to give her wife and Jameson some space. "Where's your mom off to?" she asked.

"She's making some calls."

"Think they'll be okay?"

"Who?" Marianne asked.

"JD and your mom."

Candace was much calmer than Marianne had expected. That told her that Candace was working on something. She almost pitied the men who had verbally assaulted Jameson's character—almost. "I wouldn't worry too much about Mom and JD."

"That had to be brutal," Melanie observed.

Marianne smiled. *Not as brutal as it's going to be, I'd bet.*

———————◆—●—◆———————

"Did you see Jameson?" Candace asked Cassidy.

"I did. She wanted to run a couple of things by me about her speech."

Candace nodded.

"Are you all right?" Cassidy asked.

"Not even a little bit."

"That's what I thought. Want to talk about it?"

"Yes, just not now."

Cassidy understood. Candace needed to stay focused, not only for herself and for the task that awaited her; she also needed to keep her anger in check for Jameson.

"Anything you want to review before I head downstairs?" Cassidy asked.

"No. I think I'm all set."

Cassidy clasped Candace's hand. "You will both be amazing."

Cassidy turned to leave. Candace pulled her back.

"Thank you, Cass. Your friendship—it means more to me than I think you know."

Cassidy did know. She and Candace had been friends for years. Working together had grown that friendship immensely. She smiled at the governor. They spoke daily about everything from the campaign to politics in general, their wives, their children, their parents, and the past and future. Cassidy had many friends. Candace did as well. They both tended to play other roles for the people closest to them: parent, child, mentor, even lover. While Cassidy was sure that Candace cherished all those roles just as she did, everyone needed an equal, a friend that was a confidante—a companion without any other part to play. She reached over and hugged Candace.

"I do know," Cassidy said. "I feel the same way."

Candace smiled. "It's been a long time since I had a best friend who was…"

"Just that," Cassidy finished the thought. "I know. Me too. I'll see you after the confetti falls."

"You will," Candace said.

"Aren't you going to go see JD before she leaves?" Michelle asked.

"No."

Michelle was shocked.

"She asked me not to," Candace explained. "It's been an emotional day, Shell." Candace could tell Michelle was still confused. She directed Michelle to sit beside her on the bed. "Sometimes, when we are together it's hard to separate emotions," she said. "I can only speak from my point of view. I love her so much, Shell—so much that just looking at her hurts sometimes. In a way that I think everyone hopes they will experience, but as much as loving her gives me clarity, it can also cloud my ability to focus."

Michelle smiled. Her mother's candor amazed her. "I think I get it."

"I would love to see her—give her a good luck kiss. I think my presence will make her nervous. I'll head down just after she does."

"I'm sorry about everything that happened today."

"We all are," Candace replied. "This is our moment to show everyone who we are as a family."

"That's kind of what JD said when she was getting dressed."

Candace grinned. "So? Let's show them."

Jameson felt a hand press into her back. "You are going to blow them all away," Marianne whispered.

Jameson turned around and smiled at her step-daughter. She didn't always voice her feelings. Marianne had been a rock for her all afternoon. She'd known when to give Jameson space and when Jameson needed her presence. That's why everyone needed a best friend.

Marianne wasn't certain what she saw brewing in Jameson's eyes.

"I'm not always great at telling people how I feel," Jameson said.

Marianne tipped her head curiously.

"You're my best friend," Jameson said. "Not like Scott or Steve. There was a time I would never have imagined saying this."

Marianne grinned.

"But you are. I just want you to know that."

Marianne leaned in and kissed Jameson's cheek. "I'm glad Mom found you," she said. "I feel the same way."

Jameson nodded and took a deep breath. "Did you see her?"

"Mom?"

Jameson nodded again.

Marianne almost laughed. Jameson looked like a love-struck teenager. "She's not far."

Another nod served as Jameson's reply. She inspected herself. "Do I look okay?"

"You look great, JD."

"You don't think I should have made them let me wear something more—I don't know, frilly?"

Marianne laughed. "Frilly?"

"You know what I mean! Girlie!"

Marianne shook her head affectionately. Jameson would do anything for Candace. Jameson's navy pantsuit complimented both her looks and her personality. All Candace would ever want was for Jameson to be herself. Marianne gave Jameson's hand a gentle squeeze as the video playing on the giant screens wound into its final moment. *I can't wait to see Mom's face when you take that stage.* "I'll see you in a few," Marianne promised.

"Unless I pass out first."

"You won't."

Marianne stepped away and bumped into Dana.

"How is she?" Dana asked.

"She's JD."

Dana sidled up to Jameson. "You ready?"

Jameson nodded. "Who invented heels?" she muttered. "Masochists."

Dana chuckled. *Yep, she's JD.*

◆━●━◆

Marianne slid in next to her mother behind the stage. Jameson was just walking out to greet the crowd. Marianne's attention fell on her mother's expression. Candace's eyes twinkled with affection and pride. She was sure that watching her mother watch Jameson would be every bit as entertaining as Jameson's words.

Jameson waved to the crowd and stepped up to the podium. She let her eyes fall on the several teleprompters that would roll through her speech. *You can do this, JD.* Jameson held up her hand as a signal for the crowd to quiet.

"We love you, JD!" A round of clapping and renewed cheers erupted.

Jameson felt the sentiment lodge in her chest.

"I love you too," she called out to the audience.

Candace smiled. "She's already got them."

Marianne put an arm around her mother. "She sure does."

Jameson chuckled at the continued cheers. "Okay," she spoke into the microphone. "Settle down so we can get to the main attraction."

The crowd laughed. Jameson waited a beat for the laughter to fade.

"Most of you know by now that my claim to fame is my wife—unless you ask her. She'll tell you it's my ability to order the correct Chinese food."

Michelle laughed loudly. "That was *not* in the speech."
Candace shook her head. *Lunatic.*

Jameson smiled broadly. "The world knows a stateswoman. And, Candace is that. She is the most intelligent and thoughtful person I've ever met. She sees people as people no matter where they live, how they've struggled or how much success they've enjoyed. She doesn't see problems; she sees opportunities. You can listen to all the news and all the experts weigh in on her talent and experience. You can read a million articles about her agenda and how it will or will not work. That's not my field of expertise." Jameson took a breath. "I can't give you an assessment of those things. I can tell you that Candace is someone who finds solutions. I know that because I've watched her do it a million times. I can tell you that she's a woman who can bring people together in ways that cultivate the most unlikely friendships. Before Candace was a congresswoman, a senator or a governor, she was someone's daughter, sister, friend, wife, and mother. It's all those pieces of her that have made her the compassionate leader she is."

Marianne watched as Candace's teeth gripped her bottom lip. Not for the first time, she marveled at the love she witnessed in her mother's eyes.

Jameson took a deep breath. She knew the script. She also felt she needed to be honest. "They'll tell you that I'm biased. I am. The truth is I love Candace more than anything in this world. I've watched her hold our children and grandchildren through loss. I'm still amazed every day at the way she manages to balance all the demands placed on her and remain attentive to the needs of our family. She always has time for the people she loves. She doesn't make promises unless she intends to keep them, and she doesn't shy away from responsibility. She knows how to say, 'I'm sorry," and when she does, she means it. I didn't fall in love with Senator Candace Fletcher. I fell in love with a woman who loves Chinese take-out, stows away fortune cookies, and hates it when I climb on ladders."

Candace laughed and wiped a tear from the corner of her eye.

"I fell in love with a mother whose eyes sparkle every time one of her kids calls her, 'Mom.' I fell in love with a person who makes me laugh without warning and listens to all my crazy rambling when she still has hours of work to complete. That's the Candace I know. And, it's all those parts of her that will make her the best president this country has ever had. She'll listen. She'll stand up for what she believes in. More than all the things you read or you've heard—she cares. She sees each and every one of you as an extended part of her family, as someone she wants to see cared for and appreciated. It's not a slogan. It's who she is."

Marianne pulled her mother closer. "She's right."
Candace pushed back her tears. "If she doesn't stop soon, they'll be watching a raccoon on stage."
Marianne giggled.

"The truth is," Jameson said, "sharing the person you love with the entire world isn't always easy." She took a deep breath. "I've never told this story, not even to our kids."

"Oh, Lord, what is she up to?" Candace wondered.

"I mentioned that Candace has a stash of fortune cookies. It's a bit of a joke in our family." Jameson paused. *That and Bible study, but we'll leave that one out.* "What no one knows is that I proposed to her with a fortune cookie." Faint laughter rolled through the large hall.

"She did not!" Jonah commented from behind Candace.
Candace grinned. "She did."

"I'll tell you what the fortune said. It said, 'A ship in the harbor is safe, that's not what ships are built for.' You see, I'm an architect. I understand foundations and ceilings. Those are stationary structures. Candace taught me that relationships are like ships. Life is like a ship. I told her that day that you could build a strong, majestic ship but it's not worth its weight or grandeur if you never set sail. You have to trust that it will be able to navigate rocky waters. You might be asking what that has to do with all of this. I'd say everything. Candace is a masterful navigator for all the reasons I've shared. That's why I am so proud to share her with all of you. If you don't believe anything else I've said, believe this: Candace Reid will guide this country forward with compassionate strength no matter how deep or ferocious the waters may appear. She will never quit on you—never."

"This is it, Mom," Michelle said.
Candace nodded and took a deep breath.

"You couldn't find a better person if you sailed the world a thousand times over. And, I couldn't be prouder to introduce the woman I get to call my wife and your next president, Governor Candace Reid!"

Candace sucked in one more breath and stepped out on the stage to thundering applause. She waved to the crowd and smiled. A few steps and she was looking into Jameson's eyes. She cupped Jameson's face with her hands and brought their lips together tenderly. "I love you."
Jameson beamed with pride. "I love you."
Another long embrace and Jameson handed the crowd to her wife.

"Holy shit," Jonah said.
"She was amazing," Marianne commented.
"She is amazing," Michelle chimed.

Marianne nodded. "They both are."

Candace steadied her breathing. Jameson's words were still ringing in her ears. She'd heard a good deal of the speech and she was positive Jameson had gone off the original text more than once. Now, it was her turn. *Here goes.*

Michelle nudged Jameson. "Stop holding your breath."
"I can't help it. I think I'm more nervous watching her."
"She's a pro, JD."
"She's just Candace."
Marianne smiled. Jameson spoke the truth.

"That's a hard act to follow," Candace chuckled. "I sometimes wonder if my wife should be the one running this campaign."
The crowd laughed.
"Now you know some of my worst kept secrets," she continued to more laughter. "What Jameson didn't tell you is that the reason I have the strength to stand here tonight is that I know when I walk off this stage she will be waiting for me."

Jameson swallowed hard.
"Do either of you know how to stick to a script?" Michelle laughed.

"You've had the chance to hear from my daughters, Michelle and Marianne this week. I'm amazed you're all still here," Candace quipped.
A collective chuckle emerged from the crowd.
"You've heard President Wallace impart his wisdom, and you've gotten a chance to know Nate Ellison a little better. Let me tell you, I am excited to have him as a partner. We have a lot of work ahead of us. And, in my experience, the best way to approach a long trip is a lot of planning and even more teamwork. I didn't reach this stage alone, and we will not reach the destinations we seek without each other."

Jameson listened as Candace continued her speech. She'd read Candace's speech and had thought it was amazing on paper. Candace breathed life into it as only she could.

Candace took a deep breath. "You heard Jameson a few minutes ago talking about our life—my life. When I look out at all of you, I see mothers and daughters, fathers, sons, friends, lovers, explorers and dreamers. That's who we are. I could sit here and revisit what Mr. Wolfe says in his speeches—what he envisions for America. We envision a drastically different future. There's a reason for that. We see our role in shaping America differently. This is not *my* journey. This is *our* journey. When I look at my children and my grandchildren, I see the same things each of you does when you look at yours. I see my hope for the future. I remember where I came from. I ask how time can pass so quickly, and I long to leave something meaningful to them. My heart aches for a world that allows them not only to be dreamers, but to be the explorers whose dreams can blossom into reality. That is the reason I am standing on this stage tonight, grateful and humbled to accept your nomination for President of the United States of America."

Jameson's eyes glistened as her smile grew wider. She scooped up Cooper and hugged him. "Your Mommy is something else, Cooper."

"What is she?" Cooper asked innocently.

Jameson burst out laughing and kissed his cheek. He looked at her with confusion. She laughed harder and kissed him again. "You should be very proud of her."

Cooper grinned and looked back at the screen in front of them. "Mommy's beautiful," he commented.

Jameson sighed. "She certainly is, Coop."

———— ◆●◆ ————

Candace's speech wound into its final moment.

"I've been blessed in my life—some might say more than any-one has the right to be. I had parents and grandparents who did more than provide what I needed. Each imparted wisdom about life and love that I still draw on every day. My grandfather always told me that those of us who are given abundant blessings are called to extend those bless-ings to others. My children, grandchildren, and my wife remind me of the truth in that lesson daily."

Candace smiled.

"I know how it appears. Candidates travel to cities and towns to tell you who they are and what they will do for you. It *appears* to be all about me. For me, the speeches fade and the lights dim when a mother squeezes my hand and tells me her son is abroad serving our country. Cheers and cameras disappear when a young man looks me in the eye and tells me that he had to drop out of school to care for his aging mother, and that he has no idea how they will afford her care. The ques-tions shouted by reporters and the prodding of my staff fade into silence when a father asks me how he is supposed to feed his family now that the factory he's worked in for twenty years has closed. Speeches and campaign stops, policies, and even elections are not about the people who stand before you; it is all about *you*. It is all about *us*. Moment to moment, with every word we speak, every action we take, and even every word we *fail* to speak—with every kindness we fail to extend or choose to offer we shape our future. Let's create one steeped in more than tolerance. Let's build a future that enables us to embrace one an-other, to endeavor to create a gentler world full of eager explorers. And, then let us watch as the next generation leads us to places beyond our imagining. Together we begin that journey. Together we become a bless-ing to America just as America continues to bless us. Thank you. Now, let's start moving toward that future together! God bless you and God bless America!"

Candace walked to the front of the stage and waved to the crowd. Her heart fluttered perceptibly. *It's real.* She wasn't certain she had believed that any of this was real until now. Her smile was genuine but beneath her exterior tears threatened to spill over—tears of grateful-ness and complete awe. In all her years, all the campaign speeches, the long hours sifting through policy, the hands she had shaken, babies she had held, and stories she had listened to, Candace had never seriously considered this moment as a possibility. She allowed herself the indulgence of the moment. Few people had ever or would ever stand where she now stood. It took her breath away.

"Go on," Dana instructed Nate Ellison. She turned to Jameson and Janine Ellison. "Give them a few beats and join them. Shell, you know the drill."

Candace turned and offered Nate Ellison a hug.

"That was fucking amazing," he whispered.

Candace laughed at his colorful observation. She took his hand and the two waved to an exuberant crowd. She turned slightly and caught sight of Cooper and Jameson walking toward her hand in hand. Her heart skipped several beats. *I love you.* She accepted a kiss from Jameson without any hesitation and bent over to hug Cooper.

"You're beautiful, Mommy."

Candace grinned. "Thank you, sweetheart. And, you are very handsome." She took both their hands just as the rest of the Fletcher-Reid clan meandered onto the stage.

Dana watched in the distance.

"That is some family," Glenn commented.

Dana smiled.

Glenn studied Dana as she continued to watch the display on the stage. He'd always known that Candace and Dana shared a close bond. He suspected that Dana and Cassidy were the only people on Candace's team that Candace trusted completely. Affection lit Dana's eyes. It was easy to admire Candace Reid. He realized that Dana also loved the woman. In many ways, Candace was everyone's mom. He'd found himself envying Candace's family from time to time. He did not enjoy a close relationship with his parents. He wondered what Dana's story might be. He gripped her shoulder gently. "We're all lucky to have her."

Dana nodded. "I just hope people who haven't met them realize how lucky they are to have *that* family standing up there."

"They will."

CHAPTER NINE

July 3rd

Jonah grabbed a cup of coffee and sat down at the kitchen table. Pearl watched him out of the corner of her eye. He'd shown up unexpectedly that morning with JJ. Pearl asked where Laura was. Jonah told her that Laura had plans to take their daughter, Sophie to see her mother for a few hours. Pearl was sure that something was bothering Jonah. He could be tight-lipped, but she had a guess what was on his mind. She was positive that he had arrived hoping to find Jameson. Jameson had left earlier that morning to meet Nate Ellison and his family at the airport.

"Talked to Jameson recently?"

Jonah shrugged. "Not that much—no. She's been kind of busy since the convention. I don't want to bother her."

"I see."

Jonah spun the coffee mug in his hand.

"She'll be back soon," Pearl offered.

Jonah shrugged.

Pearl took a seat at the table across from him. "Why don't you just tell her you want to spend some time with her?"

"She's got enough to deal with."

Pearl nodded. Jameson's uncle had continued his campaign against her. Jerry Donnelly seemed to enjoy any and every bit of attention anyone was willing to give him. It had been a struggle for Jameson. Maureen was not only furious, she was devastated. Jameson had done her best to rise above it all, but Pearl could see the evidence of the toll it had taken on Jameson. Candace had decided to take a few days away from the campaign trail and Pearl knew the biggest reason was to give Jameson a break. She also knew that Jameson missed Jonah.

"Just tell her you'd like to spend some time together," Pearl suggested.

Jonah shrugged again. "I asked her for some help on one of our new projects."

"That's an excuse."

Jonah shrugged yet again. Pearl wondered if he'd reverted to the ten-year-old boy she remembered.

"Jonah," Pearl addressed him firmly.

He looked up at her.

There's that little boy. "I think Jameson would appreciate hearing that."

"Grandma, JD has Coop and Mom and all this other bullshit to deal with."

Pearl laughed. "You're right."

Jonah looked surprised.

"She does. She has plenty of bullshit to deal with," Pearl agreed.

Jonah's jaw dropped.

"So, don't you go adding to it with yours."

"I don't…"

"You don't what? Asking Jameson to help you with something that you don't need help with—that's what I would call bullshit."

"She knows how…"

"She knows that you and Mel can handle that firm. If she didn't, she wouldn't have signed it over to you. She's got enough people in her life not being honest *about* her. She doesn't need her son being less than honest *with* her."

Jonah looked down. "That's not who I…"

"That is who you are to her. I love you, but you are acting like a wounded ten-year-old. I know that you've had a rough time the last few months too. Jonah," Pearl called his attention.

Jonah reluctantly met Pearl's gaze.

"I'm going to tell you what I know, and I want you to listen to me."

Jonah nodded.

"Your mother is doing something right now that few people will ever have the guts to do. We are all trying to support her. And, all of us have had to deal with things we'd prefer not to. None of us like seeing her attacked or seeing each other hurt. She can handle the attacks on her." Pearl saw Jonah ready to speak and cautioned him silently. "I said, I want you to listen to me. It's not easy for your mother. She wants to protect all of you. But it's even harder for Jameson. She's the closest to your mother. She sees what you don't. She even sees what I don't."

"I know."

"Do you? You don't think Jameson views you as her kid? Why? Because of how old you are or because she has Cooper now?"

"It's not that. I don't know. I just…"

"You know, you kids didn't really grow up with two parents. Your father is a decent man, Jonah. His life never existed at home. If you want to know the truth, I think that's what pulled your parents apart more than anything else—even your mother…."

"Even mom being gay, you mean."

"Yes."

Jonah nodded.

"You see Cooper with your mother and Jameson and a little part of you is jealous."

"I'm not jealous of Coop."

Pearl chuckled. "Yes, you are. Don't look at me like that. You and Jameson have a lot of things in common, Jonah. You might be surprised at what some of those things are."

"JD doesn't need my issues."

"Jameson loves you. You know that."

Jonah shook his head. "Grandma, all this stuff that her uncle has said and that… That…"

"That asshole?" Pearl guessed.

Jonah's jaw dropped.

Pearl laughed. "I know the word, Jonah."

"The point is that I can take care of myself. I don't want her to think…"

"Uh-huh. So, you tell her you need help at work instead of telling her the truth?"

"That's not…"

"You don't need her help at work. You need her. Tell her that. Sometimes, I think Jameson feels a little helpless."

"Helpless? Grandma, JD takes care of everyone, even Mom."

"She doesn't see it that way. You forget; Jameson had to pick up the pieces after Rick died. She had Spencer and Maddie almost full-time for months. She had a business that was her responsibility to run. She had Shell looking to her for guidance. Marianne needed support—you needed a place to land. Things have changed. She does have Cooper. That doesn't mean she doesn't miss you fools."

"She sees us all the time."

"Not the same. Marianne has Scott. Shell's married with the twins. You and Laura have your family. She doesn't have a company to run anymore. She's on the road with your mom or she's in Albany. She doesn't even have this house to look after now. Sometimes, Jonah, I think Jameson could use to know that she's still needed. Ask her to spend a day with you. Just ask her. Tell her you miss her. I think you might be surprised at the reaction you get."

Jonah sighed. "I don't want to disappoint her."

Pearl smiled. "I wouldn't worry about that," she said. "Now, if you are going to hang around here all day, you are going to have to get to work. I'm trying to cook one-handed. Half the State of New York will be here for this annual debacle before you know it."

Jonah chuckled. "Just tell me what you need, Grandma."

"Don't you worry; I will."

Duncan Reid handed his son a cold bottle of beer. He was thankful for a brief escape to the local watering hole in town. Whenever Toby visited, the two made a point of sharing a pint at The Tin Roof.

"Thanks, Dad," Toby said.

"JD was happy when I told her that you were coming tomorrow."

"Miss the annual barbecue? No way."

Duncan laughed. Candace and Jameson's annual Fourth of July barbecue was an event that everyone looked forward to. Most years, the backyard was filled with friends and family—a deliberate attempt to escape the spotlight that invaded Candace and Jameson's life. This year, Duncan was aware there would be a small media presence. The journalists invited and the two photographers granted access had been hand-selected by Candace with Jameson's approval. He'd heard his daughter-in-law's pledge that the slightest feel of intrusiveness would result in a revoked invitation.

"Are they actually letting reporters come?" Toby asked.

"A couple," Duncan replied.

"What does JD think of that? I mean, with everything that's been going on lately, I would think she'd want them as far away as possible."

"I'm sure they both do."

"But?"

Duncan took a swig from his bottle. "I don't think they have that luxury this year."

"I guess. How is JD holding up?"

"You know your sister. She talks a good game."

"I can't believe Uncle Jerry."

Duncan groaned. "I'd like to…"

"Yeah, me too. What is his issue with JD anyway? I don't get it. JD didn't have anything to do with what happened to Craig."

"No. He's always been a son of a bitch," Duncan said. "It's his way or no way."

"Well, he could keep it to himself," Toby said.

"He's never been good at that," Duncan replied with disgust. He took a greedy swallow of his beer. His brother-in-law had been free with more than his opinions over the years. Duncan had no use for a man who would hit his children or his wife. He'd tolerated the man because of Maureen. After Craig's death, Jerry had appeared in their kitchen. He'd been drinking and decided that Maureen would be the target of that night's rage. It had been the last time Jerry Donnelly had stepped into Duncan Reid's home.

"Hey, is it true what you said about the governor's wife?"

Toby and Duncan turned their attention to an unfamiliar voice a few feet away.

"What's that?" a voice asked.

"That you and her—you know."

Toby hopped off the barstool he'd been occupying.

"Let's just say I doubt she screams that way with her old lady."

Toby shoved two people out of his way. He came face to face with Jed Tyler.

"You son of a bitch!" Toby yelled. He grabbed Tyler by the shirt.

Duncan scurried to grab hold of his son. He pulled Toby backward.

"What's your problem? Jealous?" Tyler baited Toby.

"You fucking raped my sister, you asshole!"

Toby lunged forward again. It took every ounce of strength Duncan had to pull him back.

"Toby, leave it! He's not worth it."

Jed Tyler brushed himself off. "Your sister? Which one was that?"

Toby struggled against his father's hold. Duncan spun Toby around. He looked at the familiar face of a local friend. "Brett," Duncan asked his friend. "Get Toby out of here, will you?"

Brett ushered Toby toward the door.

"Let me go," Toby shook off Brett's hold.

"The only place you're going is to the door," Brett said. "Your father's right. That asshole isn't worth it."

Duncan Reid had never enjoyed fighting. It was rare that he needed to. His mere presence could be imposing. Years of working construction had kept him fit. He was nearly 6'4, muscular and no one would have guessed that the sixty-eight-year-old man was a day over fifty-five. His temple twitched with anger as he deliberately approached Jed Tyler.

"Got something to say, old man?" Tyler grinned.

"To you?" Duncan said.

"You're the one standing here," Tyler said.

"You're lucky Toby reached you first."

"Oh? Why's that?"

"Because if I had, all the men in this bar wouldn't have been able to stop me."

Tyler laughed. "Give it your best shot."

Duncan appraised the man before him and shook his head. "Like I said, you're not worth it."

"Not what the lady said."

Duncan's gaze grew menacing. He had no idea how Jed Tyler landed in the bar he frequented. He'd been around enough to guess that it hadn't been by accident. Most of the people here were lifelong friends of Duncan's. A few were friends of Jameson's as well. In fact, the only two he didn't recognize as frequent patrons were Tyler and the man he was talking to.

"I doubt any lady has ever enjoyed the pleasure of your company," Duncan said. "The screaming part? That I believe." He took a step back and smiled. Duncan threw a fifty-dollar bill on the bar. "Do me a favor, Jack," he addressed the bartender without looking at him. "Buy the bar a round on the Reid family."

Jack pushed the fifty-dollar bill back at Duncan. "The Reids are family," Jack said. "This round's on the house."

Duncan picked up the money. "Thanks, Jack."

"Tell JD that the governor has The Tin Roof's vote," he said.

"Here, here!" a few voices echoed the sentiment.

"Get out of here," Jack told Jed Tyler and his friend.

"No, no," Duncan said. "Let them stay. If there's one thing my daughter-in-law has taught me, it's to be cordial to everyone—even ass-holes." He smiled at Jed Tyler. "Enjoy your drink, Mr. Tyler." He nod-ded to Jack and turned on his heels to leave.

"She'll never win, you know!" Tyler called across the room.

Duncan continued toward the door. "She already has."

Candace handed Cooper a juice box. He accepted it with a smile and returned to coloring the picture in front of him. She sat back down on the sofa next to him. "What else?" she asked the group seated around her.

"There is some disagreement on the idea of raising tolls," Dan said.

"There's some disagreement on everything," Candace said. "I don't love the idea of raising prices on anything." She sat quietly for a moment, considering all the arguments she'd heard.

"Mommy?" Cooper whispered.

Candace turned her attention to her son. "What is it, Cooper?"

"What's a toll?"

"A toll is something a person pays for driving on a road or sometimes over a bridge," she explained.

Cooper's lips gripped the straw in his drink. He sucked some more juice into his mouth and then looked back at her. "Why?"

"Why?" she asked.

"Why do people pay to drive?"

Cooper had begged Candace to let him stay with her while she conducted meetings that morning. Jameson had argued that it might be a distraction. Candace didn't see it that way. None of her meetings were set to deal with pressing issues. She was looking to catch up on the de-tails that she'd missed during the fervor of the convention and the weeks leading up to it. She'd been far more concerned about Cooper's poten-tial boredom than any distraction he might provide. He was naturally and genuinely curious about the discussion around him, even if it seemed boring to the people engaged in it. Being a part of his mother's day made him feel important. Candace knew that.

"Well, Cooper," Candace began. "That's a good question. People pay to do all kinds of things."

"Yep, like for ice cream."

"Right."

"But why?"

This is not an easy question. "Well, money is one of the ways we keep control of the world we live in." *Or, it's supposed to be that way.* "Money is one of the ways that we show what things have value to us."

"Like ice cream?"

The group in the room all giggled.

"Yes, Cooper. You know, when you go to get an ice cream with Momma, the ice cream Momma buys you had to be made and it had to travel to get to you."

Cooper was puzzled. "Like from the cows?"

Candace smiled. "That is where it starts. Cows give us the milk we need to make the ice cream."

"Do the cows get money?"

They probably should. "No, sweetheart. The cows don't get money, the people who take care of the cows do."

"Why? They don't make milk."

Candace loved to listen to Cooper. "No, but they make sure the cows have what they need to eat, and they give the cows a place to sleep, and that all costs money."

"Oh."

"And, then a person has to spend time taking that milk and mixing it with other things to make your ice cream. Another person drives it to the store. Then someone has to scoop it into the cup for you to eat it."

"And put in the chips!"

"And, put in the chocolate chips too—yes, that's true."

"But, Mommy we have to drive to get ice cream."

"Yes, we do. And, just like the ice cream has all those people who help make it, so do the roads. And, that's why we have tolls." *Something like that.*

"Momma says everything costs too much."

Candace laughed. *I'll bet she did.* "Well, Momma's not wrong."

Cooper shrugged and returned to coloring his picture.

Oh, how I love you, Cooper. Candace shook her head. "See what other options there are. I'm open to ideas," she told her staff.

"Anything else, Governor?" Dan asked.

"No. I don't think so. I think that's enough for today. I'm suddenly craving ice cream."

Cooper looked up excitedly.

Candace winked at her son. "You all enjoy your holiday. I'll see you next week." She bid farewell to her staff and turned back to Cooper. "So, what do you say? How about we stop for an ice cream on the way home?"

"Just you and me?" Cooper asked.

Candace's heart ached in the best of ways. "Just you and me."

Cooper nodded excitedly. "But, Mommy…"

"What is it, Cooper?"

"What about Jeff and Gil? They have to have ice cream too."

Candace nodded. Gil Barclay was the agent in charge of her security detail, and Jeff Lamkin was assigned to Cooper full-time. "Well, I'll tell you what, Gil and Jeff are in the kitchen right now. Why don't you go tell them what the plan is? You can offer to buy them both an ice cream."

"'Kay!"

Candace watched Cooper run off in search of the two Secret Service agents. She understood that if she made the offer, it would be politely declined with a customary, 'No thank you, Ma'am.' If Cooper made the overture, the two senior agents were likely to acquiesce. She sympathized with the two men. The Fletcher-Reid family was both large and larger than life. It was the agents' duty to keep Candace and her family safe. That required a unique blend of physical closeness and emotional distance. She did not envy their task. To Cooper, the frequent faces that accompanied their family had become friends. He was full of questions and stories. She imagined it would be difficult for anyone to avoid falling in love with her son. She certainly had.

"Governor," Gil Barclay rapped on the open door.

"I'm guessing that Cooper found you."

He nodded. "You want to stop at Andy's on the way back to Schoharie?"

"Is that a problem?"

"No, Ma'am."

"But?"

"It is an open area."

"I know. No one is expecting us there. I think we'll be fine."

"From a planned threat, yes."

"Gil…"

"Governor, you need to take these precautions seriously—not just for yourself."

Candace groaned. She knew the agent was right. She also knew that her ability to do these things would end if she were elected. "Gil, if I win this election, the days of deciding to stop for an ice cream with Cooper at will are all but over for the next four years. He's a little boy. I need to do as much as I can with him now. Do you understand?"

"I do," he said. "Promise me that you will leave the moment I ask."

Candace held his gaze. "You have my word."

"I'll send Jeff ahead."

Candace nodded. "Gil?" she called after him.

"Yes, Governor?"

"Tell him to be inconspicuous."

"Yes, Ma'am."

Candace threw her head back and sighed. *It's just an ice cream.*

<hr>

Jameson stepped out of the car and waited for Nate Ellison and his family to exit. "I should warn you," she said. "Things can get a little crazy when all the kids are here."

Ellison smiled. "No worries, JD. I think Janine has been looking forward to this almost as much as the boys. She enjoyed talking to Marianne at the convention."

"Marianne's the best," Jameson said as she led the group toward the house.

"You two are close?" he asked.

"We are. It wasn't always that way." Jameson chuckled. "I'm not sure either of us would have envisioned how close we are now—not when I first started seeing Candace."

"Must be a little strange, being so close in age, I mean."

"Sometimes it is," Jameson admitted. "Not as much now as it used to be. Family is family. We have our ups and downs like everybody else. I wouldn't trade any of it, though."

"Ever think about adding more?" Ellison teased.

"If you mean Candace and me—no. The way Candace's kids reproduce we'll need a state of our own pretty soon."

Ellison laughed.

"There you are!" Pearl stepped out onto the back porch.

"Here we are," Jameson said.

Pearl stepped down and extended her good hand. "Nice to see you again, Senator."

"Nice to see you, Mrs. Johnson," he greeted her. "But really, Nate is fine."

"Well then, you can call me Pearl or Grandma. I seem to answer to just about anything these days."

Jameson rolled her eyes. "Just make sure you don't trip over anything."

"You are a regular comedienne, Jameson," Pearl replied dryly. "How about you let me show the Ellisons to their rooms?"

"I can," Jameson began to protest.

"I know you can," Pearl said. "The natives are getting restless," she said.

Jameson shook her head.

"Marianne got home a couple of hours ago and Spencer's been asking every five minutes where you all are."

"Who's us all?" Jameson asked.

"You, Cooper, and Nana."

"Candace isn't here yet?" Jameson asked.

"Nope. She called and said she and Cooper had something important to do before they came home."

Jameson frowned. *What on earth is she up to?*

Pearl looped her arm around Nate Ellison's and looked at Janine. "You have the pleasure of staying in Shell's old room," she said. She looked at the youngest of Ellison's sons. "You must be Grayson."

He nodded.

"Candy thought you might like to stay with Cooper and Spencer."

Grayson's face lit up. "Can I?" he asked his mother.

"Sure."

"And, you're Derek?" Pearl guessed.

"Yes, Ma'am."

"There are no Ma'ams in this family," Pearl told him with a wink. "You can call me Pearl or Grandma Pearl, just don't call me ma'am. Makes me think of some old lady."

Jameson snickered.

"Something funny?" Pearl asked her.

"No, Ma'am."

Pearl glared at Jameson. "Watch it."

Janine Ellison giggled.

Pearl looked back at Derek. "Forgive Jameson. She fell and hit her head once. Hasn't been the same since."

Jameson rolled her eyes.

"Candy thought that you might like to share a room with her friends' son, Dylan. Of course, if I had to bet, half the boys will be out in Jonah's old tent tomorrow night." Pearl leaned into Janine's ear. "I'll let Shell explain that one to you later."

"Pearl!" Jameson scolded the older woman.

Pearl flashed an impish grin. "Come on," she said. "Let's get you settled. We'll see if you still want to be part of this nuthouse after the next two days."

Jameson shook her head as Pearl disappeared into the house with the Ellison family.

"Where's Pearl off to?" Jonah's asked when Jameson stepped into the kitchen."

"Nice to see you too," Jameson laughed. "She's on a mission as usual," Jameson said. "Didn't think I'd see you until tomorrow."

"Laura spent the day with her mom."

"Does she have the kids?"

"Sophie. JJ is upstairs with Maddie."

Jameson regarded Jonah thoughtfully. "Everything okay?"

"Yeah, sure."

"Uh-huh."

"Can I ask you something?"

"Can I get a beer first?" Jameson asked. She pulled a cold bottle from the refrigerator. "You want one?" she asked.

"Sure."

Jameson handed Jonah a beer. "What's up? Issues at work?"

"No," Jonah said. "Nothing out of the ordinary."

"Okay?"

"I was kind of wondering if maybe you had some time next week. You know, I thought maybe we could go fishing or something."

Jameson took a sip from her beer. "Sure." She chuckled at the surprise on Jonah's face. "Your mom is home until the middle of next week. Everybody will be cleared out of here in a couple of days. Why don't we go on Friday?"

"Seriously?"

Jameson nodded. "If your boss will let you have the day off, that is."

Jonah laughed. "I'm sure Mel won't mind."

"How about Laura?"

"She won't mind either. Maybe she'll have a chance to spend some time with Mom."

"I'm sure your mom would like that."

"Really?"

Jameson laughed. "What's up with you? You know your mother loves Laura."

"Yeah, but you guys have been so busy. I just figured you'd want to be alone after the barbecue."

"Don't worry about us," Jameson said. "Your mom and I are good. Besides, I miss our camping trips. Fishing works for me."

"How is Mom?"

"Looking forward to the next few days, I think."

"You mean escaping," Jonah guessed.

"As much as she can. It's not like she'll have a full day off," Jameson said. "She'll just be doing it all from here. Unless the shit hits the fan again."

Jonah didn't want to upset Jameson. He had been worried about her. He and Laura were two of the only people who had known her story about Jed Tyler until Tyler appeared on the television. Jameson had confided it to Laura after Laura disclosed her brother's abuse. "JD, I don't want to pry."

"I'm okay, Jonah."

"Are you sure?"

Jameson smiled. "I wasn't for a few days. I'm okay. Nothing anyone says changes the truth."

"Yeah, well, I'd still like to kick his ass."

"Stand in line." Jameson raised her glass in a toast.

———◆•●•◆———

Cooper sat at a picnic table delighting in his hot fudge sundae while Candace delighted in watching the mess of chocolate that covered his lips.

"Mommy?"

"Hum?"

"I think that girl likes you."

"What girl? Candace asked.

"Momma says it's rude to point."

Candace forced herself not to chuckle. Lately, everything seemed to be about what Momma said. Jameson had been spending most days with Cooper. And, Cooper seemed to hang on every word she said.

"Momma's right again. What girl, sweetheart?"

Cooper looked over Candace's shoulder. Candace turned just as a young girl shyly looked away.

"Oh," Candace commented. She guessed the girl was about eight or nine.

"She looks nice," Cooper said.

"She does," Candace agreed.

"Can we say hi?" Cooper asked.

Candace sighed. *Gil will have my head.* She looked in Cooper's pleading brown eyes and knew there was no way she was going to refuse him. She nodded and looked to grab Gil's attention.

"Governor? Everything all right?"

"Fine. It seems we have an audience," Candace said.

"Did you want me to clear the area?"

"No."

Gil immediately guessed what Candace was about to request. "Governor Reid, I…"

Candace held up her hand. She gestured behind her. "The girl sitting with her mother behind us," she said. "Why don't you go see if it would be all right if Cooper said hello?"

Gil looked over at the family seated behind Candace. He'd noticed that the girl and her mother seemed to be interested in Candace and Cooper. The little girl looked away quickly, clearly embarrassed. *Another fan.* He held Candace's gaze firmly. "You're not going to make my life easy, are you?"

"Not likely."

He shook his head. "I'll take a walk over. If all seems well, I'll come back for you."

"They're less than 10 feet away," Candace said.

"I know."

Candace sighed. "We'll say hello, and we'll go."

Sure, you will. Gil nodded. "Stay here until I get back." He stepped away. "Harmony is looking to move," he told his team.

Jeff Lamkin shook his head. "Just keep your eyes open."

Gil walked up to the table. "Excuse me," he began. "Sorry to disturb you."

"We didn't mean to bother the governor..."

"No, Ma'am. That's not why I'm here. Governor Reid's son noticed your daughter."

The girl blushed.

"He'd like to say hello. If you'd be agreeable to that."

The girl's mother nodded. "We'd be honored."

"Very well." He stepped away. "How do we look?" he asked his team.

"No issues," the answer came.

Gil stepped back to Candace. "Governor?"

Candace dipped a napkin in her cup of water and wiped Cooper's face. "I think there's as much fudge on you as there is in you."

Cooper grinned.

Candace turned to the Secret Service agent. "So?"

"We're all set if you're ready." He looked at Cooper.

"I'm ready!" Cooper hopped down from his seat and grabbed his mother's hand.

Gil led them the few steps away to the next table.

Candace stepped up and smiled. "We're sorry to intrude on your ice cream," she apologized. "Cooper wanted to say hello."

"You're not intruding. Thank you for coming over, Governor Reid." The woman went to stand.

"No, no, please sit down," Candace said. She sensed the nervousness from the table's occupants. "I'm not the governor right now," she said. "I'm just Cooper's mom. Candace," she said as she extended her hand.

"Donna," the woman said. "Donna Franklin, and this is my daughter Madison."

Candace smiled. "Madison? My granddaughter's name is Madison."

The girl grinned and blushed.

"This is Cooper," Candace made the introduction.

Cooper waved. "Hi."

"Hi," Madison replied.

"You have a sundae too," Cooper said.

"Yeah," she said.

"Me too. Mommy had a cone. 'Stasho. It's green." Cooper wrinkled his nose. "Momma says ice cream shouldn't be green."

Candace rolled her eyes. "Did she now?"

"Yep."

Donna Franklin laughed. "Sounds like my husband. He doesn't like anything green."

"Neither does Jameson," Candace said. "Except asparagus. Strange."

"'Sparagus is good for you, Mommy. Momma says."

Momma has a lot to say these days. "We didn't want to disturb you. Just wanted to say hello."

"Thank you for stopping. Madison has been wanting to meet you."

Candace smiled at the young girl. "Well, I'm glad we collided then. It was lovely to meet you both."

Madison blushed again.

"You know, I will bet Cooper would love to have a picture with you. What do you say we all take one together?" Candace suggested.

"Really?" Madison asked.

"Sure. Do you have a phone?"

Donna retrieved hers and Candace took hold of it. "Selfie?" she asked.

"Shell takes funny selfies," Cooper said. "She's my sister."

"Shell does a lot of funny things," Candace said. "Believe it or not, I've gotten pretty good at this." She snapped a few pictures and handed the phone back to Donna.

"Thank you so much," Donna said. "I'm sure you have better things to do than bother with us."

Candace smiled. "Not at all," she said. "Cooper and I have a party to get ready for, don't we?"

"Yep! Dylan's coming," he said. Cooper idolized Cassidy Toles' son, Dylan. He'd been talking about seeing the teenager for days.

"Yes, he is," Candace agreed. "And, I will bet Momma and Spencer are wondering where you are."

Donna Franklin looked at Cooper. "It was nice to meet you, Cooper." She turned to Candace. "If it matters, you have our family's vote."

"Thank you for that. It matters a lot," Candace said. "Nice meeting you both. Enjoy your sundaes."

Cooper waved goodbye. "Bye, Madison."

Madison waved.

Candace took Cooper's hand. "Momma doesn't think my ice cream should be green?" she asked.

"Nope. She don't like green."

"She doesn't like green," Candace gently corrected him. She chuckled softly. "You can tell me all about it on the way home." *I'll just bet I can find something in green she likes.*

CHAPTER TEN

J ameson rolled over and pulled Candace closer.

"Morning," Candace said.

"Call it off," Jameson groaned.

"The barbecue?"

"No, morning."

Candace laughed. "Tired?"

"More like I just want to lie here with you and forget there's a house full of people."

Candace closed her eyes. "I promise, we will do that soon."

"Mm-hum."

"I promise, Jameson."

Jameson kissed Candace's head. "It's okay."

"No, it isn't."

"It is." Jameson meant it. "So? You were up with Alex late last night. What was that about or is it better if I don't ask?"

"It was about Nate."

"What about him?"

"Just about his background."

"Uh-huh. I don't want to know."

"It's nothing for you to worry about."

"That's crap code for I should worry."

Candace giggled. "No, it isn't."

"Okay."

Candace turned in Jameson's arms. "It isn't." She kissed Jameson tenderly. "I will tell you this; I'm grateful to have Alex and Jane."

"I know you are. I'm glad you have them too."

"You are?"

"Yeah. I know they are watching out for you."

"They are."

"Candace?"

"Hum?"

"You don't have to tell me, but what did Alex say?"

Candace took a deep breath. She'd told Jameson about Nate Ellison's background—what she knew.

"Like I said," Jameson began.

"No. It's not that I don't want to tell you."

"What is it?"

"There's just a lot of holes," Candace said. "It's like everything I learn, I end up with more questions than answers."

"About Nate?"

"About everything."

Jameson tucked a strand of hair behind Candace's ear. "I know I'm not an expert on any of it. I'm here—if you need me."

"I know. I love you for that."

"Just for that?" Jameson asked.

"I can think of a few other things."

"Yeah? Want to share?"

Candace pushed Jameson back and straddled her hips. "Only if you can keep quiet."

Jameson's eyes danced. "Absolutely."

"Are you sure? Because this is Top Secret."

Jameson swallowed hard when Candace's hand drifted up her shirt.

"No talking. No whispering."

Jameson was fairly certain if Candace continued what she was doing, there would be no breathing. Candace was toying playfully with her nipples, and nipping at her neck.

"Maybe you can keep the secret," Candace whispered. Her lips moved to claim Jameson's with a fiery kiss.

"Mom!"

Candace's head fell into the crook of Jameson's neck, and she groaned.

"Mom!" Shell's voice bellowed again. "You said you wanted to make breakfast together! Marianne and I are waiting."

Jameson stroked Candace's back. "Well, at least we know one thing."

"What's that? That we can never make love in the morning?"

"No. Don't make Shell your National Security Adviser."

Candace laughed. "Noted."

"Mom!" Shell called again from outside the door.

Candace threw on her robe. "I'm coming!" She opened the door.

Michelle arched her eyebrow. "Really, Mom? Can't you leave the Bible Study for after the fireworks?"

Jameson pulled the covers over her head and laughed.

"I'll be down in a minute," Candace said through gritted teeth.

"I'm sure JD is thrilled."

"Shell!" Candace and Jameson yelled simultaneously.

"We'll just start without you." Michelle waved and walked away.

Candace closed the bedroom door. "Honestly."

"Well?" Jameson asked.

"What?"

"She said they'd start without you," Jameson grinned. "I'd rather not."

"Rather not what?"

"Start without you," Jameson deadpanned.

Candace laughed. She dropped her robe and climbed back onto the bed. "You really are a lunatic." She kissed Jameson sweetly.

"What about breakfast?" Jameson asked.

"They know how to toast bagels and scramble eggs."

Jameson pulled Candace closer. "Everyone will wonder where you are."

"No, they won't."

"No?"

"No. Shell will probably give a press conference before the coffee is brewed."

"You do realize that this house is full of curious ears."

"Consider this a classified briefing, Jameson. Silence is your ally."

Jameson closed her eyes. "My lips are sealed."

"I hope not," Candace said as her lips trailed over Jameson's neck. "Now, where was I?"

———◆●◆———

Jameson was enjoying the buzz of activity in the backyard. An impromptu game of soccer had started behind the barn. Jameson found the display amusing. Cooper seemed to listen to everything Dylan said. Alex and Cassidy's daughter, Mackenzie seemed to have charge of Spencer. Jameson wondered how the game would end.

"Full yard," Claire Brackett took a seat beside Jameson.

"Yeah, it is. I was just thinking that I can't believe how many kids are here."

Claire laughed. "What are you doing, trying to keep up with Alex?"

"What?"

"Well, in your case most of them are grandkids." Claire shuddered. "God, imagine when Alex's kids start having kids?"

"I like it."

Claire looked at Jameson. "Kids?"

"Yeah," Jameson said. "The first year we did this, we only had Spencer. Now? Marianne has Maddie. Jonah's got two, and so does Shell."

"Uh, so do you."

"Yeah, I guess I do."

"Can't be easy with Candace on the road so much," Claire guessed.

"It isn't. We make it work." Jameson decided to change the subject. "How are things with you? You and Hawk going to make things official?"

"I think so," Claire said.

"Yeah? Maybe you'll be adding a couple to this chaos."

"Kids?" Claire asked.

Jameson smiled.

"Hell no, I won't!"

Jameson laughed. "I seem to remember you said that about marriage too."

"Yeah, well. No kids here. No thanks. I don't need any of my own."

"No?"

"Nope. I have Alex and Cass's kids."

"Not the same."

"Close enough for me, thanks."

"Claire? Can I ask you something?"

"Sure."

"What do you know about this stuff with Lawson Klein?"

Claire sighed. "You really want to go there?"

"Yeah, I do."

Claire hopped to her feet. "Let's take a walk."

<hr />

Candace led Nate Ellison through a small flurry of activity and into the house. She passed Alex along the way and acknowledged her with a smile.

"I thought we'd escape the chaos for a few minutes," Candace said.

"Sounds good to me."

Candace guided Ellison into the study and closed the door. "Scotch?" she asked.

"Scotch?"

"If you ask my wife or Pearl, it's my Achilles heel," she quipped. "If you ask me, it's sanity in a glass."

Ellison laughed. "I'll go with your theory."

"Good idea." Candace poured them each a glass and gestured for him to have a seat. "Whenever I bring someone in here, I feel I should offer them a cigar," she said. "Sorry to say, that's one poison I never developed a taste for."

"No?"

"No, Although, I swear I smell the aroma in here late at night sometimes."

"It's an impressive room."

"Not as impressive as the man who occupied it," she said. "Or the woman who brought it back to life."

He nodded. "What's on your mind, Candace?"

Candace sipped her scotch. "Truth," she said. "And lies."

"I'm not sure I follow."

Candace's demeanor remained relaxed, but she held his gaze firmly. "Everyone has secrets, Nate."

"I suppose they do."

"There's nothing to suppose; they do. Everyone has a right to certain secrets."

"I agree."

"But secrets are a funny thing. No matter how much effort anyone puts into keeping them, sooner or later they see the light of day—even when they're kept for the best of reasons."

Nate Ellison listened, wondering where Candace was taking the conversation.

Candace offered the younger man a smile. "You're wondering what I am driving at."

He sipped his scotch silently.

"One of my worst kept secrets," Candace began, "is my priority." She smiled at the confusion in his eyes. "My first priority will always be my family. It's the greatest hindrance to what may become my presidency. I know that. There are times when my obligations as a leader must take precedence over everything else. That will become a frequent reality if we make it to the White House."

"I don't think you're unique in that regard."

"Perhaps not. That isn't the point. Compromise is part of life, so is sacrifice if you hope to achieve anything meaningful."

Ellison nodded. "How do I fit into this picture?"

"I learned early on in my career that recognizing the challenges ahead is the best way to ensure you are prepared to navigate them. There's a difference between compromise on your terms and being compromised by someone else."

"You're talking about loyalty."

"Not exactly." Candace took a moment to sip her scotch. "There's loyalty and there's blind loyalty. The former is an asset. The latter is a weakness that can be exploited."

Ellison continued sipping his scotch, gauging the woman before him. He'd only begun to get to know Candace Reid. She was a talented politician and policymaker. She was personable, and as far as he could tell, she was honest. He'd been impressed at the way her staff responded to her, and her ability to re-direct a conversation without the participants realizing what she had done. And, he had watched her with those closest to her. Loyalty was something Candace Reid commanded without deliberate effort. That told him that she was sincere and that she kept her word. Now, her presence possessed an air of more than control. Her bearing denoted confidence and determination. This, he understood, was the future president speaking to him.

"One thing that a president cannot afford is to be exploited, particularly not by those closest to the presidency. I think we both know that exploitation always comes from the closest corners."

"And, you want to be sure we are on the same page."

"I want to be sure that no matter where your career began, and no matter who has helped pave the way for you to sit here now, that you understand whose agenda you serve."

Nate Ellison set down his glass. *She knows*. "How did you find out?"

"You'll find that I like to cross all my 'T's' and dot all my 'I's.' I've been at this a long time. I have my adversaries. I also have friends."

"What are you asking me?"

"I'm not asking you anything. I don't expect you to share the details of your past. I do expect that your agenda remains firmly in line with my administration. I am open to your ideas and I welcome your experience—all of it. The presidency serves the people. That is the purpose of the presidency. There will be times that I am forced to make decisions I would prefer I was not faced with. There will be times that I will have to defer to the intelligence and military experts, and there will be times when I will deny their requests and advice and choose a different path. That's what a president must do. We both know that there will be people in every corner seeking to undermine my success for their gain. That cannot be you."

Ellison nodded. "I'm curious."

"Go on."

"If you knew that I had an intelligence background, why did you ask me to join the ticket?"

Candace smiled. "Because you were the right choice."

"And, you still feel that way?"

"We wouldn't be sitting in this room if I didn't. You should know that my eyes are open," she said. "In front of the cameras, on the stage all people see is a campaign. Behind the scenes, we need to be prepared for more than an election. And, Nate? We can't afford to allow Bradley Wolfe a chance at the White House."

"I agree."

"I can promise you that what you share with me will stay with me."

He nodded again. *How much do you know?* "Something tells me you know what you need to know."

"I know more than you expected me to."

Ellison chuckled. "I should have guessed."

"Why is that?"

"Your friendship with Agent Toles isn't a secret."

"No."

"And, Agent Brackett?" Ellison shook his head. "You do know about her background?"

"I told you; I have friends."

"Do you trust them?"

"I do."

Ellison sighed. "They report to different corners than I did."

"Did?"

Ellison picked up his scotch and sipped for a moment. "Once you're in the game, they never let you out—not really."

Candace listened.

"Someone always wants something. Sometimes it's information. Sometimes it's a more tangible operation."

"I understand."

"Money, Candace—in the end, it always comes down to money—who has it, who doesn't, who's moving it, who's receiving it and where it needs to go."

Candace nodded. "I'm aware."

"I can see that. You're worried that my agenda might differ from yours."

"It does."

Ellison nodded.

"But it can't."

He raised his glass. "Understood, Madame President."

"Not yet."

"You have my word," Ellison said. "I'm on your team."

"I hope so."

Ellison drained his glass and set it aside. "Let's talk about Lawson Klein and why he's in Bradley Wolfe's corner."

"I'm listening."

***

Jameson took a seat on a log. Claire plopped down beside her.

"This your secret getaway?" Claire wondered.

"One of them."

"You're worried about Candace."

"Wouldn't you be?"

"Sure," Claire replied. "She seems like she has a grip on things, JD."

"I'm more worried about people trying to get a grip on her."

"You mean Klein?"

"I mean anyone."

Claire nodded. "She has Jane and Alex in her corner."

"I know, but that's…"

Claire laughed. "Trust me, JD; that's the Holy Grail."

"What do you mean? Alex is your partner."

"Now she is. It wasn't always that way."

"I've heard."

"Yeah, but you've heard pieces—if I had to guess."

"So? Fill in the blanks for me," Jameson said.

"You don't want to know most of it."

"Tell me what I need to know then."

Claire sighed. "If you want to understand Lawson Klein, you need to understand that he's nothing more than an expendable pawn on a worldwide chessboard. He's a fly, JD—a nuisance."

Jameson listened.

"He might think he's in charge, but someone is always playing him. They'll keep moving him until they don't have any use for him anymore."

"Wolfe?"

"Nah, I doubt it. Look, people think that we have all these adversaries—the country, I mean."

"And, we don't?"

"No, we do. It just isn't as simple as it looks. Russia, China even North Korea—there's the public narrative and then there's the agenda behind it."

"Yeah, okay. What does that have to do with Candace?"

"Everything and nothing. If she gets elected, it will become her problem. The more she knows, the more she won't know."

"That doesn't make me feel better."

"Look, me and Alex—Jane, Cassidy—we all sort of were led to this life. Kind of like Candace was led to hers and you to yours." Claire sighed. "Our families were all part of the intelligence community in some way, just like Candace's grandfather was in politics, and yours builds things."

"And?"

"That goes back more than one generation, JD. This mess we live in isn't something we created. The problem is there are more people perpetuating the mess than trying to fix it. And, a lot of them believe they're doing the right thing."

"What is the right thing?"

"Depends on who you ask," Claire said. "Klein's not your biggest problem. He's not Candace's either. It's like that asshole who was on the news talking about you."

"Don't remind me."

"Yeah, that had to suck," Claire observed. "He didn't do that all by himself."

"Yeah, I'm sure he was well paid."

"Right? But who paid him?"

"Klein, probably."

"Maybe. Maybe not. You have to think beyond that. It's the same with all this stuff about Candace and Russia—about John and Russia."

"That's what worries me. They're trying to hang Candace for…"

"I wouldn't worry about that. She's got just as many people in her corner. JD, that attack on the embassy—it was done to create a narrative too."

"A narrative? Jesus, twenty-two people were killed."

"Price of doing business."

Jameson's caustic chuckle made Claire sigh.

"It's the truth. I know what you want me to do. You want me to give you details," Claire said.

"I want to be able to support Candace. Alex told me some. I feel like everyone leaves out the pieces that matter."

"Depends on what you think matters."

Jameson shook her head.

"You want my advice?" Claire asked.

"You're going to give it to me anyway."

"No, I won't."

"Go ahead."

"Listen, if you want to know all the gory details about Lawson Klein, I can tell you what I know. I can tell you all about what happened in Moscow. I can even tell you about John's assassination and how Cassidy's ex met his end—If that's what you want to know."

"But?"

"But that won't help Candace."

"How do you figure?"

"It's like Alex. She tells Cass enough. Cass has learned what enough is."

"What does that mean?"

Claire took a deep breath. "What we do, JD—me and Alex? What we've done? It makes you see the worst in people—even yourself. A lot of times every choice you have sucks."

Jameson listened intently.

"Candace—she strikes me as someone who sees the best in people."

"She does."

"Mm. Where she's choosing to go? That's not gonna be so easy."

"So, let me help."

Claire laughed. "You think knowing about all the crap she sees and hears is the answer?"

"Isn't it?"

"I don't know," Claire answered honestly. "I think she's a lot like Cass. The thing is, she's made a choice to know the details. That's gonna make it hard for her to see the best in people. Alex always says that going home to Cass and the kids is what helps her keep perspective. Cassidy knows enough, more than she'd probably like. What she doesn't know, what she doesn't see lets her keep seeing the best in people. That's what makes it possible for us to do that."

"Us?"

"This will sound weird. Somehow, I think you'll understand. Cassidy is like my mom in some strange way. My mom died when I was thirteen. What most people don't know, JD is that I watched while my father strangled her."

Jameson's heart dropped. "Jesus."

"I told you. Things can be ugly in the world. In my world and Alex's, they get uglier than most people ever see. You need someone who sees the other side. Otherwise, you can get sucked into it."

Jameson sighed and shook her head. "I just want to keep her safe."

"You do. It's just not the way you think you should," Claire said. "I get it. Listen, Klein is a dirtbag. He's helping to funnel money to some of the most disgusting people on earth—people who sell people, JD—people who kill people for sport. That's the truth. Candace will have to face those realities if she gets elected. That's why Cassidy and Jane told her what they have. That's why Alex told you what she thought you should know. Like I said, I'm not Alex or Cassidy. If you want to know, I'll tell you. Just be sure it's what you think is the right thing for both you and Candace."

"I get it. Claire?"

"Yeah?"

"Do you think she'll get elected? Seems like Wolfe has these people you're talking about in his corner. He's got that whole outsider thing going for him."

Claire shrugged. "I'm sure he has a lot of them banking on his victory. I said it's ugly. I never said we didn't work with good people. There's a lot of people in her corner, JD. As far as being an outsider?" Claire laughed. "That's a load of shit. He's not a politician. He is a someone's pawn. That makes him part of the game. Candace is the outsider," she said. "It's been a long time since there was an outsider in that role. Longer than you might imagine," Claire said.

"Doesn't that put her at risk?"

"You want me to lie to you?"

"No."

"Yeah, it does."

Jameson closed her eyes against a wave of nausea.

"Everybody in that office is at risk. It gives her the advantage, though."

"Is that supposed to make me feel better?"

"Nope. I told you when we first met, I don't bullshit. People can accuse me of a lot of things, JD and most of them would be true. I've never been a liar. And, I will tell you this much. I don't have a lot of friends. The ones I do have? I don't take kindly to anyone threatening them. That's one thing Alex and I have in common. Don't worry so much about Candace. Trust her."

"I do."

"Good. Trust that you both have people watching out for you."

"I appreciate that."

"You can call me, JD. If something doesn't feel right—you can call anytime."

"I will."

"Good. So, got any more beer?"

Jameson nodded. "Not sure there's enough after this conversation."

"Scotch?"

"I know where some might be hiding."

"Lead on."

* * *

"I hear you and Claire disappeared for a while. Something I should know?" Candace teased.

"I think we both know that you have more information than I do."

Candace sighed.

"I'm sorry. That didn't come out right."

"Yes, it did. Jameson, there isn't anything I wouldn't tell you."

"I know that."

"Do you?"

"Yeah, I do. Claire sort of spelled that out."

"What did she tell you?"

"Nothing specific. I just wish I could help you."

Candace smiled. "You do help me."

"I hope so."

"You do." Candace looked across the backyard. She thought a change in topic was in order. "Can you believe how many kids are still awake?"

"I can't believe how many kids are in this yard."

Candace laughed. She let her head fall onto Jameson's shoulder. "Jonah tells me you two are going fishing."

"Yeah. I hope that's okay. I know we had talked about spending the week together."

"We are spending the week together. Besides, it'll give me a chance to spend some time with Laura and the kids. Cassidy invited Marianne and Scott down for a visit. Cooper asked if he could go."

Jameson snickered. "He worships Dylan."

"Yes, he does. Marianne said it's okay with her if we don't mind. They're leaving Friday morning. They'll be back Sunday afternoon."

"Are you okay with it?" Jameson asked.

"Not really," Candace confessed. "It's not about me. It's good for him. He's blossomed so much, Jameson. Remember how nervous he used to be meeting people?"

"I do."

"Who's going to travel with them?" Jameson asked.

"I don't know. Alex said she'd work that out with Gil."

"I'll bet she did."

"Are you okay with it?" Candace asked.

"Yeah, I am."

"Need a break?"

"What?" Jameson asked.

"Honestly, I don't know how you are still standing," Candace said. "You've been chasing after Cooper and me for over a month."

"I don't see it that way."

"I know."

"But I'll admit I like the idea of an entire day alone with you. Can we banish visitors?"

"Consider it done," Candace said.

"Seriously?"

Candace kissed Jameson's cheek. "Yes."

"I was thinking about our first barbeque," Jameson said.

"Seems like forever ago," Candace commented.

"Do you remember the kids fighting about our kids?"

Candace laughed. "The kids we said we'd never have?"

"Yeah, those."

"I remember. You told me the kids had you knocked up and your mother had us headed to the altar."

Jameson gently pulled Candace to look at her. "I love you, Candace."

Candace's gaze narrowed.

Jameson's voice remained steady. "No matter what happens with this election, I don't want you to forget that."

"Jameson."

"I'm serious. I told you that day there wasn't anything I wouldn't do if you asked me. Even if I didn't think I'd be any good at it, I'd try."

"I remember."

"There is one thing I would never do."

Candace waited.

"I would never leave you, and I would never lie to you. Not even if you asked me to."

Candace caressed Jameson's cheek. "I would never ask you to." She kissed Jameson tenderly. "Never."

"What's up with Mom and JD?" Michelle wondered.

Marianne exchanged a smile with Cassidy.

"It's a little early for Bible Study, isn't it?" Michelle observed.

"Bible Study?" Cassidy inquired.

"Shell is traumatized by the knowledge that Mom and JD do the same things she does with Mel."

Cassidy sniggered.

"I am not. I'm traumatized by the fact that I've heard it. Don't pretend you're not," Michelle said.

Marianne rolled her eyes.

"It happens," Cassidy said. She looked at Michelle. "Don't think your kids won't be feeling the same way one day."

"No way," Michelle said.

"Taking a vow of chastity, are you?" Marianne goaded her sister.

Michelle grumbled.

Marianne and Cassidy laughed.

"What are you laughing about over here?" Alex asked.

"Sex," Cassidy told her wife.

"Parental sex," Marianne corrected.

Alex shook her head. "My parents never had sex."

"You keep telling yourself that, love," Cassidy said.

Alex mumbled.

"See?! Alex understands," Michelle said.

"What do I understand?"

"Come on, you never heard your parents doing it?" she asked Alex.

"No!" Alex shuddered.

Cassidy noticed Dylan approaching from behind Alex.

Alex looked directly at Michelle. "No one should hear their parents having sex—ever. There's not enough therapy or alcohol for that."

"Good to know I won't need to go broke on shrinks and beer," Dylan chimed.

Alex's jaw dropped.

Cassidy burst out laughing.

"Just kidding, Alex," Dylan tried to let her off the hook.

"No, he's not," Michelle said. "Look at his face! See? It's trauma-tizing."

Dylan laughed.

"Did you need something, honey?" Cassidy asked her son.

"Apparently, I need therapy since Alex won't let me have a beer."

"Stop talking," Alex said. "Please."

The group fell into a fit of laughter at Alex's horrified expres-sion. Despite her best effort, Alex joined them.

———————◆●◆———————

"This place gets crazier every year," Maureen said with a chuckle.

"Sure does," Pearl agreed. Candace and Jameson's family went far beyond biology. The deep bonds of friendship and love allowed it to grow beyond traditional definition. "Good thing Candy will have a big-ger yard soon." She detected the worry in Maureen's eyes. It had been a difficult week for Jameson. As a mother, Pearl understood Maureen's concerns. Pearl worried about Candace the same way. She was confident in one outcome—their family would stick together even if heaven itself fell. "Don't worry about them," Pearl said. "The thing about this family is the crazy is what keeps us sane."

Maureen's eyes fell on Jameson. Jameson was holding Candace close. Cooper was climbing into Candace's lap. She heard Michelle yell at Jonah in the distance and the laughter that followed. She smiled. "Truer words," she said. *Truer words.*

FRIDAY

"I can't believe we haven't caught a thing."

Jameson grabbed a beer from the cooler. "Should've gone down to the river instead."

Jonah set his fishing pole aside. "So, you're kidless for a couple of days, huh?"

Jameson shrugged.

"Uh-oh, not happy about that?" Jonah guessed.

"You mean Coop being away for a couple of days?"

"Yeah."

"I'm not unhappy about it."

Jonah nodded.

"Jonah? Want to tell me what's going on?"

"What do you mean?"

"I'd like to think I know you pretty well. What's up?"

Jonah had been mulling over Pearl's advice for days. He still wasn't sure what to say to Jameson. "Nothing is up."

"Right. Did I do something to upset you?"

"No," Jonah answered quickly. "Why would you say that?"

"Maybe because you asked me to go fishing but you've barely spoken two sentences since we got here." Jameson handed Jonah a beer. "Maybe that'll help."

"I'm not upset, JD. I guess I feel bad about asking you to spend the day fishing."

"Why?"

"Coop for one thing."

"What does Cooper have to do with you and me going fishing?" Jameson wondered.

Jonah made no reply.

Jameson rubbed her eyes and groaned. *JD, you idiot. How did you not see this?* "Jonah."

"You've got so much going on. Coop's little. The last thing you need is my shit," Jonah said.

"I must've missed something. When were you giving me shit?"

"You know what I mean."

"No, I don't." Jameson sighed. "You think because your mom and I have Cooper that I don't have time for you?"

"That's not it."

"Yeah, I think it is."

"No. You've got a million things going on."

"Yeah? So do you. None of those things are more important than you are—not to me."

Jonah picked up a stick and started drawing in the dirt.

"I'm sorry, Jonah."

"For what?"

"For being so preoccupied lately. If you want to know the truth, I don't want to bother you."

"Bother *me*?"

"You're running the firm. You've got two little ones and you have all the bullshit Laura's father has dropped in your life. I figured if you had time or you needed me, you'd let me know."

"About that."

"What?" Jameson asked.

"Did Laura's dad have anything to do with what happened the day of Mom's speech?"

Jameson shook her head. "I don't know. It's not important, though."

"Bullshit, it isn't."

"Jonah."

"What? Screw that, JD. First, he comes at Mom, then Laura, then he goes after Coop—now, you? I don't give a shit if he is her father. I hate that guy. I mean that. I hate him."

"He's not exactly my favorite person either."

Jonah bristled. "And, that asshole Tyler? I wish I'd been with Toby when he ran into him."

"No, you don't."

"Yeah, I do."

"I'm okay, Jonah."

"It's bullshit—all of it. You don't get it."

"What don't I get?"

"It's like I told you before, I can't do anything."

"I'd say you're doing a lot," Jameson replied. "The firm is thriving. Laura loves you. The kids are happy. What do you need to do?"

Jonah shook his head.

"Jonah?"

"What if I fuck it all up?"

"Which 'it' do you mean?"

"Any of it—all of it. The only reason the firm is doing so well is that people still see it as yours."

"That's not true."

"Yes, it is. You built it. What if I ruin it?"

"That's not going to happen," Jameson said. "I don't want to hear it. You and Mel were handling almost all of it well before I stepped aside. Where is this coming from?"

Jonah let out an exasperated sigh. "I have no idea what I'm doing."

"With?"

"JD… What if I…"

"What if you what?"

"What if I end up like him?"

"Who?"

"What if I end up like my father?"

"Your dad isn't such a bad guy."

"No, but he wasn't such a great father either."

"He loves you, Jonah."

"You sound like Mom."

"Your mother doesn't lie."

"I barely saw him. I still barely see him." Jonah twirled the stick in his hands. "Shit. How am I supposed to be someone's dad when I feel like a little kid half the time?"

Jameson's expression softened. "Welcome to the club."

Jonah looked up.

"Oh, you think you're the only one? I hate to break it to you; you're not. Your mom still runs to Pearl. You don't think I've cried on my mother's shoulder or bitched to my dad about things? Jonah, if there is one thing being with your mom has taught me it's that none of us ever really grow up. At least, not when it comes to wanting to run to our parents. That doesn't change when you have kids."

"Maybe not."

"Come on, what's really bothering you?"

"Pearl thinks I'm jealous of Cooper."

Jameson nodded. "Are you?"

"Maybe. I just wonder what it would have been like to have them both around—to have you both around."

Jameson smiled. "Thanks for saying that."

"You're thanking me? For being an asshole?"

"You're not an asshole. I get it. Not in the same way, but I think I understand. I was lucky. My parents were both there for me. It's not like things were always perfect, but they were always there for all of us. So, I don't know what that's like—having an absentee parent. I do know what it's like to feel you missed something with someone you love."

Jonah was curious.

"I missed this huge chunk of all your lives. Sometimes, that's hard," she said. "Your mom feels that too. She wonders what life would have been like if her mother had been different."

"She had Grandma Pearl."

"She did, but that doesn't mean she didn't miss her mother. It's like Laura being close to your mom. That doesn't replace Mary or her father, no matter how much she dislikes what he does."

"I know."

"It's true for Cooper too. Cooper loves us. We didn't replace his mother. It's a new relationship. Someday, he will have this conversation with someone—what would his life have been like had she been different? It doesn't mean he doesn't love us. It's just human."

"I guess I just miss this," Jonah said.

"Fishing?" Jameson teased.

"Hanging out."

"Me too. You can always come to me, Jonah—me or your mom. It doesn't matter how old you are or what is going on in our lives. And, before you say anything, that won't change if your mom gets elected. That won't ever change."

Jonah nodded. "Can I ask you something else?"

"Shoot."

"Do you ever wish you and Mom... I mean, that you could have had us together?"

"All the time."

"I'm glad Jonah is spending the day with JD," Laura told Candace.

"Me too."

"He doesn't say much, but I can tell he misses her."

"She misses him too. What about you? How are you doing?" Candace asked.

"Better than I think anyone believes."

Candace nodded.

"I can't let my father have that control over me anymore. I'll never understand him. It's funny. I think I've just started to accept that you can love someone you don't like very much."

Candace was impressed by her daughter-in-law's wisdom. Love didn't come with conditions. Relationships did. That was a reality in life that Candace knew few people ever fully grasped. No matter how much you loved someone, sometimes you had to let them go. Sometimes, a person you loved was not someone who made your life better. Those were some of the most painful moments in life.

"That's true," Candace said.

"I don't know how to explain it," Laura said. "If my father wasn't who he is, I probably wouldn't know Jonah. My life would be totally different. Don't get me wrong, there are parts of my life I could do without. But I love my family. I would never change that."

"Believe me, I understand." Candace giggled when Sophie pushed away her bottle. "This family has certainly grown."

"Good thing the White House has so many bedrooms," Laura said.

Candace laughed. "They'll be lucky if it stays white if we make it there."

"Do you hope that you do?"

Candace kissed the baby's head. "The truth?"

"Yeah."

"Most of the time, I do."

"And, the rest of the time?"

Candace placed Sophie on her shoulder. "Part of me wonders why I can't be content with this."

"Burping babies?"

"Being Nana," Candace replied.

"You'll still be Nana when you're president."

"True, but that won't be the role that occupies most of my time."

"I don't think it's the amount of time you spend with them that matters," Laura said. "You're always Nana. Just like JD is always Jay Jay. I guess I shouldn't speak for anyone else, but I think we all know you're there for us when we need you."

"We are. Sometimes, I wonder if you feel you have to ask."

"Ask?"

"For us to be there. For me to be there."

"I don't think that would be any different if you retired altogether," Laura said.

"No?"

"No, I don't. I mean, it's not unlike having JJ and Sophie."

Candace was curious. "How so?"

"The other day, JJ told me that Sophie needs us more. I understood what he meant. I had to explain to him that Sophie needs us differently, not more. I think that's just the way life is. You have a lot of people who look to you," Laura said. "But that's part of the reason they do look to you. We all get that."

Candace moved Sophie to her lap. Sophie smiled and giggled at her Nana.

"See? Sophie agrees. Can I tell you something?" Laura asked cautiously.

"You can tell me anything."

"You really do need to give yourself a break, Mom. Sometimes, Jonah and Shell? They don't see how much of a toll everything takes on you. Marianne and JD do. I see it too. It's not the campaign. It's because you feel guilty about running it. Don't. We do need you. That doesn't mean other people don't need you too. They just need you differently."

Candace had thought when Laura arrived that their visit would center around Laura's life. She wasn't surprised. She'd been impressed by Laura's intelligence and thoughtfulness the moment Jonah introduced them. "You know," she said. "Jonah is lucky to have you as his partner."

"I don't know. I'm glad that things worked out for us, though."

"Mm. Do you still think about pursuing the political arena?"

"Someday," Laura said. "I'd like to think I could make a difference."

"I've no doubt," Candace said. "When you're ready, you let me know."

"I don't expect you to…"

"I'm not saying that because you're my daughter-in-law or because I love you. You have a lot to offer, Laura. I've always known that."

"I think you might be biased."

"I'm definitely biased. That doesn't make it any less true. You let me know when you have some idea what you might like to do—whenever that might be."

"Do you really think I could do it?"

"I don't think so. I know so." Candace smiled. "How do you feel about leftover Chinese food?"

"Love it, so does JJ. All he ever asks for is chicken fingers and fortune cookies."

Candace looked at Sophie. "We'll break you in soon enough," she promised. "Let's go find your big brother and raid Nana's refrigerator. What do you think?"

Sophie giggled.

"No doubt who she's related to," Laura said.

"I keep telling Jameson it's biological. She doesn't believe me."

"I'll make sure to let her know it's been passed down—strengthen the argument."

Candace laughed. *You will do well one day, Laura. You will do well.*

CHAPTER ELEVEN

August 18ᵗʰ

Glenn shook his head. "The polls have narrowed, Candace."

"And?"

"You can't ignore this story about Jameson any longer."

Candace glared at Glenn.

"You can be as pissed at me as you want. It's not going away."

"It's a load of crap."

"And?"

"I'm not subjecting Jameson to that."

"Subjecting me to what?" Jameson walked into the room.

Candace bit her lip to suppress her rising frustration.

"Well?" Jameson urged.

"It's nothing," Candace said.

Jameson looked at Glenn. His expression was a dead giveaway.

"Would you excuse us, Glenn?" Jameson requested privacy.

Glenn picked up a few files and headed toward the door.

"Close the door," Jameson told him. "Feel like telling me what that was all about?"

"No."

"Why would that be?"

"Jameson, let it be."

"I don't think so."

"Jameson."

"Don't do that. We've been down this road before. You don't get to make decisions about what's best for me without my input."

"This is different."

Jameson sat down on the coffee table that faced the sofa Candace occupied. She had a guess what Glenn and Candace's discussion pertained to. "I do read the paper and watch the news," Jameson said.

Candace shook her head.

"It's time," Jameson said. "It's not going away."

"No."

"You don't get to make this decision."

"It's my campaign."

"It's my life and my reputation."

"Jameson, this is not something you need to talk to anyone about."

"I think we're beyond that now. Look, we both knew that our relationship would factor into this election. We knew they were going to come at us."

"This is not the same," Candace argued.

"Yes, it is. The Russia story hasn't gained them any ground. Hammering me has."

"You have nothing to defend."

"No, I don't. I'm not going to defend myself. Glenn wants me to do an interview—one on one with this on the table," Jameson said.

"How did you know…"

"I have ears, Candace."

Candace threw her head back. "I can't ask you to do this."

"You didn't."

"Glenn asking is the same thing."

"I'm offering," Jameson said.

"I don't like it."

"I don't like it either. I need to do this."

"Why?" Candace asked. "For my campaign or for you?"

"Both."

Candace sighed and covered her face.

Jameson took Candace's hands and pulled them from her eyes. "Hey, we are in this together. Okay? It's okay."

"It's not even a little bit okay."

Jameson moved to the sofa and pulled Candace into her arms. "It is. You have to stop thinking I'm made of glass."

"I don't think that."

"Maybe not. You can't make decisions that affect me like this without talking to me. That's not fair."

"I feel responsible."

"For Wolfe's people being assholes or for Jed Tyler?"

"You know what I mean," Candace said.

"Stop taking this on yourself. It's not your fault. This is on them."

"And, it hurts you."

"I'm okay."

Candace held Jameson's gaze. "Are you sure?"

"Completely."

Candace fell back into Jameson's arms. "Please tell me this is all worth it."

"It will be."

"Do you really believe that?" Candace asked.

Jameson held Candace tighter. "Yeah, I do."

AUGUST 28th

"Relax, Mom. JD will be fine."

Candace was unconvinced. Jameson was taping a live interview with Katie Brennan. Candace had known Katie for years. She trusted her as much as she trusted anyone in the media. She also understood that journalists had a job to do. Dana had suggested that Jameson appear on the morning talk show before endeavoring to talk to anyone else one on one. Katie Brennan was fair-minded and intelligent. She had endured her share of scrutiny when she married her wife a few years earlier. Katie had suggested that a live segment would be advisable. Although she endeavored to keep her political opinions out of interviews, it was public knowledge that Katie Brennan was a passionate advocate for civil rights who leaned left. She had even called Candace. A live interview would reduce at least some of the blowback that might claim the interview was staged. All of that should have eased Candace's mind. But she understood that Katie Brennan was no rookie. Katie would press Jameson appropriately albeit respectfully. There were no do-overs, no edits in a live segment. Why she had agreed to allow Jameson to do this continued to perplex her.

"I should never have let her do this."

"I don't think you had much choice," Michelle said.

Candace shot her daughter a harsh glance.

"Hey, don't get mad at me."

"I'm sorry, Shell."

"She'll be fine. Katie is in your corner."

"Katie is a TV host with a job to do."

"She's also a thoughtful journalist."

"Who needs ratings."

"And is a lifelong Democrat. Relax, Mom. Dana couldn't have picked a better place for Jameson to appear. Plus, JD has become a pro."

"This isn't the same, Shell. It's a different ballgame."

Michelle was growing frustrated with her mother. Lately, Candace had been on edge. Jameson had seemed confident that morning when she left for the studio. And, Michelle knew that Candace had spoken with Katie. She couldn't understand what was driving her mother's obvious displeasure. "What's up with you?"

"What are you talking about?" Candace bit.

"That. No offense, Mom, you've been in bitch mode for days."

"I don't like this."

"Okay. This? You mean Jameson giving this interview?"

"What else would I mean?"

"I don't know. What are you worried about? Is it that JD will fall apart or is it because you think if she does it will hurt you in the polls?"

Candace's face grew hot. "Watch it, Shell."

Michelle shook her head. "Yeah, sure." She walked away.

"What was that all about?" Dana asked Candace.

"Nothing."

"You okay?"

Candace made no reply.

Dana nodded. "I'll let you be."

"You all right?" Katie asked Jameson.

"I'm good."

Katie sighed. "Listen, I've been told this is fairly painless."

"Good to know."

"You ready?"

Jameson nodded.

Katie adjusted her earpiece and waited for the signal. She offered Jameson an encouraging smile before turning to the camera.

"I'm delighted and honored to introduce you to this morning's guest. There's a lot more to Jameson Reid than being married to New York's enigmatic governor. I've already discovered that she loves coffee as much as I do. She's taken some time out of her hectic schedule to be with us this morning. I don't think she needs any more introduction than that, so let's get right to it. Thank you for giving us a little time on this hot Monday morning."

Candace took a deep breath. She'd been dreading today. Michelle's words were ringing in her brain. Had she been in "bitch mode?" Maybe she had. More than one unexpected issue had landed on her desk. There had been two officer-involved shootings in New York City that were under investigation and causing stress for both the community and law enforcement. That had exacerbated the narrative about Jameson. Jameson's uncle had taken to calling her a traitor to her roots and her family. He'd spouted that her Uncle Patrick would be ashamed of her choices—aligning herself with a governor who preferred criminals to cops. After all, Jameson was the granddaughter and niece of blue bloods. His attacks didn't end there. He accused Jameson of turning her back on her Catholic upbringing, and that she'd led her cousin to follow a dark path that led to his death. He did much of it with Jed Tyler in the background, maintaining that Jameson was a "token lesbian," riding the governor's coattails to easy street. The entire thing made Candace sick. Jameson's father, brother, Scott, and Jonah had all expressed their desire to "beat the shit" out of both Jerry Donnelly and Jed Tyler. Jameson had spent long hours reeling them in. That was just the tip of the iceberg.

Alex had called Candace to let her know that the investigation into Lawson Klein's relationship with Petru Rusnac had been re-opened. And, it wasn't only the FBI following the trail. Alex didn't know everything. She did suspect that there was money filtering into the DNC from abroad. And, she suspected that the plan was to create a trail to Candace. Candace had acted immediately. It was a complicated situation. Cutting off the funds that were being deposited might hinder any chance of locating the source. If she failed to close the hole, she risked questions about her leadership ability and her integrity as the leader of the party. If she did shut it all down, she might never learn who was behind the plan. That was something as president she would need to know.

Amid all of it, Cooper had fallen prey to a nasty ear infection. The pediatrician told her and Jameson that he suspected Cooper had suffered a few during his early years that had not been treated properly. Cooper would likely be prone to them in the future. Candace was being pulled in a thousand directions. She was on stage for what seemed to be twenty-four hours a day. She couldn't afford to appear rattled on a stage or in front of a camera. She realized as she replayed her interaction with Michelle, she had taken her frustrations out on those closest to her. *You've got some fences to mend, Candace.* She took another deep breath and listened as Jameson engaged with Katie Brennan.

"I can't imagine the last month has been easy for you," Katie said.

Candace smiled. *Open-ended questions—good.*

"You mean with my uncle and Jed Tyler doing the two-step?"
"Is that what you call it?" Katie asked.
"I'm not sure what to call it."
"You didn't expect it?"
"No. The truth is my uncle has been estranged from the family since my cousin Craig died."
"You were close to your cousin as I understand."
"He was my best friend growing up, he and my cousin Scott. They both fell into partying when we were in high school."
"And you didn't?" Katie asked gently.
Jameson chuckled. *"I was too busy being the geek,"* she said. *"And trying to stay in the closet."*
Katie smiled.
"They got caught breaking into a house. It threw the whole family into chaos. Two of my uncles were cops at the time. It wasn't pretty."
"I can imagine."
"It's a badge of honor, you know? Being part of the Donnelly family. That's how we were brought up. So much so that Scott and I both were given Donnelly as our middle name."
"What would you say to your uncle if you could? If he was listening right now, what would you want to say?"
Jameson shook her head and sighed. *"You know, I've thought about that a lot. I think I would want him to know how much he's hurt my mom. I don't like to revisit the past too much. What happened to Craig tore our family apart. But the truth is, he hurt Craig too. Craig just wanted to please him. He was a kid. He made a mistake and it ended his life. I wish that I could have stopped it somehow. I wish I'd known what he was doing. I was away at college. Maybe if I'd been there…"*

A tear rolled over Candace's cheek. No matter how much time passed, and no matter how much healing occurred, a part of Jameson would always wonder if she could have somehow saved Craig. *Oh, Jameson.*

"I think we all have those moments in life," Katie said. *"How do you feel about what's been happening in New York? One of your uncles recently retired from the NYPD. Your wife had been reserved in her support of the officers under investigation."*

"She's also reserved in her absolution of the people who were shot. Candace doesn't jump to immediate judgment like most people do. That's why she has the job she has."

"What about you?" Katie gently pressed.

"I think that walking the streets as an officer is a tough job. I think that when you are out there, you have less than a second to decide whether to pull the trigger. You don't have the benefit of analyzing videos or listening to stories about the person you are confronting. It's you or them. You want to go home to your kids. That's what I think."

"Have you ever shared that with the governor?"

Jameson chuckled. *"Many times."*

"And, what does she say?"

"She understands. There are also people out there who carry a badge who shouldn't," Jameson said. *"My Uncle Patrick always said that a cop's worst enemy was a bad cop. He used to say that criminals come in every shade, even blue."*

"Sounds like an enlightened man."

"I don't know. He'd lived through things."

"And, the governor?"

"Candace? She's lived through plenty. She waits for the facts to come in. That doesn't mean she doesn't have feelings. She does. She gets that two families are suffering. And, she knows that the cop who takes a life because he or she fears for theirs will never be the same again. She's talked to those cops. She's talked to the families of the cops who are killed in the line of duty, and she's had to comfort the families of unarmed teenagers who've been killed by a cop. She doesn't have the luxury of jumping to conclusions. There's too much at stake."

Katie nodded. *"I have to ask; you must have had some idea that people would call your relationship into question."*

"Sure. I just didn't expect anyone to question my sexuality."

"Fair. Now that someone has, does it make you question this path you're following?"

"You mean being married to Candace?"

"I mean being married to someone seeking the presidency."

"No."

Katie looked genuinely surprised. "Not even a little?"

"No, not even a little."

Michelle stepped back into the room and watched as Candace wiped the tears from her cheek. She stepped up and placed her hands on her mother's shoulders. Candace reached back and held Michelle's right hand.

"She loves you," Michelle said.

"I know."

Jameson continued. "I've never regretted anything about being with Candace. I've regretted losing my patience a few times. I've had to apologize more than once for letting my mouth run away from my head. I've never had a second thought about our marriage or any part of it. That includes the decision for her to run this campaign."

"Even with the pressure it's caused?"

"It's no more pressure than those families we were just talking about. It might be different; it's not more."

"I'm curious," Katie said.

"You don't say?" Jameson quipped.

Katie chuckled. "Tell me why you think Candace should be president?"

"How long is your show?" Jameson replied.

"Not as long as I'd like," Katie replied.

Jameson nodded. "There are so many reasons, I'm not sure how to narrow them down."

"Give it your best shot."

"Most people have never had the chance to meet Candace. I have an advantage. Our family has an advantage. We know her. Sure, she's smart. She's experienced and well-educated. She's informed—all those things you hear people on the campaign trail talk about—all the things that shows like this one discuss. There are plenty of people who are intelligent and educated, even prepared. I've met them. I've

never met anyone like Candace. She doesn't do this because she's trying to prove something about herself. She does it because she wants to make a difference. I've seen her up in the middle of the night trying to find a way to get people to the table and pass some piece of legislation. That's after she's spent hours trying to comfort our son while he suffers from an earache. She doesn't think she has all the answers, but she does believe there are answers. And, she won't quit until she finds them." Jameson took a breath. "And, if it matters, she is the funniest person I've ever met. She's real. She's not perfect. She's real."

Katie smiled at Jameson. "And, if she loses?"

"Life will go on for all of us. That's what she would say. It will. We'll all get up the next day just like we did today and we'll go on. Win or lose, things will be different. In a family as big as ours you learn to expect the unexpected."

"How does the family feel about all of this?"

"We have our moments," Jameson said. "It's not a magazine cover." She chuckled. "Four kids, six grandchildren, spouses and parents, brothers—there are a lot of personalities and everyone has an opinion about everything. We sat down with all the kids before Candace decided to do this. It's not easy sharing her with the world. It is worth it. She has too much to offer for any of us to hold her back."

"Last question. Let's pretend that you land in the White House for the next eight years, what do you hope life will be like when you leave?"

"For us or for you?" Jameson asked.

"I told you," Michelle said. "She's a pro."

Candace squeezed Michelle's hand.

"Both," Katie said.

"For you, I hope it will be a little bit better. I hope that you will feel that Candace's presidency improved your life in some way. I don't know what that will look like. I'm not the policy expert. Maybe you will have to worry less about your kids' education or who you love. Maybe the environment will be cleaner. In some way, I would hope you would feel the difference."

"And, for you?"

Jameson smiled. "I look forward to an entire week with no talk shows, no speeches, no advisers calling in the middle of the night, and no crisis beyond a crying baby or a need to grind more coffee."

Katie laughed. "Crying babies?"

"Not mine," Jameson clarified. "The way Candace's kids are adding them, I wouldn't be surprised if I'm changing diapers into my sixties."

Candace shook her head with amusement. "Why should it be any different for her?"

Michelle laughed along with her mother. "Feel better?" she asked.

Candace tugged on Michelle's hand and pulled her over to the sofa. "I'm sorry, Shell."

"It's okay, Mom."

"No, it isn't. I've been a bitch."

"Nah, just in bitch mode."

"There's a difference?"

"A big one. I know you have a lot on your mind," Michelle said. "Just remember that we are all here for you. You're always so busy worrying about everyone that you forget that sometimes."

"Been talking to Jameson?"

"Maybe, but I don't need JD to see what's going on. I've worked with you for years now. I get it. You can't let the strain show to most people."

"That doesn't excuse me hurting you—any of you."

"You didn't."

Candace raised her brow.

"You didn't. You might have pissed us off a little."

Candace laughed. "Well, I will try not to do that in the future."

Michelle let the apology lie. She didn't need an apology. "What's next on your agenda?"

"Funny you should ask," Candace said.

"Why is that?"

"I was thinking coffee."

"There's a coffee maker right there." Michelle pointed across the room.

"Well, I was thinking you and I might escape this room for an hour or so."

"Gil will love that."

"He's used to it," Candace said.

"You enjoy driving him crazy, don't you?"

Candace winked. "Not at all."

Candace heard the door open and immediately went to greet Jameson.

"I thought you had a meeting with the mayor?" Jameson asked.

"I canceled."

"Why?"

"Something unexpected came up." Candace closed the remaining distance between them and kissed Jameson lovingly.

"Was my interview that good?"

"I'm sorry."

"I missed something," Jameson said.

"No, I did. Michelle set me straight."

Jameson's face contorted in confusion.

"Stop," Candace swatted her.

"Shell set you *straight?*"

"Okay, I get the joke."

Jameson grinned.

"I've been a bitch."

"Shell called you a bitch?"

"No, she said I was in 'bitch mode.' I called me a bitch." Candace chuckled when Jameson made no reply. "Good to know you agree."

Jameson put her arms around Candace's waist. "I love you even when you are a bitch."

"You're enjoying this, aren't you?"

"Maybe a little," Jameson confessed.

"You were amazing today, Jameson."

"I just told the truth."

Candace smiled. "Yes, I know."

"Did you really cancel your meeting?"

"I did. I was hoping you might be agreeable to heading back home early."

Jameson was confused. Candace had made a speech the previous night at a benefit supporting The Human Rights Coalition. It had timed perfectly to Jameson's appearance on *Coffee with Katie*. Candace had agreed to a meeting with the mayor in the afternoon and she had planned to take her calls from the hotel that evening. They would drive back to Albany the next morning.

"How early?" Jameson asked.

"Nowish."

"Now?"

"If we leave by noon, we'll be in Schoharie before dinner."

"Worried about Coop? Marianne said he seems to be back to himself."

"I'm not worried," Candace promised. "Truthfully?"

"Please."

"I could use a night at home, Jameson—not in Albany, not in a hotel room—at home."

Jameson placed a kiss on Candace's forehead. "I'll get our things packed."

"I already did."

"Did you tell Gil?"

"Done," Candace said. "I told him when Shell and I went to have coffee."

Jameson chuckled. "You aren't going to make it easy for him, are you?"

Candace shrugged.

"I'm glad you're taking a breath."

"Me too," Candace confessed.

"Although, I'll confess, I thought for a minute you had something else in mind."

"Did you?"

"Maybe."

Candace let her hand travel over Jameson's breasts. "Take me home, Jameson."

Jameson felt a familiar lump form in her throat. "I'll get our bags." She cleared her throat and walked away.

Candace grinned. Jameson's face had flushed with desire in an instant. *Works every time.*

———————◆●◆———————

"We're still trailing," Wolfe said.

Ritchie shrugged. "It's to be expected."

"What are we doing about it?"

"There's a plan in place."

"There had better be," Wolfe warned.

"Stick to the script, Brad."

"Why? Has that worked yet?" Wolfe grinned. He walked out onto the stage effectively dismissing his closest adviser.

———————◆●◆———————

"Mom!" Marianne called into the kitchen.

Candace followed the sound into the living room. "What is it?"

"You and Jameson have got to watch this."

Jameson sauntered into the room. "Watch what?"

Marianne pointed to the television."

"Oh, boy," Jameson groaned when she saw Bradley Wolfe's face.

"There's a clear choice here, folks. Lesbians on parade or a man who hasn't missed a Sunday in church in his life."

Cheers blared through the auditorium.

"Guess we know what his new line is going to be," Jameson said.

Candace's expression remained impassive as she listened.

"Now, I don't know much about lesbians. I will say this much; Jed Tyler can't be much of a man. I don't buy an ounce of his story."

An audible gasp of surprise could be heard in the crowd.

Wolfe held up his hand. "No, no. Let's win on the facts. I don't have a problem with what Mrs. and Mrs. Reid want to do. I just don't think they should be the poster girls for what our daughters should aspire to."

Jameson shook her head. "Still think my interview went well?"

Candace silently took hold of Jameson's hand and stroked the back of it with her thumb as she watched Wolfe continued to speak.

"Here's something the governor and I do agree on."

"This ought to be rich," Marianne commented.

"We agree that America needs to get back to basics. We don't agree on what those basics are. Put people first? Which people, Governor? The people who came here illegally and take away jobs? How about the criminals? We should show them more empathy? The terrorists? Are they deserving of a fair chance? Which people? I say it's the mothers and fathers who get up every day and try to support their families. The ones who go to church. Why can't we just say that? Since when do we call church-going folk bigots? Who is the bigot here? Me? I don't think so. I've helped all kinds of people. I've spent my life building companies."

Marianne rolled her eyes. "More like buying them and then selling them."

"Companies that pay people. What has the governor spent her life doing? She's spent it living off your dollars. Take a look at your tax dollars at work. Ask yourself who you trust with those dollars? Someone who works for a living or someone who makes her living on your backs?"

Candace reached over for the remote and clicked off the television.

"Mom?"

"I was thinking that we should cook out on the grill tonight. Let the kids play in the pool for a while now that Cooper's ear is better," Candace said.

"Mom?"

Candace smiled. "It's his campaign. He gets to run it any way he chooses."

"What are you going to do?" Jameson wondered.

"Right now, I am going to go pour us some wine while you get the kids into their bathing suits."

"Candace, if you need to…"

"What I need is to sit by the pool with Marianne while you swim with the kids. Then? Then I want to have burgers and dogs on the grill and watch some of that *Scooby Doo* nonsense you've managed to get our son addicted to."

Marianne chuckled. "I'll get the kids ready," she offered and headed for the stairs.

"I know you want to step away," Jameson said.

"It will still be there tomorrow."

As if on cue, Candace's phone buzzed. She took a deep breath and answered it. "Hello, Glenn. Yes, I saw it. What do you mean, how do I want you to respond? Don't." Candace sighed. "That's right. Don't respond at all. Worried? About what? About Bradley Wolfe telling the world Jameson and I sleep together? I think that's been covered ad nauseam. Uh-huh. You can do that. No, I'm not coming to Albany now. No, I'm not getting on a call. Leave Dana alone. Because, Glenn, I said so."

Jameson chuckled.

"Mm-hum. I will be there at noon tomorrow. No, not earlier—at noon. Goodbye, Glenn. No. No, you won't." Candace held the phone away from her and rolled her eyes. "Sorry, hold on." Candace covered the phone slightly and raised her voice. "What was that, Jameson?"

Jameson listened with amusement.

"Sorry, Glenn. Jameson needs me. I'll see you tomorrow. Right. I know you will. Noon. Right. See you then." Candace tossed her phone onto the sofa. "Honestly."

"You know it would be okay if you needed to talk to him."

"I don't. I told you what I need." Candace stretched to place a kiss on Jameson's cheek. "Just make sure you pick a short movie," she said with a wink. "I'd like to get to bed early."

Jameson watched Candace strut off to the kitchen. For the second time that day, she fought to swallow the lump in her throat. *It never gets old.*

CHAPTER TWELVE

September 28th
Georgia State University—First Debate

C andace sat quietly in the small room she'd been ushered into. She could hear the buzz just outside the door but she chose to ignore it. She'd only arrived in Georgia that morning after a whirlwind of appearances and a campaign rally a day earlier in Florida. Glenn was pressing her to dedicate more time to three specific states: Florida, Ohio, and North Carolina—all which he believed were in play for Candace. Candace had seen the analysis. She heard the poll results for each state and for the general election. She was running three points ahead in most polls nationally. She'd warned her team against a false sense of confidence. A great deal could shift in a month. She listened to Glenn's counsel. She listened to Michelle and Dana, to Grant and Doug. She'd even made it a point to consult with Nate Ellison on the finer points of the campaign as the clock ticked down. The two people whose advice and guidance she invested herself in were Cassidy Toles and Jameson. With so many competing ideas and opinions, she needed peo-ple she trusted to be honest with her—brutally honest if necessary. She'd been relieved and delighted when Cassidy had agreed to travel with her for the debates. While it was not a speech, debating required practice and preparation. Cassidy understood Candace's voice. Candace would enlist every ounce of help that she could to nail the three debates ahead of her.

"Okay if I come in?" Cassidy peeked into the room.

"Tell me you have wine," Candace said.

"I promise I will buy you a glass after. Nervous?"

"Aware," Candace said.

"Remember what we talked about," Cassidy advised. "He's going to pummel the idea that he's built things. This is *your* forum, not his. These are the voters' questions, not the moderator's. That's your advantage. Don't let him pull you to his narrative. Pivot back to yours."

Candace took a deep breath. "How did Jameson seem?"

"She walked in with a big smile," Cassidy said. "If she's nervous, she's not showing it."

Candace grinned. *She's nervous.* "Shell keeps saying she's a pro."

"She pays attention," Cassidy said. "That's how we both learned."

"True." Candace heard a knock on the door. "Come in."

"Excuse me, Governor Reid. They're ready."

Cassidy reached over and hugged her friend. "You are so far out of his league, he'd need the starship Enterprise to catch you."

Candace chuckled. "Thanks for the vote of confidence."

Cassidy winked. "See you in ninety minutes."

"With wine."

"With wine," Cassidy promised.

Candace took a deep breath. *Here we go.*

Jameson took Teresa Wolfe's hand and shook it amicably. "Nice to see you," Jameson said.

Teresa Wolfe offered Jameson a smile. "Jameson," she said. "It's good to see you too." She looked down at Cooper. "Hello, Cooper."

"Hi," he replied a bit shyly.

"Lots of lights," Jameson explained.

"I understand," Teresa said.

Jameson nodded and shook Bradley Wolfe's only daughter's hand. She'd never met Isabel Wolfe, though she had heard her on the campaign trail. "We haven't met," Jameson said.

"No," Isabel said.

The smile on Isabel Wolfe's face was strained, and Jameson couldn't determine in the few seconds they had if it was due to dislike or regret. "Well, it's nice to meet you," Jameson said. "Come on, Coop." She moved to find her seat a few rows away.

Marianne nudged Michelle as they approached the Wolfe family. "Behave," she whispered.

"Tell Jonah that," Michelle whispered back.

"You too," Marianne turned around and whispered to Jonah. He smiled.

Jameson watched as the three stooges greeted Bradley Wolfe's family. She forced herself not to laugh. She was sure that to anyone looking in, all three appeared genuinely friendly. She could detect the desire to scream in all of them. Despite her best effort, she chuckled softly.

"Where's Mommy?" Cooper whispered to Jameson.

"She's behind the stage, buddy. She'll be out in a few minutes."

Cooper yawned. He looked at Jameson hopefully just as Marianne took her seat.

"Do you want to sit in between me and Marianne instead?" she asked.

Cooper nodded.

"Okay."

Jameson had immediately regretted bringing Cooper when she saw the lighting design for the stage. While the lights were not moving, the entire theater was highlighted by blue and red lights. Lights remained a trigger for Cooper. He recalled them from the ambulance that whisked his biological mother away. Jameson and Candace had been gradually working on his anxiety. Jameson recognized that while Cooper's coping skills had improved dramatically, some things would likely always cause him stress. She conveyed her concern quietly to Marianne on the way into the theater. Moving Cooper between them would help him to feel safe.

"Hey, Coop." Marianne leaned over into his ear. "Are you okay?"

Cooper shook his head.

"What's wrong?" Marianne asked.

Cooper looked up at the red and blue lights.

"I know," Marianne said. She reached over and took his hand. Cooper reached for Jameson's at the same time.

Jameson looked at Marianne helplessly and was met with a smile. The moderator, Dan Fitzgerald walked out onto the stage. Jameson whispered in Cooper's ear. "Here comes Mommy." She watched as his expression brightened. *Yeah, I know how you feel, Coop. I know how you feel.*

⚬

Candace had grown tired of pivoting. She felt that she had held her ground, stuck to the issues. Cassidy was right; this was her forum. Nonetheless, Wolfe had come at her whenever possible. The digs were thinly veiled, backhanded insults that he dressed in sarcasm. Candace had failed to take the bait. She wished she could see her family, but the lights made it nearly impossible for her to see anyone except the person who stepped to the microphone. She'd answered questions about education, welfare, and immigration. One young single mother had asked how each candidate would ensure she could find affordable healthcare for her family. So far, everything had been textbook. Candace kept waiting for the curveball that didn't come. Debates sought ratings too. The media would be looking for some sensational nugget to capture viewers' attention for the next twenty-four hours. The end was in sight. *Of course—save the 'mess' for last.*

"We're onto our final question for each candidate. This question will be about your personal perspective and it comes from Dean Rigby. Mr. Wolfe, you will answer first. Governor Reid, Mr. Rigby will ask you a question to follow. There is no rebuttal period for this question. Mr. Rigby will be allowed one follow-up question."

Candace kept her eyes on the microphone stand.

"Good evening," the young man at the microphone greeted the candidates. "Mr. Wolfe, you've said that you are a Christian man. You've called both Governor Reid's morals and policies into question. I'm also a Christian. Doesn't our faith call us to heal the sick, feed and clothe the poor? Doesn't it demand that we treat others as we wish to be treated? This country is diverse in every way. Do you believe that extends to every person or only some people? As a Christian and as a president, once this election is over, how will you live those values?"

Candace nearly choked. In a million years, she would not have expected that question to be posed to Bradley Wolfe. She wondered what was in store for her.

Wolfe paced to the front of the small stage. "Let me start by saying that I appreciate your question. You're right. My faith does tell me that I am supposed to help those who are not as lucky as I have been."

Candace wanted to roll her eyes.

"When I'm president, I'll do what I've always done."

"God help us all," Michelle muttered. Jonah kicked her.

"I'll build new systems that give people the chance to help themselves. I don't think it's our responsibility to provide everything for everyone. It's our job to make sure they can provide for themselves. That's what gives people pride."

Michelle bit her lip. "Which is a cardinal sin, you moron." This time, Marianne kicked her.

"The other part of your question was about treating people the way you like to be treated, right?" He took a breath. "I'll go out on a limb and guess that your question refers to what I've said about Governor Reid's relationship. I'll repeat that here. I don't have a problem with what the governor does in her personal life, but I do have a problem with it being a campaign slogan. Part of being Christian is learning to live according to God. I think a president has to live up to that example. Last I checked, homosexuality was a sin. She deserves forgiveness like anyone. That doesn't mean that she should be a leader. As president, I'll make it so that people can find ways to take care of their families. We need to get back to basics. Respect your parents. Pay respect to the people who serve the country. Respect the flag. Respect your teachers. Work hard. I don't think it's unfair to hold people accountable," Wolfe said. "I'd expect no less."

Candace sat on her stool praying that her expression did not betray her.

"Do you have a follow-up for Mr. Wolfe?" Dan Fitzgerald asked.

"I do. Mr. Wolfe, do you believe that Governor Reid is less qualified because she is a lesbian?"

"I believe she is less suited because she is a lesbian."

"Asshole," Michelle sputtered.

"Understatement," Jonah whispered through gritted teeth.

The moderator stepped back in. "Governor Reid, the final question is for you."

Dean Rigby stood again. Candace hopped off her stool and walked closer.

"Good evening. Governor Reid."

Candace smiled.

"My question for you is similar. You've avoided discussing your marriage in any detail with the press or on the campaign trail. While it is true that legally you have the right to marry anyone you choose, many people in this country, particularly religious people feel that your choice betrays American values. Is there anything you can share that might change their perception? They have been highly critical of you and your family in personal ways. If you are elected, how will you serve their needs and stay true to your convictions?"

"Oh, boy," Michelle whispered.

Marianne took her sister's hand and glanced over at Jameson. Jameson was intent on Candace.

"Well, Dean thank you for your question. It's certainly not the easiest one," Candace began. Faint chuckling met her ears. "Another two-part question. Your observation is fair and accurate. I haven't discussed my marriage in any detail. That's because I haven't seen the need. My 'coming out' was not private, as you might have heard."

Another rumble of suppressed laughter emerged.

"There isn't much that I can *say* about my marriage that is going to change the mind of anyone your question refers to. In my experience, people change their perception when they get to know someone—not from a debate or an interview—over a glass of wine, at a playgroup, in the office, even in church. Both Jameson and I were raised going to church every Sunday. We still attend when we can. I suppose, I have a different view of what faith teaches us than Mr. Wolfe does." She took a breath. "What could I tell them?" Candace smiled warmly. "I will tell you this, I love Jameson. I love her because she's the kindest person I know. She's generous and honest, and she helps me to remember what matters most in life. What matters most is who we love. That's why people vote—believe it or not. They want to have a say in making their lives better. They want the best chance for the people they love—their parents, children, friends, coworkers, and in more cases than we give credit, their employees. It doesn't matter if someone disagrees with me or if they don't like me. As president, my job will be to remember that every person matters to someone. Every person deserves an equal chance at achieving his or her goals, at thriving in their life. To me, that includes the right to commit their lives to the person they choose, to worship as they choose, to have the career they desire. Has this campaign gotten personal? Without question. Does that hurt? Yes, it does, and not just me. My family is just like everyone else's. We have our ups and downs, we argue on occasion, we battle illnesses and we pay bills. It's not lost on me that we are fortunate. I've never worried about my next meal or how I would pay for school, neither has Jameson or our three grown children. We have witnessed the struggle through Cooper's eyes. I want

245

every child—every person to go to sleep secure that there will be enough for them to eat the next day, and that they have the chance to make their dreams reality. How do I *do* it? I get to work."

"Mr. Rigby?" Dan Fitzgerald's voice broke the momentary silence.

"Governor, Mr. Wolfe said that he thinks you are less suited to be president because you are a lesbian. Do you think he is less suited because he is critical of who you are?"

"Do I think he is less suited to be president because he has an issue with who I am? No. There are a lot of people who have issues with who I am. Some because I am a woman, some because I am a lesbian, others simply because I had the good fortune to come from a family that possessed wealth. One thing about serving in elected office, there is always more criticism than consensus. I think I'm better 'suited'—as Mr. Wolfe put it—because I understand that gaining consensus requires just as much listening as it does expressing my opinion. People don't have to like everything about me to work with me. They don't even have to agree with *who* I am or how I live my life. They need to agree on one thing—to try to do what is best for the people we are all elected to serve. A president isn't elected to serve the people who cast their votes his or her way. A president assumes the responsibility for the entire nation. I can assure you, I understand that."

Dan Fitzgerald looked in the camera facing him. "That concludes tonight's debate. I want to thank both our candidates...."

"Well, that was interesting," Jonah commented softly as Fitzgerald made his closing remarks.

"Do we really have to go shake his hand?" Michelle groaned.

"Yes," Marianne said.

"I'd rather..."

"Play nice, Shell," Marianne whispered.

"I don't have to like it."

Jameson slipped into bed behind Candace and wrapped her in an embrace. "You never cease to amaze me."

"Let's hope the pundits are as kind." Candace turned to face her wife.

"Glad it's over?" Jameson asked.

"I am. Two more to go."

"Are you worried?"

"No. I just hope that I don't let everyone down."

Jameson brought her lips to Candace's. "Impossible."

"I wish that were true."

Jameson kissed Candace again. She traced a fingertip across Candace's brow. "Quiet, now."

Candace closed her eyes and reveled in the tenderness of Jameson's touch. They'd slept apart for the last five nights while Candace campaigned in the south. She'd missed the comfort of Jameson's arms. Jameson could quiet her questions and ease her anxiety. Feeling Jameson close to her, Candace's heart commanded her head. Here she could escape the world, lose herself in the presence of the woman she loved—in Jameson's kiss, in her touch.

"Jameson?"

"Hum," Jameson hummed in Candace's ear.

"Make love to me."

Jameson moved to look in Candace's eyes. Sometimes, the blue of Candace's eyes deepened to a hue that reminded Jameson of a brewing storm, signifying an inevitable thundering of passion and desire. She brushed Candace's hair aside and gazed at her lovingly. Candace left her breathless without any need of words or the slightest touch. Her lips brushed across Candace's forehead tenderly. Her hands moved to divest Candace of the clothing she wore. Candace began to speak. Jameson silenced her with the softness of her lips.

"Shh," Jameson cooed. She sat back and pulled her shirt over her head.

"I need you, Jameson."

"I'm here," Jameson promised.

Candace closed her eyes. Her hands continued to roam over Jameson's back and hips, back to the nape of her neck. Finally, they gripped the elastic of Jameson's shorts. The need to feel Jameson moving against her overpowered thought and reason, as if she might be swallowed whole by Jameson's presence. "Jameson…"

Jameson began to glide sensually against Candace. Her hands caressing Candace's body in slow circles, lingering at the sound of a passionate sigh. She could lie here forever feeling Candace and never wish for anything more.

"I hate being apart," Candace whispered. She did. Jameson provided comfort, acceptance—a place to soar and a place to fall. She guided Jameson's lips to hers. Her fingertips traced the outline of Jameson's face, committing it to memory as a blind person might, only sensation to guide her exploration. Warmth spread over her body and began to flow from her freely. The ache in her chest traveling to every nerve in her body and settling in her core. Her back arched, begging for anything to satisfy the need that swelled within her. Two strong fingers met her unspoken request. Her head fell back onto the pillow.

Soft. Wet. Inviting. Yielding yet demanding. Jameson followed the gentle sway of Candace's hips as they met her well-timed rhythm. Slow. No, fast. Soft. Jameson's tongue bathed Candace's straining nipple in a flurry of sensation. Candace's body bent to her will.

Candace's head rolled side to side against an endless array of sensation. It would never be enough. Her hands found Jameson's face, pulling her higher. No questions. She needed no permission. Candace turned them about. Her hair spilling into Jameson's face as Jameson struggled to stay inside her. Deeper. Candace's head fell back. Never enough. It would never be enough. She gathered her strength. Jameson's face flushed with desire. Her nipples straining in the cool air. Candace's mouth surrounded them one by one, back and forth. Soft. Hard. Deep. She prayed it might never end.

Warm. Gentle. Jameson's lips parted with anticipation. Her fingers continued their gentle assault, pressing deeper, twisting and probing. She became captivated by the sounds that mingled in the air between them. Quivers erupted from them both, tiny prickles of pleasure brought on by painful anticipation. Should she beg? She startled at the sensation of sudden loss and watched in rapt fascination as Candace's mouth moved to hers. No questions. Candace hovered above her. And, then warmth again. Warmth spreading everywhere—over her and through her. Softness above her, heat moving lower in long, languid strokes—giving and taking and giving some more. Jameson surrendered to the storm. Faint rumbling turned swiftly to thunderous pounding through her into Candace and back again. Another unexpected crash finally gave way to the soft pattering that followed the shaking from above and settled within. It was the perfect storm, the kind you met with outstretched arms, hoping it would overtake you.

Jameson opened her eyes. The stormy blue of Candace's irises sparkled now like tiny diamonds, clear and bright, hopeful and grateful. She traced Candace's lips with her fingertip. "Perfect," she whispered.

"What?" Candace asked.

"You," Jameson said. "Now. It's perfect."

Candace kissed Jameson reverently. "Such a romantic."

"No." Jameson's eyes began to mist over. "I know how lucky I am."

A smile curled Candace's lips. "I love you, Jameson."

"And, I love you."

Jameson pulled Candace into her arms. She wouldn't seek to fill up the moment with words. As if the universe understood, a faint pitter-patter on the roof drifted to her ears. "Perfect."

OCTOBER 16th
DETROIT MICHIGAN

"When does Jameson arrive?" Grant Hill asked.

"Tomorrow morning," Candace replied.

"Have you talked to her?"

"This morning, why?"

"No reason."

Candace lifted her brow.

"I was just curious how she felt things were going there," Grant said.

"There?"

"She's been with Jane for the last two days. She must have a pulse on things."

Candace nodded. Jameson had been campaigning with Jane Merrow in Arizona and New Mexico while Candace traversed Wisconsin and Michigan. Marianne and Shell had both been covering ground on the east coast at rallies. Nate Ellison was off in the south making the case for Candace. Candace wasn't leaving any stone unturned. Some of her advisers were frustrated by her insistence on covering broad ground. Grant fell into that category. The argument they presented Candace was that she needed all her assets in the states where she had a realistic chance of winning. With just three weeks remaining before voters would go to the polls, Grant and Glenn had argued passionately that Candace needed to narrow her focus. She maintained a two to three-point advantage in the national polls, nowhere near what anyone deemed a comfortable edge. Candace had listened to all the points they presented. She maintained her determination to campaign broadly albeit through surrogates.

"The energy is high. You know that."

"Candace, I know you don't want to hear this."

"Then don't say it."

Grant sighed. "You're not going to take Arizona, and New Mexico is a wrap. You have to know that."

Candace shrugged. "I wouldn't rule anything out as possible. Why are you and Glenn spinning over this?" she asked. "Shell was in Pittsburgh yesterday. I'm here in the Midwest. Jameson will be in North Carolina on Thursday and I'll be in Ohio."

"And, you have Nate heading to California which is a lock for you while you insist on heading to Texas on Friday where we both know Wolfe is going to devour you. Three weeks, Candace—three weeks."

"I know how much time there is on the clock, Grant."

"I don't understand why you won't listen."

"I am listening. I just don't agree."

"You need to pull those close states into your column."

"Grant," Candace addressed him firmly. "Do you think that my ignoring three-quarters of this country sends the right message?"

"Yes—to the people who are still sitting on the fence; yes, I do."

"Maybe to those people it does. It sends the message that the most important thing to me is getting their votes."

"Isn't it?"

"It's important."

"It's imperative," Grant argued.

"And, the votes in Arizona and Texas aren't."

"Candace, be reasonable here. Those states are not going to land in our column."

"Probably not."

"Forgive me if I can't follow your logic."

"Grant, you and Glenn keep accusing me of not listening to you. I think I could make that same argument." She held up a finger. "I don't want you to simply hear the words I am saying, I want you to *listen* to them. Can you take a breath and do that?"

Grant groaned.

"First, I don't agree with you about the map. You are convinced that we've locked Nevada and lost Arizona. I don't agree with you on either count. You think that because a state has less electoral votes, I should place it on the backburner. You want to play this the same way it's been played every four years."

"Because it works!"

"No, it *worked*. That is the problem in this country, Grant—one of them. Just because something worked yesterday does not mean it will work tomorrow."

"I know how you feel about governing. You have to get elected first."

"You think this differs?" Candace took a breath and shook her head. "People forget, you don't know what works today until tomorrow comes."

"What does that mean?"

"It means that we can't evaluate the success or failure of something until we've reached the other side. You are using pure hindsight to guide your recommendations."

"What would you suggest we do?"

"I think that's clear. Look at this election," she said. "No matter how much hopeful chatter there might have been, four years ago most people would not have imagined I would get this far. A woman who is a lesbian running for the highest office in the land? No. That was a pipedream of the aspiring liberal. And, Wolfe? You couldn't find someone more my opposite. Neither of us fits the mold cast for the model you are following. We have to cast a new one if we want to cross this finish line first."

Grant scratched his forehead. "And if you're wrong?"

Candace smiled. "Then it's on me—just as it should be. You know, when I brought you on board a lot of people judged my decision based on your past."

"What does that have to do with this?"

"Nothing directly. It goes to what I am trying to make you understand. What seems obvious is seldom as simple as we want to believe. There's a reason Bradley Wolfe and I are where we are. You think that is about our campaigns. You might even think it's about us. It is—to an extent. Beneath it all, it's because of the people who go to the polls—even the ones who won't."

"The ones who won't?"

"Absolutely. You don't think they're still talking at the watercooler? Bitching at the bar? Posting on their Facebook pages about us?" Candace covered Grant's hand with hers. "When the watercooler and the bar were the places people commiserated, your plan might have worked. Stick close to home. Home isn't just the kitchen table or the office anymore. Media is the watercooler, Grant. Everyone is watching from everywhere. Polls? They sample a small group of likely participants. I'm more concerned about the larger group they'll never touch."

Grant sighed. "It's your call."

"Yes, it is. You need to trust that I don't make it lightly."

"I want this for you," he said.

Candace smiled. "I know you do. Do me one favor?"

"If I can."

"Stop thinking you know what's best for me better than I do."

"That's not what…"

"It is," Candace interrupted him gently. "In a few weeks, we'll know whether what I decided today was the best thing for tomorrow."

"You're okay with that?"

"I have to be. I don't have the benefit of hindsight and foresight is always an educated guess. Whatever happens, we'll go forward. There isn't any other choice."

"Ms. Reid?"

Jameson turned to the sound of a young voice. She smiled when a pair of wide eyes greeted her. The moment Jameson's eyes met hers, the young girl blushed. Jameson had to remind herself not to laugh. She imagined the girl to be about sixteen.

"Hi," Jameson said.

"I was wondering if I could get a picture?" The girl's voice quivered slightly as she made the request.

"Sure," Jameson said. She suppressed a chuckle as the girl fumbled with her phone. "How about I take it?"

"Really?"

"Sure. I'm pretty sure my arms are longer," Jameson joked. She snapped a few photos and handed the phone back.

"Thanks."

"What's your name?" Jameson asked.

"Sarah."

"Thanks for coming out to support Candace."

"I wish I could vote for her." Sarah's blush deepened.

"I know that will mean a lot to her. She likes to see young people get involved. Hopefully, you'll get your chance in another four years." Jameson winked. "Nice meeting you, Sarah."

"Holy shit! You got a picture with her?"

Jameson laughed at the eruption of squeals behind her.

"Another fan?" Jane bumped Jameson lightly. "You might be converting more than votes."

Jameson rolled her eyes. "Don't say that too loud. I can just imagine that in Wolfe's next speech."

"Candace better watch her back," she teased Jameson some more.

"I'd rather watch hers," Jameson quipped.

Jane burst out in laughter. *No wonder she loves you so much, JD.*

OCTOBER 17th
DAY OF THE FINAL DEBATE

"You've said that Governor Reid wants to punish the wealthy to prop up the poor. Do you think that's fair?"

"It's the truth," Wolfe said. "This is the problem with the liberal mentality. They want to play Robin Hood—steal from the rich to give to the poor. Robin Hood wasn't a hero; he was a thief."

"Can you believe that guy?" Michelle asked. She switched off the television.

Melanie shrugged.

"Mel?"

"He's a jerk."

"But?"

"But what?"

"Don't tell me you agree?"

"No, I don't agree that your mom wants to punish the rich."

"But."

"Shell…"

"I don't believe this. You think he's right."

"I don't think he's right. I think that he has a point, though."

"What point is that?"

"I just think that there's some truth to the fact that the Democrats tend to make the successful people into villains."

Michelle's caustic chuckle sent a shiver up Melanie's spine.

"I didn't say I agree with Bradley Wolfe," Melanie said.

"Yeah, you just did."

"You know, Shell sometimes you really can be a jerk."

"Excuse me?"

"Well, you can. I love your mom, you know. I think Wolfe's an asshole. That doesn't mean I have to agree with your mother on everything. She wouldn't expect me to."

Michelle shook her head. "I think we should stop talking about this."

"Why? Because I have the nerve to express an opinion that you don't like?" Melanie shook her head. "I don't think that poor people are lazy, Shell. I also don't think that wealthy people are all selfish assholes who want to take advantage of people."

"Mom never said that."

"No. But sometimes the party line sounds that way. Not everyone who is poor is a victim, Shell. Not every CEO or Wall Street banker is an overdressed thug."

Michelle's jaw dropped. Melanie seldom commented on politics.

"That's not what Mom thinks. That's not what the party thinks either."

"Maybe not. You're so close that you don't hear the way it sounds sometimes."

"Maybe because you're hearing something that isn't there."

"It doesn't matter."

"What does that mean?"

"The twins will be waking up any minute. I should check on Spencer and Maddie before they do."

Michelle shook her head when Melanie walked away. *What the hell was that all about?*

"Nana?"

Candace turned and smiled. Spencer had asked if he could stay with his nana while Michelle picked up Marianne and Scott at the airport. "Come over here," she called to him.

Spencer picked up his pace and collapsed into Candace's lap.

"Spencer? What's wrong, sweetheart?" Candace held her grandson close while he cried. "Sweetheart, why are you crying?" Candace rocked Spencer gently. He rarely cried. Something had clearly upset him. "Spencer?"

"Everyone is mad," he choked on his words.

"Who's mad, honey?"

"Shell."

"Shell is mad? Why is Shell mad?"

"She yelled at Mel."

Candace sighed. Marianne and Scott had a fundraising dinner to attend for the clinic that Scott was spearheading in Albany. Michelle and Melanie had offered to take Spencer and Maddie for a night and meet them in Detroit for the debate. Michelle had been taking short trips to campaign for Candace. And, she had continued to help Jameson with writing speeches and preparing for interviews. Candace imagined it was taxing for Shell. She also guessed that the constant movement and stress of the campaign had to be difficult for Melanie. Melanie had responsibilities at the architectural firm, two babies to take care of whenever Shell was away, an elderly grandmother whom she helped care for, and Shell's needs as well. The campaign was draining for everyone. She and Jameson had taken turns snapping at the other in recent weeks as well. It was a symptom of fatigue. It didn't herald impending doom. She was sure as she held Spencer that he had picked up on the adults' stress in his life.

"It's okay," Candace assured him. "You've yelled at Cooper before, haven't you?"

"Yeah."

"And, you've gotten upset with Maddie a few times."

"Yeah," he grumbled.

"But you still love them."

Spencer looked at his nana through swollen eyes.

"I know everything has been a little crazy lately, hasn't it?"

"Yeah."

"That happens sometimes. Don't worry so much, sweetheart. I hate it when you are upset."

Spencer's downcast expression tugged at Candace's heart.

"Spencer?"

"You and Jay Jay are gonna leave us."

Candace took a deep breath and released it slowly. "We would never leave you, Spencer."

"But you'll be far away," he said.

"That might happen," she admitted. "But it won't be forever. We always come home, don't we?" She kissed Spencer on the head. "Do you remember when Cooper first started visiting us? He was so afraid we would forget about him, so you gave him your frog?"

Spencer looked at her curiously.

Candace smiled. "You knew that Cooper would be back because you knew that we loved him. No matter where Jay Jay and I go, we will always be there for you."

Spencer's tears started to flow again. Candace pulled him close. His life had changed dramatically since Scott and Marianne became involved. She sometimes lost sight of the fact that as much as he adored Scott and loved his mother, she and Jameson played a much more central role in his life than they did any of their other grandchildren. He was the first. He also had endured loss. She and Jameson had given him a foundation through that. It created a unique bond. In many ways, Spencer would always see them as parents more than grandparents. He lived with them. They cared for him. As she listened to his uncharacteristic whimpers, she felt both his sadness and his fear. Tears gathered in her eyes.

"Oh, Spencer. I love you so much," she said. "So much," she promised. "I'm sorry that we haven't had more time together."

Jameson opened the door and froze. She closed the door softly, turned to Jeff Lamkin, and whispered in his ear. Then she crouched down to Cooper. "Coop, Jeff is going to take you down to Jonah's room; okay?"

"Why's Spence crying?"

Jameson smiled. "I don't know, buddy. I'm going to go talk to him right now, okay?"

Cooper frowned.

"I think maybe I need to talk to Spencer with Mommy for a few minutes. Is that okay?"

Cooper nodded.

"Okay. You go with Jeff." Jameson took a deep breath and opened the door again. "Hey."

Candace looked at Jameson regretfully. No further explanation was needed. Jameson made her way to the pair and knelt beside the chair Candace occupied.

"Hey, Spence." Jameson put her hand on Spencer's back. "What's going on, bud?"

Spencer began to cry harder. He missed Jameson. He used to go places with her. It seemed like forever to him since he'd been with his Jay Jay.

Jameson was taken aback when Spencer threw himself into her arms. She closed her eyes and held him. "Hey…"

Candace's eyes looked to the heavens. Spencer was articulate, bright and animated. He'd always been that way. He was only five. In the last few months, everyone's life in their family had been altered. In many ways, Candace now realized, Spencer's had been turned upside down the most.

"Spence," Jameson tried to calm her grandson. "Whatever it is, it's okay."

"You're leaving me."

Jameson gripped Spencer firmly, but lovingly. "Spencer, that would never happen. Even when I am away, I'm always thinking about you." That was the truth. She loved Spencer. She missed him sorely. After his father's death, Jameson had become almost a full-time parent to her grandson. It had been difficult for Jameson to step back as Marianne regained her footing. Now that Scott was in the picture, Jameson was needed even less. She understood that was as it should be. She missed Spencer. Even when he was in her care, most of his time was spent playing with Cooper. That was also normal and healthy for both the boys. Jameson was grateful they had each other. She loved them both, and she missed the time that she and Spencer had shared.

"Yes, sir," he sobbed.

"No," Jameson repeated. She placed Spencer back in Candace's lap. "Listen to me. I know that I've been away a lot—so has Nana. But, you know, you've been pretty busy too."

Spencer looked at her and bit his lip.

"You love spending time with your mom and Scott. Lots of times when Nana and I are home you and Cooper are busy doing things together."

Spencer looked down into his lap.

"And, that's okay, Spence. But see? You might be busy, but you still love me and Nana."

He looked back at her.

"I wish we could always be together—you and me and Nana and Coop, Maddie and your mom. Even Aunt Shell." Jameson winked.

Spencer giggled through a sniffle.

"Do you know that I remember the first time I met you?"

Spencer was curious. "It was Christmastime. We walked into your house, and you were on your dad's shoulder. You were still a baby," Jameson said. "Nana took you, and you giggled. Then you smiled at me," Jameson said. "And, you know what? I knew right then that I loved you just as much as Nana did—just as much as I love Nana."

Candace smiled. *Oh, Jameson.* Jameson possessed the most sensitive heart of anyone Candace had ever known. She had no doubt of the sincerity in Jameson's words. Hearing them meant as much to her as she knew it did to Spencer.

"We haven't always lived in the same house," Jameson said. "For a long time, you lived pretty far away from us. You don't remember a lot of that. I do. I missed you then. Nana missed you. We wouldn't leave you, Spencer. You can talk to me or Nana anytime. And, I promise, we will find a way to be there for you." Jameson grinned. "You know, you spent a lot of time hiding from me and Nana."

Spencer smirked.

"We always found you, didn't we?"

"'Cept when I hid in the cabinet. Shell found me then."

Candace chuckled.

"I remember," Jameson said. "I don't want you to worry. I'll make you a promise right now. You and me and Nana, we'll spend a whole day together, just the three of us in a few weeks. Okay?"

"What about Coop?" Spencer asked with concern.

Candace replied. "Oh, I think Cooper might enjoy spending a little time with his grandma and grandpa."

Jameson smiled gratefully. Cooper adored Maureen and Duncan Reid, and they were equally in love with him. She was positive her parents would welcome a weekend with their grandson. "Sounds like a pretty good plan to me," Jameson said. "What do you think, Spence?"

Spencer nodded. "Jay?"

"Yeah, buddy?"

"Can I stay with you and Nana and Coop tonight?"

Jameson nodded. "As long as your mom and Scott say it's okay."

Spencer nodded. "I'll call Mommy."

"Mommy will be here soon. She and Aunt Shell should be in the car by now," Candace said.

"But I can call?" Spencer asked.

Jameson took out her phone. "Yeah, Spence—you can call." She dialed the number and handed Spencer the phone.

"Mommy?"

"Spencer?" Marianne was surprised to hear her son's voice.

"Yep. Can I stay with Nana?"

Marianne was puzzled. "Spencer, Nana's pretty busy."

"Nana says I can. Jay says so too."

"Is Nana there?"

Spencer passed Candace the phone.

"Hi."

"Mom? Is everything okay?"

Candace's fingers riffled through Spencer's blonde waves. "Everything is good," she said. "We were just wondering if you'd allow us the pleasure of Spencer's company tonight."

"Mom, you have the debate. Don't you want some space? I thought maybe Scott and I could take Coop and…"

"We'd love for Spencer to spend tonight here."

Marianne heard the resolve in her mother's voice. "You'll fill me in later?"

"Absolutely," Candace promised.

"Okay."

"See you in a bit," Candace said. She looked into Spencer's hopeful eyes. "Well, I guess you are stuck with us for tonight."

Spencer grinned. He looked back at Jameson. "Where's Coop?"

"He's with Uncle Jonah."

"Can I get him?"

"Go get some shoes on and we'll find Cooper."

"'Kay!" Spencer hopped off Candace's lap and sprinted for the other room.

"And, he's off," Jameson said. She looked at Candace. "I didn't see that coming."

Candace sighed. "I should have seen it."

"Don't start beating yourself up."

"I'm not. Spencer told me he heard Shell arguing with Mel."

"You think that's what triggered this?"

"I think we are all tired," Candace said.

"Yeah, I guess we are. Are you okay?"

"Yes—and, no," Candace said. "I knew this was going to be tough, Jameson."

"But?"

"I needed to do this."

"I know."

"I don't like how much it has already hurt all of you."

Jameson reached over and took Candace's hands. "We're all okay," she said. "If it wasn't this campaign, some other crazy thing would be happening."

Candace chuckled.

"And, I don't think we're all hurting," she corrected Candace. "Maybe sometimes we all miss the ordinary chaos a little. In a few weeks, we'll be figuring out a new normal—whatever happens."

"I love you, you know?"

"I know. I love you." Jameson stood to her full height. "You have a debate to get ready for, and I have a mission to complete with Spencer."

"Want to trade?" Candace asked.

"Nope. Although, I think Coop and Spence might be able to help you."

"Oh?"

"Yeah. Ever heard them debate about which superhero can overpower a T-Rex? It's brutal."

Candace laughed. "You really are a lunatic."

"It's how I survive," Jameson said. She went off in search of Spencer.

I have no doubt about that. None at all.

"Governor Reid, Mr. Wolfe brings up a point many people agree with. How long can the government be expected to support someone? Who's paying for all these entitlement programs? Is it fair for the wealthy to carry everyone else?"

Candace smiled. "There's no simple answer to those questions. There are layers of issues involved. Social Security and Medicare are considered entitlement programs. We pay into those over the course of our working life with the expectation that we will have access to those programs when we retire or become incapable of working. Welfare is considered an entitlement—food stamps. Those programs were designed as a bridge, not as a crutch. I would be the first person to admit that we need to make sure they are utilized in the way that was intended. With that said, if the government fails to provide a satisfactory education for young people, if it declines to invest in the health of its people, then the ability for those who have become dependent on those programs to cross that bridge is diminished greatly. When you ask about whether the wealthy should 'carry' the burden, you're referring to taxation. The answer to your question is, no. People mistake the suggestion and belief that those who enjoy wealth should pay their fair share as an attack on success. Our tax codes are stacked in favor of the wealthy. They are laden with loopholes and scapegoats for the richest people in our country. Most of the people you are alluding to would thrive even if we removed every preferential treatment the tax code provides them. So, no; I don't believe in overburdening the wealthy. I don't believe in vilifying the poor either. I believe in leveling the playing field, if only slightly. There will always be those who have advantages. It's a president's and Congress' responsibility to create opportunities for people at both ends of the spectrum and everywhere in between. So, yes, wealthy people will have to pay more than they are now. How long do we support people? I think the question to ask is how do we provide stronger bridges instead of the weak crutches we currently employ so that people can support themselves."

Melanie smiled. "See? Your mom and I do agree."

Michelle took her wife's hand. She leaned in Melanie's ear. "I'm sorry, Mel."

Melanie squeezed the hand holding hers. "I still love you."

Thank God.

———————— ◆ ● ◆ ————————

"What do you think?" Jameson asked Candace.

"I think we should get the boys back to our room and eat some junk food and finish that *Scooby Doo* movie you were all watching earlier."

Jameson took Candace's hand. "I don't know why anyone bothers to debate you."

"What?"

"Pretty sure the world's problems could be settled over junk food and *Scooby Doo*."

Candace laughed.

Jameson narrowed her gaze.

"What?" Candace asked.

"I thought for sure you'd call me a lunatic on that one."

Candace shrugged. *I don't think you have any idea how right that may be.* "Let's go," she told Jameson. Candace beckoned Spencer and Cooper to her.

A reporter shouted for Candace as the foursome headed through the pressroom. "Governor Reid, are you anxious to get back and see how the country feels about tonight?"

Candace gave Jameson a nod. Cooper and Spencer held each of her hands as she stepped to a line of cameras. "I'm certainly interested," she said. "But I'm afraid I have to pass on CNN and FOX's offers. I have a date with *Scooby Doo*." She smiled at the boys and led them away.

"She really is too much sometimes," Dana laughed.

Cassidy smiled. "That's why she's going to win."

CHAPTER THIRTEEN

ELECTION DAY

Candace sat silently in the SUV. She kept her gaze out the window as the car wound down familiar roads to her polling place. Jameson reached over and took her hand. Candace hadn't spoken a word since waking. She exchanged a smile with Jameson when Jameson placed a cup of coffee in front of her. She offered Jameson a nod when Jameson asked if she was ready to go. Jameson understood Candace's need for silence. When the SUV stopped, and Candace emerged, the blinding lights of cameras, blaring sound of cheers and deafening shouts of reporters would begin. It would not end until long after the results came in. She squeezed Candace's hand when the car rolled to a stop and heard Candace sigh.

"I'm so proud of you," Jameson said. "So proud to be with you."

Candace leaned over and kissed Jameson lovingly. She wiped a small smudge of lipstick from Jameson's lips. "I love you," she said. "More than anything."

Jameson smiled. Candace's door opened. Jameson squeezed her hand again. "Let's go get you elected," she said.

Candace smiled. She took a deep breath and slid from her seat. "Thank you, Gil," she acknowledged the Secret Service agent. He nodded. Candace looked out at the crowd and the line that had formed to enter the school. Cheers greeted her ears. She waved enthusiastically and felt Jameson's hand press into the small of her back.

"We love you, Madame President!"

Candace laughed. "Not yet," she called back.

Candace shook a few hands on her way into the school, accepting well-wishes and thanking people for coming out to vote. She stepped into a large auditorium and up to the table to check in.

"Governor Reid," a volunteer greeted her.

"Thank you for being here," Candace said. She recognized him from local politics. He was a staunch Republican. Next to him sat another familiar face. Someone she'd seen at this polling place for many years. She smiled at the woman. "Good to see you, Greta." The woman handed her a paper ballot. "Thank you. Make sure they give you both lots of coffee," she said. She was surprised when the older man chuckled. "I hope so. It's gonna be a busy day, I think, Governor."

"I hope so," Candace said. She stepped away toward one of the small partitioned tables.

Jameson accepted her ballot and stepped to the spot next to Candace's. She wondered what Candace felt as she looked at the ballot with her name. Jameson's stomach went into a series of somersaults. She had to remind herself to breathe as she filled in the bubbles.

Candace took a deep breath and looked at the paper in front of her. She traced over the ballot, took one more deep breath and began to fill in the bubbles. She stared at the line of black dots that fell across the paper. *Well, that's it.* She picked up the ballot and walked the short distance to the machine. She watched it disappear and smiled at the attendant.

"Wait," he said. He handed her a small sticker that read 'I Voted.'

"Thank you," she said.

"Good luck, Governor."

"Thank you. Thanks for spending the day helping here."

"We all have to do our part."

Candace nodded. "Yes, we do."

<hr />

"Have you heard from JD or your mom?" Scott asked Marianne.

"JD called a while ago to talk to Coop and said that they're planning on spending some time here after they vote. They'll head to the city this afternoon."

"Huh. I thought they'd be headed right there."

Marianne smiled. "No. I think Mom wants some quiet. Dana is meeting them here with Grant. Glenn and Doug are in the city already."

"Mom," Spencer grabbed Marianne's shirt. "Nana's on TV!"

Marianne smiled and let Spencer lead her into the other room. She watched as Candace emerged from casting her vote. She sucked in a nervous breath.

"Worried about her?" Scott asked.

"No," Marianne answered honestly. "I just hope she wins."

"Really?"

Marianne nodded. "Not for me, for everyone else."

Jonah turned when he heard Laura close the door. "How did it go?"

"I managed to fill in the right bubble," Laura joked.

Jonah nodded.

"You okay?"

He nodded again. "I think it just hit me."

"That your mom might be the next president?"

"Yeah."

Laura put her arms around his neck. "Pretty amazing, wasn't it? Seeing her name there."

Jonah smiled.

"You're worried," Laura observed.

"I just wonder how she's holding up."

Laura kissed him softly. "Your mom will be okay, Jonah—no matter what happens today. I'd worry more about the people who need her the most."

"You mean like Cooper and JD?"

"No."

Jonah nodded. He pulled Laura close. *Please, let this all work out.*

"Jonah, why don't we head to Schoharie and see how they're doing?"

"They're in the city."

"No. I talked to Marianne. Your mom and JD aren't leaving for the city until around three."

"We need to get the kids ready for tonight, and…."

"Jonah, we're already packed. We can drive to the city just as easily from there."

"It's further and…"

"And, you'll feel better when you see her."

Jonah's eyes closed in resignation. "I don't want to intrude on…"

"Go get JJ. I'll get Sophie ready to go."

———◆●◆———

Melanie giggled. "Shell, stop pacing."

"I can't help it."

"It's not even 11:00 A.M. We won't have a floor left by noon."

Michelle stopped and flopped onto the couch. "I hate this."

Melanie took a seat beside her wife. "Babe, why don't we just head into the city early. You can see your Mom and…"

"She's not going to the hotel until later."

"What?"

"Dana called. She said Mom and JD were headed back to the house after they voted. She's meeting them there at two."

"I'll get the twins dressed."

"What?"

"Well, if you're going to wear a hole in someone's floor, I'd rather you do it there. JD will know how to fix it."

Michelle watched Melanie's figure retreat. She let her head fall back and took a deep breath. *God, help me get through this day.*

———————◆◆●◆◆———————

Candace poured herself a cup of coffee and sat down at the kitchen table.

"Avoiding the news?" Pearl guessed.

"Something like that," Candace replied.

"You know, I remember your granddad doing the same thing."

"What's that?"

"Sitting in this kitchen while everyone else buzzed around trying to figure out what was going to happen. He had something stronger in his cup as I recall."

Candace laughed. "Don't tempt me."

"It'll wear off by the time you have to make an acceptance speech."

Candace smiled.

"Suddenly worried?" Pearl asked.

"No. Aware."

"Did you write a concession speech?"

"Nope."

"Good."

"Mommy?" Cooper slid into the kitchen in his socks. "Jonah's here."

"Jonah's here?" Candace was surprised.

"Yep."

Candace looked at Pearl.

"Don't ask me," Pearl said.

Candace followed Cooper into the living room.

"Coop!" Spencer yelled excitedly. "Aunt Shell is here!"

"Shell is here?" Candace looked at Marianne.

"I have no idea," Marianne said.

"Hey," Michelle opened the door with Brody in his carrier. "Hey, Jonah. I didn't know you were here."

"Am now," he said.

Jameson came down the stairs and looked at Candace with confusion. "Did I miss something?"

Candace's eyebrow arched.

Jonah and Michelle spoke at the same time.

"Dana said you'd be here."

"Marianne told Laura you'd be here."

"Uh-huh," Jameson said.

Candace chuckled.

"Hey, is there anything to eat?" Jonah asked.

"Pearl made lasagna yesterday," Marianne said. "It's in the fridge."

Jonah grinned. He handed his mother Sophie, took Laura's hand and headed for the kitchen.

"Hey, wait up," Michelle said. "I haven't eaten all day." She handed Brody to Jameson.

"Think I'll join them," Scott said.

Marianne shrugged and followed.

The next sound was Pearl's voice. "What is everyone doing in my kitchen?"

The door opened, and Melanie walked in with Amanda. "Where is everyone?"

"Kitchen," Jameson said.

Melanie freed Amanda from her carrier and put both their jackets in the hallway closet. She smiled at Jameson.

"Oh, no. I've got one already," Jameson said.

"So? You have two hands." Melanie handed Jameson Amanda and started for the kitchen.

Jameson looked at Candace. "Why did we come here again?"

Candace shrugged.

"Marianne!" Shell yelled. "That is so gross!"

"I don't want to know," Jameson said. She took a seat on the sofa with the twins in her arms. Candace sat beside her.

"Mommy?" Cooper slid back into the room.

Candace looked at him curiously. "Can me and Spence have chocolate milk. Shell said you're in charge."

Could've fooled me. "Sure, you can, Cooper."

Cooper pumped his fist in the air and ran off.

"Still think this is quieter than the city?" Jameson asked.

Candace smiled and let her head fall on Jameson's shoulder. *It's exactly what I needed.*

8:00 P.M. EST
NEW YORK CITY

Candace sat with Cooper's head in her lap. Her hands played with the tight curls on his head while he slept. She watched the television in front of her. Behind her, a flurry of activity continued. She could hear competing news coverage as the polls closed on the east coast. Everything was out of her hands now. It was in the hands of the voters. She had spoken to them; now, they would give their answer.

"Most polls on the east coast have closed. Exit polling shows some tight races. Let's see what is happening in real time. Trevor?"

"All the polls except for Governor Reid's home state of New York are closed now. New York officially closes at 9:00 P.M. There are still lines in many states. Anyone in line at closing will be allowed to vote. I can tell you what our exit polling shows." Trevor Booth made his way to a familiar map. *"As we expected, Governor Reid is riding ahead of Bradley Wolfe in New England. I would expect her to sweep those states with a healthy margin. The most interesting thing to watch right now is Florida where polls closed about an hour ago and the first official returns have started to come in."*

Booth brought up a map of Florida. "The cities have yet to come in, but this is what you should watch. Right here—See this? This is Polk County. Polk County is a decidedly red county. It's also a county where there is a significant vote. Right now, Governor Reid is running neck and neck with Bradley Wolfe. If she can hold that, even if she loses by a small margin, her chances of taking Florida are excellent. Florida has 25 electoral votes. Wolfe wants this. If Candace Reid pulls out Florida, the math for him could get difficult."

Candace took a deep breath.

"That's a good thing," Jameson reminded her.

"I'll feel better when we see Pennsylvania and Ohio," Candace said.

Jameson nodded. "Can I get you something?"

"Scotch?" Candace winked. "I'm okay, honey. I swear."

Jameson nodded. "I'm going to go grab something to drink."

Candace smiled and turned back to the TV.

"Yes!" Glenn's voice boomed through the room. "Keep your fingers and toes crossed. Ben just called from Philly. He thinks Pennsylvania is in our column."

Candace took a deep breath. *Let's hope so.*

———◆●◆———

"How's she doing?" Marianne asked Michelle.

"Waiting," Michelle said. "She's quiet."

"Are you worried?" Marianne asked.

"If Ohio comes in for her or Florida—either one—it's going to be tough for him. Both are close."

Marianne nodded. "What do you think?"

"I'm trying not to."

11:00 P.M. EST

Candace needed to step away. She had just made her way to check on Cooper when a round of whoops and excited screams erupted. Cooper stirred.

"Shh." Candace kissed his head. "Go back to sleep, sweetheart."

Candace heard Glenn's voice as it carried. "Where is she?"

"What is going on?" Candace asked.

"They just called Florida for you," he said.

"It looks like we're ready to call another state. We've been watching Ohio for hours. It looks like Ohioans have made their wishes known. Trevor?"

"They certainly have. It looks like we can call Ohio for Governor Candace Reid."

"Yes!"

"Oh, my God!"

Candace took in the first full breath she had in hours. She looked at the television at a map that had grown significantly bluer.

"Candace?" Grant grabbed Candace's arm, snapping her from a momentary daze.

"Yeah."

"I don't want to get your hopes up."

Candace smiled.

"I just talked to some of my contacts. I'm pretty sure North Carolina's going blue too."

Candace's genuine surprise was evident.

"I'm not kidding," he said.

"I've been trailing there."

"Yeah, well, you're not trailing tonight," he said. "It's close. I think you just might pull it out."

Candace sighed nervously. Doug and Glenn had been convinced she had a shot at North Carolina. She'd always considered it a long-shot. A lesbian winning in North Carolina seemed unlikely to her.

"He's not beating you by the margins he needs to in the rural areas. He's beating you—not enough if your margins hold in the cities. Your margin in Wake is massive. If you hold or pass 60%, I think he's done."

Candace nodded. She wasn't ready to get her hopes up. She'd already been declared the winner in all of New England, New York, Pennsylvania, DC, Illinois, Maryland and now Ohio and Florida. She knew the math. North Carolina would put her at 190 electoral votes. She was confident about the west coast. North Carolina would make it next to impossible for Wolfe to win. She clasped Grant's hand. "Let's see."

11:30 P.M. EST

"Just about 11:30 PM here on the east coast. We have another two states we are ready to call. The first we expected. Until now we've said it was too early to call. We are calling the State of California for Governor Candace Reid. The other has been a nail-biter, but we feel confident now that we can also call Michigan for Governor Reid. The math is getting harder for Mr. Wolfe, Trevor."

Trevor Booth went to his map. "It certainly is. The race we are watching closely right now is in North Carolina. That was considered an uphill battle for Governor Reid. Most of us would have guessed we would have called this one for Bradley Wolfe by now. It's so close that we can't call it until the rest of Wake County comes in. Right now, the governor is standing at 249 electoral votes. She only needs 270. If she pulls out North Carolina, she would only be eight votes shy of that magic number. A win in Washington, Minnesota or Wisconsin would put her over. She's leading right now in all three."

"God Damnit!" Wolfe screamed. "What the hell is going on?"

"Calm down. She's not going to take North Carolina," Jed Ritchie said. "A lesbian in the tip of the south? Relax."

Candace sat surrounded by her family and her staff. Jameson held her hand. Glenn had given them the warning that his sources told him some big news was about to break.

"It has been an interesting night. Some surprises and some close races. We're about to make some important calls right now. Based on the results we have in, we are calling the State of Arizona for Bradley Wolfe."

Candace held her breath. Wolfe had taken the thick of the south as expected and he had taken Missouri and Wisconsin by a narrow margin.

We're also ready to call the States of Minnesota and New Mexico for Governor Reid. And, what seems to have everyone buzzing right now, we now feel confident that we can call the great State of North Carolina for Governor Candace Reid. If my math is right, Trevor that means that we can predict that Governor Candace Reid of New York will be the next President of the United States."

Candace heard the cheers erupt around her. She sat perfectly still, staring at the map on the television screen. No one's words registered until she heard a sleepy voice.

"Mommy?"

Candace smiled at Cooper. "We woke you up."

Cooper collapsed into her. "Everybody's yelling," he said.

Jameson laughed. "Mommy just became the next president, Coop."

Cooper rubbed his eyes and looked at Candace. "Do we have to go to the White House now?"

Candace chuckled. "No, sweetheart, not right now. We do have to make our way to a party."

Cooper brightened.

"Oh, that woke you up," Candace said.

"Why don't you go to the bathroom and brush your teeth, Coop," Jameson said. "I'll be right there." She turned to Candace. "Congratulations." Her lips met Candace's tenderly.

Candace held Jameson's face.

Jameson smiled. "You have a room full of people to hug," she whispered. "I'll get Coop ready."

"Jameson." Candace tugged on Jameson's hand. "I love you."

"I love you too, Madame President."

12:45 A.M EST.
VICTORY SPEECH

Candace walked out onto the stage to a roar unlike any she'd ever heard. She walked back and forth and waved before stepping to the podium.

"So, here we are," she greeted the room. "I recall a little girl watching her grandfather greet an audience much like this one. Watching my grandfather, not just as he campaigned or made speeches, but as he talked to people, I knew that one day I wanted to be like him. I wanted to touch people's lives in some small way."

"We love you!"

Candace chuckled. "I love you too. This election has never been about me. It's always been about you. I've heard your stories. I've listened to your frustration, and I've enjoyed all the dreams that have been shared with me, some by children and some by grandparents. At every turn, every factory or meeting hall, every coffee shop and every rally, you've reminded me what this election was all about—what America is all about. You've shown me your scars, and shared with me your triumphs. I've shed tears, and I have laughed until my sides ached. I've listened. We have a lot to do. We need more of that laughter and less of those tears. And, that is what we are going to strive to achieve together. I have so many people that I need to thank. All the many volunteers who did everything from make phone calls to give people a ride to the polls. We couldn't offer them much more than some bad coffee and the promise we'd do our best to reach this day. My campaign staff and advisers, Glenn Freeman, Doug Mills, Grant Hill and my wonderful daughter, Michelle who has been more of a guide than she will ever realize. And, my amazing friend who keeps me on track, Dana Russo. Your next Vice President, Nate Ellison and his incredible family for agreeing to be part of this journey." Candace took a breath. "Most of all, I want to thank my family. I have the most amazing children and grandchildren anyone could ask for. You can call me bias. I am. I'm also right."

Affectionate laughter rose through the crowd.

"Marianne, Shell, Jonah, and Cooper—each of them has endured my lengthy absences and the scrutiny of the press. They have never once faltered in their love and support. And, you know our family has had its losses. But it also continues to grow. Spencer, Maddie, JJ, Sophie, Amanda, and Brody—you remind me every day how precious life is and how bright the future is for all of us." Candace cleared her throat. "I lost my mother earlier this year. I'm blessed that I had two women who raised me. I want to thank my other mother, Pearl for never letting me get away with too much nonsense."

The crowd laughed again.

Candace's voice softened. "And, let's be clear. There's no one I need to thank more than the love of my life, my wife, Jameson."

Cheers and clapping began to thunder through the ballroom.

Candace laughed. "I don't blame you," she said. "Jameson and I both know what it's like to feel you have to hide who you are, to fear that you will be judged or shut out of opportunities because some people view you as different. I want a world that not only respects our differences; I want a world that thrives because of them. This country has been called 'a shining city upon a hill.' In the harbor of this great city we love, a woman stands holding a torch to guide the way for weary travelers, to welcome them to a land of opportunity and prosperity. That is who we are. Every one of us is one of those travelers, seeking a place where we are not only free to dream, but where we might turn dreams into reality. Every one of us must also serve as a beacon, shining a light into the darkness toward a brighter future. Together, we will do that. And, it must be together." Candace paused. "A short while ago, I received a call from Bradley Wolfe."

A few groans emerged. Candace held up her hand.

"I want to thank him for a hard-fought campaign and for raising issues that are on the hearts and minds of many Americans. We do have differences. We must be willing to acknowledge the things that separate us if we hope to come together. Honest dialogue, listening, reaching across lines that make us uncomfortable—that is what we must do to build a stronger, fairer, more prosperous America for us all. You have placed your trust in me. I accept the responsibility with humility and gratefulness. I understand the enormity of the task before me. I cannot do it alone. Just as we reached this day together, so we also must work together to create a better tomorrow for all. The time for campaign speeches and promises is over, my friends. Now, we forge ahead not as Democrats and Republicans, liberals or conservatives—as Americans. Each day when I wake up and go to work, I will remember your faces and recall your stories. I will remember that YOU are America. That is what makes us '*the* shining city upon a hill.' God bless this wonderful country. Thank you. Thank you all."

"You were amazing," Jameson whispered in Candace's ear as she waved to the crowd.

"No, they were." Candace looked out at her supporters.

"You know it's going to get even crazier?" Jameson said.

Candace chuckled. Cooper and Spencer were waving enthusiastically to the crowd. She glanced over to see Michelle bouncing with Brody. Marianne was scooping up a sleepy Maddie, and Jonah was laughing at JJ while he twirled a streamer. "Good thing I'm used to lunatics," she whispered back.

Jameson laughed. *The White House will never be the same again.*

BOOKS BY JA ARMSTRONG

OFF SCREEN
Off Screen
The Red Carpet
Dim All the Lights
Writer's Block
Casting Call
Intermission
Waiting in the Wings
Script Doctor

BY DESIGN
By Design
Under Construction
Solid Foundation
Rough Drafts
New Additions
Renovations
Building Blocks
Road Blocks
Campaign Trail
Election Day

SPECIAL DELIVERY
Special Delivery
Small Packages
Handle with Care
Late Arrivals
Best Practice

FIRST COURSE
First Course
Main Dish

BOOKS BY NANCY ANN HEALY
ALEX AND CASSIDY
Intersection
Betrayal
Commitment
Conspiracy
Untold
Falling Through Shooting Stars

LEARN MORE AT:
www.thebumblingbard.com

www.ingramcontent.com/pod-product-compliance
Lightning Source LLC
Chambersburg PA
CBHW070322260626
47160CB00003B/925